SEA & ASH

Shadow and Ash – Book 1

Isadora Brown

www.BOROUGHSPUBLISHINGGROUP.com

SEA & ASH

ISBN: 978-1-953810-87-8

For Johnny

SEA & ASH

CHAPTER ONE

Hannah

What a wonderful day for an execution.

The sun left a trail of blood down the sky, marking tonight as the perfect evening for the Consumption. The ocean was still, as if it held its breath waiting for the first plume of smoke to fill the crisp, salty air. My bones were chilled, and I felt like a marble slab waiting to be carved by a skilled sculptor. Not even the crackling fire in my room could warm me.

Sulfur already tickled my nose even though we were an hour from the Lighting Ceremony. Bile rose in my throat, and I forced myself to swallow it. I cast my gaze to the floor where my lady-in-waiting was lacing up the white gown Father bought for me specifically for this event.

“There.” Roseanna stepped back, her chin tucked down, hands folded in front of her. “You are ready, mum.”

I murmured a gentle thank you and dismissed her with a nod before pulling on my stifling gloves and smoothed down my dress. I shuddered, knowing I had only a few moments before my sister and I were whisked away on Father’s orders. We would ride down to the Ankura square, where we’d be thrust into priority seating so close to the event we would be able to feel flames lick our skin.

A Fire Consumption was the worst. Watching a person burn alive while restrained to a wooden mount with the ocean in plain view was a particularly hellish sort of torture. I had witnessed two Fire Consumptions in my seventeen years, and one had been too many.

My fingers tingled and I closed my eyes, trying to block out the passing servants on the other side of my door as they made their way down the hall. Low gossip filled my ears, and though I could not hear what was being said, I knew instantly one of them was lying. The magick flowing in my veins told me so.

"…Jonathan Nyx is going to burn for his crimes against the Legacies."

"I met him one time, in the courtyard." *Lie.* "His eyes were as black as the devil's soul, and I nearly screamed with terror." *Another lie.*

Blocking out the lie was impossible. I dropped my head into my hands and let the pressure wash over me. I needed a moment longer to collect myself.

When the servants were far enough away, the magick inside me could no longer pick up what they were saying. I let out a strangled breath, my shoulders sagged forward, and I folded over until my stomach touched the tops of my thighs. My breath caught in my throat, and it took me a moment to collect myself.

Blasted corset.

The two times I was forced to attend a Consumption, I was fraught with the expectation I would become a victim myself. I could be locked in a cage and sunk to the bottom of the ocean, buried alive in rich soil, or burned. Regardless of the method, each was terrible, and my chest always tightened thinking it could be me.

"Hannah?" There was a gentle knock at the door, and I straightened as my older sister Elizabeth waltzed in without my permission. "You all right? You have a pinched look on your face."

I reached up to tidy my hair. "Did you need something, dear sister?" My gaze traveled over her outfit. Instead of the white we were supposed to wear, which symbolized purity, she was dressed in black. "Lizzie, are you certain you wish to wear that?"

"You sound like Fiona, so I sent her away," she scoffed, shaking her head. Even her hair was wild. Small trinkets were braided through her golden-brown tresses instead of being unadorned and neatly pulled back from her face and piled on top of her head, as mine was. "Someone is going to die, Han, and we should all be in mourning about it."

I refrained from rolling my eyes, brushing my skirts with care. "Father is not going to be happy," I pointed out.

"Father cannot dictate what I do any longer," she said, her voice firm.

"Is this about Brendan? I thought you called off the engagement months ago. Father seems to have forgiven you."

She narrowed her eyes as she always did when Brendan Pickard was mentioned. "This is not about Brendan, I assure you," she said, her voice tight.

I did not press even though I ought to. Lizzie cleared her throat and glanced away.

"The carriage is waiting," she said. "Father will meet us there. He's wrapping up collections and is waiting for Adrian Blood's."

"The brothel owner?" I frowned as we stepped out of my room together.

I was not particularly fond of Blood's Brothel. I'd accompanied Father as he made his collection rounds each week, and as uncomfortable as the place made me, I had agreed to a meeting there later this evening with a known witch.

"Yes, the one who is available only at night." Her lips curved up as we headed down the staircase. "Given his delay, Father will not be aware of my attire until it is too late for him to do anything about it."

We stepped outside and up into the carriage. Harrold, our butler, gave us a cursory glance, his thin lips tightly pressed together. There was no love lost among us, but he was loyal to my father, which I appreciated. After he assisted us, we settled into our seats and the carriage began its trek from the hills down the winding trails to town.

I glanced out my window, taking in the scenery. The hills rolled smoothly like the waves, the grass a rich green from the copious rain Ankura received every year. Some whispered magick was involved in keeping the island filled with life, but I was unsure as to its the truth. The blue sky was drowning in gray, though it was too soon to tell if there would be a storm. Nearing summer, storms became frequent and tended to be the most dangerous we received all year.

By the time the carriage reached the courtyard, I was past ready to return home. I wanted to prepare for my meeting with Marcella, but I would not be able to do so until I was truly alone.

Harrold helped us out of the carriage, and we were ushered to seats close to the wooden galley. The ocean was behind us, and though one had to follow a trail of cobblestones to reach the beach, it was within view. Our backs would face the water while we would watch death unfold.

Peripherally, I saw two men in pristine red uniforms standing on each side of the prisoner, their ink-black boots shining in the setting sun. A flour sack was placed over the prisoner's head, masking his identity. Everyone was waiting for the governor, my uncle, to arrive.

I eyed the stake in the middle of the galley and my shoulders seized. I couldn't keep looking at where Jonathan Nyx would die a painful death. My stomach turned into sailor knots.

There was always a large crowd for Consumptions. Even shop owners closed up early to attend. Men were smoking and drinking, women whispering and shaking their heads. Parents brought their children to teach them a lesson in consequences. There was a fascination about death being snuffed out before one's eyes at the hand of a mere mortal. To have such power, such responsibility, was more than disconcerting.

It wasn't only death they were here to see: it was *his* death.

A particularly strong scent of body odor overpowered the salty air, and I shifted my weight, trying to keep from bumping into anyone. Every now and then, my magick picked up hints of conversations, but I focused my attention on the prisoner in hopes it would alleviate the pulsating behind my brows.

Captain Jonathan Nyx, Pyrate Mage, was a thorn in the side of nearly everyone in Ankura. Though I was privy to his exploits, I was unfamiliar with the details. Lizzie followed his "adventures," always returning from her blacksmith and weaponry shop with gossip about the women he was with or mischief he had gotten himself into. He seemed more like a nuisance than a threat, but Patrol did not appreciate being ridiculed so publicly. Even though the king and his legion of noble supporters were on the main continent of Cardonia, he too was concerned about fear, respect, and his people taking him seriously.

"I never thought he'd actually get caught," Lizzie murmured from beside me. "Then again, Nyx apparently got caught standing over the body of a woman."

"He killed her?" I asked.

She shrugged. "I'm not sure," she admitted. "Apparently, the body was so waterlogged, it was difficult to make out who it was."

Someone pushed us from behind.

"Do you mind?" my sister asked, lifting an arm.

"Beg your pardon, mum," a woman said, encircling the shoulders of a young boy with dirt on his cheeks and mud on his shoes. "The lad's excited is all."

Lizzie softened. "Of course." She stepped to the side. "He's more than welcome to stand next to me."

I stepped to the side, a flair of annoyance filling my veins. Not because I had a problem with the boy stepping into our space, but I did not understand the notion of being excited to watch a man die, especially one touched by magick. It revealed a possible future I might be fated to should anyone stumble on to the fact I, too, had magick inside of me. The only person who knew about me was Lizzie, but only because she had an ability as well. I did not trust my secret with anyone else, not even my father. Not even my cousins, the Becketts. Those who were not touched by magick saw us as abominations, as devils who needed to be purged from society.

I glanced around at the thought of them and caught sight of the three sisters in a special room, away from the crowd but with an enviable vantage point. All three wore some form of white, with Everly, the youngest, wearing something as pure as untainted snow, while Jessa, the oldest, wore something that appeared to be a shadow of white. Kara, the middle sister, was the only one dressed in a simple white dress, with no additional features to make it fashionable. Kara scanned the audience and saw me. We nodded at each other before shouting caught our attention.

"Ladies and gentlemen," a man on the galley called out, arms stretched out, smile lighting up his plucky face. "Thank you all for coming out this evening to witness a Consumption. It has been six hundred and nine days since our last one, nearly a new record, until we discovered Jonathan Nyx had weaseled his way through the taverns, stealing ale and flirting with the women."

Angry shouts erupted behind us. I had to bite my lip to keep from smiling. Normally, such behavior was abhorrent, but there was something special about Jonathan Nyx and why he participated in such vileness. Perhaps I was giving him the benefit of the doubt because he had magick, but I wanted to believe he was not as wicked as others insisted he was.

"He is charged with multiple counts of the use of Enchantment, including…" He let his voice trail off as he unraveled a thick scroll in his hands. He held it up so he could read it with ease. "Commandeering a church and setting that church on fire. Stealing a pig and bewitching it to run throughout town. Camouflaging himself in the closet of the married Legacy Olivia Runner in order to steal large sums of riches from the Runner family during their stay on Ankura. He has swindled ale from honest businessmen and enchanted loving wives, so they committed multiple accounts of adultery against their husbands.

"He has commandeered multiple Patrol ships and hidden them on various parts of the ocean surrounding the island. He has intercepted merchant ships with his own insufferable ship, *The Prodigal Death*. He's been drunk in public on more than one occasion. He's disguised himself as a Legacy in order to enter homes and steal jewels, books, and other items of value. He's manipulated thoughts…"

My eyes shifted from the Proclaimer to Jonathan Nyx. The Proclaimer's words droned out as more charges were listed. Nyx's shoulders were slack, though his defiant stance showed there was still life in him. His shoulders were rolled back, seeming unafraid of his fate. Unable to see his face, I wondered if he was as beautiful as everyone said.

Not that it mattered, but I was curious.

I had never encountered the man before, and apparently, I should be thankful for such a thing. Lizzie claimed to have seen him sneaking sweet rolls from Madame French's bakery, disappearing down the alley that spilled into the shoreline. As much as I loved my sister, I was skeptical. She could have mistaken a drunken sailor for the elusive Pyrate Mage for all I knew.

"Will anyone speak on behalf of his soul?" the Proclaimer asked after he finished listing the charges.

Doing so would not save him, and no one wanted to be a Sympathizer to a Pyrate Mage, as they could be imprisoned or condemned to death for speaking up.

At that moment, my father made his way through the crowd. Another man, tall and pale, followed him. I recognized him immediately. Adrian Blood. He moved through the crowd like a shark among fish. Everyone stumbled around him, wanting nothing more than to get out of his way.

When no one responded to the Proclaimer's question, he took what appeared to be a metal stick and slapped the back of Nyx's knees with it. He did not scream in pain, but he stumbled forward.

"Ascend the staircase," the Proclaimer barked out.

My fingers tingled with pulsating sparks. I had never felt such a surge before. I had no idea where it came from. It was as if someone was manipulating my magick to be more than it was. I wasn't sure such a thing was even possible.

My eyes widened. My mouth dropped open. My fingertips went numb. I curled them into my palms, but that did absolutely nothing. If anything, the tingles only got more noticeable, like when I fell asleep on my arm and woke up in the same position.

What is happening to me?

I was distracted by heavy footsteps stomping on wood in time to the beat of my heart. Nyx made his way up to the galley where the stake was placed, wrapped with ribbons of dry thorns and branches.

"Now, he shall be placed in irons that will numb his magick," the Proclaimer announced and proceeded to remove the simple rope and replace it with iron.

The tingling persisted, increasing even. I let out a whimper as Father joined Lizzie and me. Adrian Blood was nowhere to be found.

When the Proclaimer finished, two Patrolmen proceeded to tie Nyx to the stake with sailor's rope, thicker and heavier than typical bindings. Once they finished, they stood back.

I swallowed. There was no way Nyx would be able to get out of that, especially with his magick numbed.

"Light the Earth," the Proclaimer announced.

The stake lit instantly, flames licking Nyx's boots. I opened my mouth, not in horror, but because whatever was happening to me was too much for me to bear.

My gaze skipped over to my cousin Kara, who was observing me with a strange expression. I didn't have time to think too much on it before something tugged at my fingers. It was unbearable, and I needed to let it go.

I shot out my arms, and blinding light filled the square. I let out a quiet sob of relief, dropping my arms once the unfamiliar sensations had drained from my body.

Women screamed. Men shouted.

The stake had been snuffed out, leaving a small trail of smoke floating into the sky.

Jonathan Nyx had disappeared.

CHAPTER TWO

Hannah

I blinked. Surely, I was mistaken. The man could not have simply vanished. I blinked again and turned.

The murmuring of the crowd got louder. A woman screamed. Someone to my left fainted. The Proclaimer turned to his right and then to his left, trying to figure out what had happened. His mouth hung open as though dislocated from his jaw, and he stared stupidly. The scroll in his hand crumpled, his grip on it tight.

If my fingers didn't still tingle, I might have found the whole thing amusing, and unnerving. As it was, I was scared. Not because Jonathan Nyx had escaped *again,* but because there was a chance I might have had something to do with it.

"Now, stay calm, ladies and gentlemen," the Proclaimer announced, raising up his hand. "Stay calm. We shall find Jonathan Nyx and bring him back for his Reckoning. Make no mistake—"

"He disappeared right in front of you," a man roared. "How can you say you'll find him?"

"What was that light?" a woman demanded. "Has Hellmouth finally opened to swallow our sinful souls?"

The crowd grew even louder until they were nearly shouting, flinging ideas and accusations like jagged rocks.

"Lizzie," my father said, leaning close to my sister. "Take the carriage and get you and your sister home immediately. I do not think this will end well."

Lizzie nodded.

I reached out and took my father's hand. "What of you, Father?" I asked. I didn't want to tell him what to do or how to handle this situation, but I didn't want him to get hurt if things took a bad turn. Judging by the way the crowd's anger and fear seemed to feed off each other, I was certain things would escalate.

My father's eyes dropped to my hands, and I immediately released him. Had he felt a spark of life when I touched him, even with my gloves on? Had I given away the fact that perhaps it was I whose powers lit up the night sky and gave Jonathan Nyx the perfect distraction to escape?

"I must assist your uncle," he said, nodding toward the building where the governor and my cousins were safely tucked away from the milling crowd. "I am sure he's not pleased Nyx has slipped through his fingers once again."

Father did not seem troubled by my touch, so I allowed myself to let out a breath of relief.

"Go with Lizzie, Hannah," my father instructed. "Do not stop for anyone or anything."

I lost my chance to argue with him as Lizzie's fingers snaked around my wrist and pulled me into the crowd. I bumped into a portly man who leaned forward to yell his displeasure at the Proclaimer. Droplets of his spit hit my cheek, and I narrowly dodged a girl crying out for her mother, her shrieks piercing the night. I stopped to offer assistance, but Lizzie yanked me forward so hard, I hit a woman in a tight corset.

"Watch it," she said with a sneer. "Yous thinks 'cause you're a Legacy, you can do what you please?"

"I'm not—"

But Lizzie continued to pull me so hard, I was afraid she would dislocate my arm from my shoulder.

"We cannot stop," she insisted. "You heard Father."

"When do you actually listen to Father?" I shot back. I rubbed my lips together, finding my footing so it was easy to avoid the crowds surging forward, demanding a Consumption of some kind, even if Jonathan Nyx was gone.

"When he's right." Lizzie kept her gaze forward, searching for our carriage. "Though rare, he does manage to be right every now and again."

I returned my attention to the screaming child, guilt ripping through my chest. My arms drooped. My feet felt like two anchors were dragging them beneath the hard dirt. I didn't wish to leave, and

I could not fathom why. My heart beat quicker. The crowd grew louder and more careless with their movements and with their words. I could hear curses and threats. I could feel people getting pushed and shoved behind me and in front of me. I knew there would be disappointment with Nyx gone, but I didn't realize it would turn into this fury.

Being among the crowd as it grew more agitated was not something I wanted to partake in.

My eyes drifted over to where my father was heading. I managed to catch a glimpse of white—probably the dress of one of my cousins—but they were already gone from view. I wondered where Kara was, wondered if she knew what had happened. Her face flashed in my mind, her odd look moments before the power had exploded from my fingertips. Before I could think further on it, Lizzie yanked at my wrist, grunting when I didn't keep up with her.

"Hannah, I cannot do this on my own," she snapped. "Considering you are not a child, could you please move your feet?"

I nodded and focused ahead of me. Dirt kicked up into the air made my eyes water and narrow. The flames from the guards and their beacons began to die off now there was no one to bring them to life, lending a chill to the air. With the sudden movement and separation of the onlookers, there was no insulation from the cold. Body heat evaporated into the night sky like ghosts at the crack of dawn, and I trembled.

Jonathan Nyx had nearly been Consumed, and yet he had managed to escape.

I feared the rush of something dormant inside me had caused the light.

My emotions were choppy and conflicted like the surface of the sea. Had I potentially exposed myself and my abilities to those who would harm people like me?

"I see the carriage," Lizzie called, thrusting her finger ahead. "We need to cross over."

A woman bumped into me, spilling her drink on my dress. I caught my balance as she cursed at me, demanding I pay for another. There were so many taverns lining the docks hoping to catch the attention of merchant sailor and pyrate alike, it was no surprise to see people with ale or rum in their hands. Surprise or no, I didn't appreciate it was all over my attire.

I stepped around a man so drunk he had fallen onto the dirt and hadn't bothered to push himself up, despite people rushing the square, afraid of Jonathan Nyx and his magick at the same time they were upset they'd been robbed of a Consumption. The Patrol armed themselves with their rifles, marching throughout the square in pairs to ensure order despite the crowd's anger. One Patrol officer hit a drunken man with the butt of his rifle, the sickening crunch overpowering the other sounds.

"Do you think Brendan is working tonight?" I asked as we made our way to the lone carriage.

"Why would you bring up Brendan?" Lizzie asked, her voice curt. Though I knew the subject matter was something she refrained from discussing, it was strange to hear her so defensive. "How should I know if he's working?"

I said nothing more, shifting my gaze. Brendan Pickard was a Patrol officer, and under no circumstances would he be okay with his men using their rifles against the crowd, even as a means to control them. Unless they engaged in violent or threatening behavior, he would try to maintain control by other means. As chaos rippled through the dispersed crowd, I felt sure he wasn't present.

Finally, we made it to the carriage. The horses were tense, rolling their eyes in panic, shifting their weight from side to side. It seemed they were ready to lift their back hooves and thrust out their legs in powerful kicks.

"Where is Steward?" Lizzie asked, throwing open the door. She spun around, her hair wild and flaring out around her. Her eyes were wide, and for the first time since I could remember, I saw fear in her golden irises.

"Lizzie," I said slowly. Noise forced me to turn. A fight in the middle of the square had gained some attention. From what I could see, it appeared to be two drunkards getting physical, probably after an argument over something inconsequential. Not even the two nearby Patrol were interested in stopping it.

"I can't find him." Lizzie turned back around. She seemed to be searching my face for something, but I couldn't say what. Finally, she nodded, chewing the bottom of her lip.

"Get in." She jutted her chin to the carriage.

My mouth fell open. "What?"

"I said get in, Hannah. For once, would you please listen to me? I don't command you often. When I do, I'd appreciate it if you would listen."

My eyebrows rose, surprised by her outburst. However, I said nothing, opened the door to the carriage, and stepped inside.

"And now?" I called once seated.

Suddenly, the carriage jerked forward. I nearly fell onto the floor. The door slammed shut. What was going on? Had someone commandeered the carriage? What had happened to my sister?

I managed to retain my balance and settled back into my seat, tightening my muscles in preparation for another jerky movement. I leaned out the window to see Lizzie sitting in the driver's seat, reins in hand, trying to guide the horses.

"Lizzie," I screamed.

"You call my name like you're reciting a prayer," she responded. I was surprised she was able to hear me. "Is there something you want, or can I concentrate on the task at hand?"

My eyes went wide when I finally realized what was going on. "Do you know how to drive such a thing?" I demanded to know. "You are going to get us killed."

"What was going to get us killed is that riot back there," she said. "We were without an escort since Father decided he must be part of the committee to complain about another Jonathan Nyx escape instead of accompanying us home safely. Steward is nowhere to be found, probably in one of the taverns dotting the harbor, two ales in and unfit to take us home. Which leaves me." She glanced over her shoulder to give me a smile at the same time a lady screamed.

Lizzie whirled around. "Pardon me," she called to the older woman who was waving

her fist at our carriage.

I winced. "Are you sure you can do this?"

"No," she said. "But we don't have much of a choice, do we?"

I pulled my head in and fiddled with an errant strand of hair. As much as I wanted to concern myself with Lizzie's abilities, I had too much on my mind. My meeting with the witch was any time now, and I wanted to change my attire into something more fitting before heading back to the square.

I picked at my skirt, fiddling with the seam. The overpowering cloudy sky blotted out the moon, and only a few of her beams lit the pathways. The ride was jerky at best, and I had to brace myself with each passing moment more from the unevenness of the road and Lizzie's inexperience maneuvering a carriage. But we were on the way home. I should be grateful for that.

I settled into my seat, trying to keep myself from letting my anxiety at Lizzie's inexperience with driving a carriage paralyze me. My mind searched for any distraction until it landed on Kara. From the way she had stared at me as power flew out of my fingers, I thought she might know I was able to do magick but was unable to control it.

Did her recognition mean Kara held magick as well, and she had helped me to release mine? Or had Jonathan Nyx been responsible? There were too many questions without answers.

I curled my fingers into a fist to stop fidgeting. Magick swelled inside me, crossed my chest, sunk to my feet, and then rose back up again. Keeping it contained in one part of my body was impossible. I was anticipating release but was unsure how it would come about. Would light fill the carriage, or did someone need to coax it out of me?

From the corner of my eye, I caught sight of two people walking on the pathway beside the Forest of Legends. A hint of light blonde hair made me pause.

Claire Turner? What was she doing in the forest, on the dirt path, and was the man walking with her Richard, her fiancé?

I tilted my head up, hoping to get a better view of them. Darkness coated the forest, giving it an ominous presence, and the grass stalks were so tall it was difficult to make out who she was with. In fact, if I did not recognize the flash of pale hair, deducing the woman was Claire would have been impossible.

I assumed my best friend had been in the square for the Consumption, as everyone in Ankura was. She would have been with her father, a wealthy merchant who did a lot of trading between the main continent and the port cities, and her mother, as well as her older sister, Lydia. Her fiancé might be with their party, although I could not be sure Richard could spare the time, considering he was a physician who always had patients.

As Lizzie slowly passed the couple, I was able to catch sight of the man. His face was hidden, but his posture was more casual than Richard's and he had more muscle. Definitely not Richard, and definitely not someone I knew. And I considered Claire my closest friend.

I opened my mouth, ready to see if Lizzie wanted to stop for them. I was almost positive she didn't see Claire and her companion, or she would have already slowed. I paused, not wanting to interrupt an illicit tryst if Claire was simply having fun. While I did not condone her behavior—if she was engaging in such behavior—it was not my business to interfere. Richard was always cordial but cold, and I knew Claire was not as enamored with him as he was with her.

Guilt gnawed at me. I liked Richard. He was good to her, a good man who would provide for her. I would have to pretend I was unaware of her mysterious partner and possibly have to lie for her.

Thank goodness no one could divine my thoughts. Lizzie might, but I trusted her not to betray my confidence.

I turned around so my gaze was on the seat in front of me. My heart thundered against my chest in time with the horses' hooves on the path. I sucked in a breath, trying to calm myself. Regardless of my attempts, the panic from earlier returned. I pulled at my fingers, at the material of the gloves, trying to keep any power from manifesting.

Maybe later Marcella would tell me what was going on, if I made it to our meeting on time.

And like that, Claire was forgotten.

CHAPTER THREE

Adrian

There was a traitor in my brothel, and I planned to discover who it was by the end of the evening. Blood's Brothel was practically empty save for the sirens who were my employees. There were six of them, with another shipment due in three days.

My gut wretched at the thought of these mer-women being transported from Underedge and delivered to me as if they were nothing more than cattle ready for slaughter. I did not like the thought of offering them to the Blood Mages who lived on this spit of land, but it was better than them feeding on humans. Humans had families. Humans—most of them, anyway—would be missed. Sirens, on the other hand, would not. As much as I didn't like it, it was true.

"You're pacing like a feline," the bartender said as she continued to wipe down the surface of the bar. Though it was quiet for the brothel, I expected this place to be bustling with potential clients, human and Blood Mage alike, in an hour or two. The disappointed audience, robbed of their fiery execution, would need a way to release their built-up tension. What better way than a different type of consumption, through feeding and fucking. "Is there anything in particular on your mind? Tell me you're not upset about Nyx escaping yet again."

My lips pulled into a tight frown. Jonathan Nyx was a Pyrate Mage who could upend my entire business and expose me and my clientele for what we were. As far as I was concerned, he was a fly and I'd thought he'd finally been caught up in a spider's web from which he could not escape. They could slit his throat so his blood fed the sharks for all I cared. That he had managed to escape yet again said more about the men who roamed the island in red uniforms than it did about Nyx himself. Patrol were incompetent imbeciles and made Nyx look cleverer than I believed him to be.

In fact, this entire Consumption was the perfect night to move the next batch of sirens from my brothel to the sea. I needed to act quickly if I was going to be successful, but if I rushed anywhere, Pepper would start to suspect something was going on. As much as I trusted her, I could not involve her in this. If I was caught, I would be penalized. I refused to let the same thing happen to her.

"I'm more concerned about my mortality," I told her, turning back to the task at hand. If anyone found out I was breaking the bargain of transporting sirens the governor and the king of Underedge entered into, my reputation would be tarnished, and I would most certainly be put to death. Especially if anyone found out I objected on a *moral* level.

"Mortality?" she asked. Though I kept my gaze in front of me, I could feel her staring at my back and I held back a smile of amusement. She had no idea what I was referring to and I was glad for it. "What mortality? We're going to live forever, Adrian, or did you forget?"

How could I forget such a thing? A Blood Mage's life span was never-ending unless someone killed me with silver or sliced my head off. I was unsure which option I preferred.

"Well, I have heard whispers someone is going to try to kill me." I positioned the chair to be exactly across its partner. Rarely did clients come to my establishment to dine, but I liked adding to the atmosphere.

Pepper had gone quiet. "You… What? Someone has the balls to try to kill *you*?"

Someone had discovered what I was doing, I was sure of it. The sirens always brought news, whispering amongst themselves, not realizing I could pick up even the faintest of words.

"You know, I find myself as taken aback by this news as you are," I told her casually. After turning the second chair a fraction so it was perfectly positioned in front of its partner, I moved to the next table. "I found silver shrapnel in one of the rooms during an inspection. At first, I thought it was one of the mer-folk, intent on revenge. Though I'm not the one issuing their transport to Ankura, they sure as hell don't like me even though I give them much more freedom than their people ever had."

This was a lie, but Pepper didn't need to know that.

"Rumors abound there'll be war with them," she said. The squeak at the bar told me she was back to cleaning.

"I would welcome it." I turned to face her, my hands behind my back, and I tried to pick up anything out of the ordinary.

Pepper was better at her job than most. The majority of the taverns lining Ankura's main square were dirty, teaming with sand, dirt, blood, and piss. Seawater clung to the wood like a shadow clinging to darkness, leaving a heady, musky, salt-stained smell, which turned the stomach and reminded sailors of an unforgiving ocean.

I made it mandatory my brothel would be well-maintained, with an emphasis on cleanliness. Pepper understood and made it a point to put out scented candles at each table, lighting them moments before we opened our doors so each room, even the bar area, was filled with pleasant scents to calm the senses and help people drop their guard. A man or Blood Mage was willing to spend more when they were relaxed.

"I'm surprised war hasn't come sooner."

"The king didn't know one of his daughters was killed by a Pyrate Mage," Pepper said.

"Why do you think Jonathan Nyx is being executed, then?"

Interesting point. Murder, especially of a royal Underedge, seemed too absurd for someone like him. I thought he had been too clever to get involved with something so sordid.

I had watched what happened to Jonathan Nyx tonight, watched how the damn Pyrate Mage managed to escape yet again. I didn't understand how one man could be so slippery. It was no doubt why they called him an eel.

"Do we know for certain it was the princess?" I asked. "I heard the body was a waterlogged woman. No identity has been ascribed to her."

"None we know of," she pointed out. "Patrol may be incompetent, but they know how to keep their mouths shut."

"Because they have not a clue as to what is actually going on." I rolled my eyes at the mention of Patrol. Ankura wasn't exactly the safest place to live, especially if one lived in town, within the square limits. The close proximity to the ocean allowed pyrates, thieves, and vagabonds to come and go without many obstacles deterring them. The governor, Warton Beckett, brother-in-law to Reginald Walker, seemed only concerned with catching those with magick.

Other crimes, especially those of humans against humans, were overlooked, especially if a bribe was offered up. The only man I knew on Patrol who was actually law-abiding was Brendan Pickard, although whether it was because he cared or because he had a stick up his ass, I could not be certain.

"I hear Walker and our dear governor have been meeting quite frequently about what to do about it," Pepper said. "Why do you think our protection fee has increased so dramatically?"

"Have they informed the main continent?"

"Not that I've heard of." She shook her head. "Even if they did, I wouldn't be surprised if Cardonia doesn't send Ankura aid. Even though the island is part of their territory, it seems like we're on our own the majority of the time."

I hoped we would not be alone for too long. The clients should begin to trickle in soon, eager to calm themselves from the day's excitement, and indulge in the services I provided.

The door flew open and I smelt him first. It was a human judging by the pungent scent and racing heartbeat. Turning, I recognized the man as someone who had begun to frequent the brothel more and more, especially in the last fortnight. There was something about him that did not belong, something that made me suspicious. He was here for more than pleasure, I was certain.

"You," I said. The back of my neck prickled. "What are you doing here?"

He hesitated, his eyes going to Pepper as though she would help him. I almost laughed. What could he possibly think she would help him with? She was busy tidying up the counter, and I didn't think she noticed him.

"I, uh." He swallowed. "I need to talk to you."

"About?"

He looked to Pepper again. This time, she met his stare, eyes narrowed.

"I know this man," she said through a growl. "He's the one who's stealing from you."

"Is he now?" My lips curved up. "Pepper, set up the storage room. Make sure the door is closed. I want to have a chat with our friend."

CHAPTER FOUR

Hannah

When Lizzie successfully reached home, I jumped out of the carriage. I didn't have much time to waste. Father was out with Patrol trying to find Jonathan Nyx. The square would be bustling with activity. If I could get out now, I might be able to blend in.

Clumsily, my fingers stumbled as I buttoned up an old overcoat that belonged to my father while glancing at my door, which, gratefully, remained closed.

The crash of the ocean outside my window caused my eyes to flicker over to the glass and my heart to jump. I shouldn't be so nervous. Traveling into town at night was something I often did with Father. But this time, I would go alone.

Though the sun had set earlier, I knew from the ocean's rough temperament a storm would be here in an hour or so. I welcomed the rain always. It allowed my mind to go blank. Deciphering lies was dampened, as were thoughts my family would not want me to know of.

Unfortunately, such a thing could not always be helped. I had never been able to control what I was able to pick up from others, though I longed for the ability to drown out the lies.

I finished pinning up my hair and took a cursory glance at my reflection in my mirror. I was unfamiliar with what one wore to a brothel for a meeting with a witch, so I settled on a simple blue dress I hoped would allow me to blend in. From my limited experience, women did not frequent Blood's Brothel as patrons much, and my presence might draw unwanted attention.

A whistle pierced the air behind me and I nearly jumped out of my skin. I turned to see my older sister leaning her willowy figure against the doorframe of my room. I hadn't heard her open the door. She scanned me, though not in a critical way. If anything, she seemed to be curious as to why I was dressing up when it was nearly time to retire for the evening.

"Meeting anyone unseemly tonight?" she asked, bouncing into the room and plopping onto the bed.

I rushed to close the door. The last thing I needed was any of the maids or the servants to hear my boisterous sister's comments. She might think she was being comical, but she was keeping me from my appointment.

"I have to make a collection call for Father, considering he is otherwise indisposed." The lie fell from my lips with ease, because I had practiced it so much. I was grateful Lizzie didn't have my magick.

"Adrian Blood does business only at night and he missed last week's collection. I'm going to see if I can bring his account up to date."

Lizzie made a guttural noise, her finger tapping her chin. Her loose nightgown looked more comfortable than what I was wearing, and for a brief moment a swell of envy washed over me. After the events of the evening, I wanted nothing more than to sleep.

I dropped my gaze, pulling at the long sleeve of my dress to ensure my wrists were covered. "I'm planning to take my leave now, Lizzie," I said, hoping she would take the hint her presence was not desired, at least for the time being. "Was there anything else you needed?"

"Father will not like it when he hears you're going by yourself," Lizzie pointed out, pushing off my bed to stand. Her golden hair—nearly the same shade as mine—fell over her shoulders in thick waves. "Especially after what did *not* happen tonight."

"Father trusts my ability to get what is owed to him," I said, choosing my words carefully. Technically, I was not supposed to be making the collection rounds at all without a guard. Adrian Blood had paid his share, and the rest of the collections had been completed last week.

Luckily, Lizzie didn't know this. She wanted nothing to do with Father's business when she had her own blacksmith shop to focus on. "Leaving a name unchecked in the ledger leaves me uncomfortable, and with Jonathan Nyx's escape distracting Father, I thought it would be best if I handled this on my own."

Lizzie grinned, her eyes turning a warm shade of gold. "I know how meticulous you are,

Hannah." She glanced out my window and her lips turned into a frown. "It's dark and it looks like it might rain. The riots could still be going on. I'm not sure it's safe to go out alone. Do you want me to accompany you?"

"I am perfectly capable of collecting by myself," I snapped. I let out a breath and turned from my wardrobe after closing the doors. My wrists were indeed covered appropriately. I had forgotten about the riots. My intent had been getting to Marcella, but now I wasn't sure the meeting was worth the risk. "Sorry. I—"

"You don't like anyone doubting your abilities." Lizzie squeezed my shoulder. I nearly jumped. I hadn't realized she had gotten so close. My focus had been on trying to hide my face. "I understand. I want you to be safe. You're my little sister. I can't help but be protective. I would tell you not to go, but I know such orders never inspired my obedience."

"I know." I turned from her trying to smooth out invisible wrinkles from my dress.

"I'll see you later tonight, then. I'll be up, so don't think of going on an adventure, especially without me. And please, Han, be safe. Do what you must to save yourself." She said no more. She didn't have to.

She flounced out of my room, her nightgown twirling around her feet, leaving me to my solitude. I bent down and began to check my boots, making sure they were laced snugly. The grandfather clock tick next to my wardrobe rang in my ears. I knew I needed to hurry. My heart fluttered and I pushed stray strands of hair from my face. I didn't want to be swept up in the angry crowd if I could help it. A young woman by herself was akin to a rabbit alone in a forest with a hungry pack of wolves looking to tear into something.

If you do not leave now, you may never get this chance again.

I forced myself to take a step toward my bedroom door, and then another. This was my opportunity to seek guidance from a known witch about the ability that plagued me since birth. This meeting had taken seven weeks and three days to arrange, and I refused to let it slip through my fingers. If I could understand why I was able to detect lies, why I was gifted with this ability—and how it was possible—it might help me understand who I was and, quite possibly, who my mother was, since Father rarely spoke of her.

When I was out the door, I went left and padded down the long hallway, which spilled into a winding staircase. I clutched the smooth banister with one hand and put the other in the pocket of my coat. I glanced around, ensuring there was no one lingering before I headed outside. I stepped carefully, hoping to muffle any noises my boots might make on the wood.

Once I reached the bottom, I all but skipped to the double doors and slid outside. I closed the door behind me, muffling the sound. Men patrolled the perimeter of the house, but as long as I held my head high, I would blend in despite being a young lady without a chaperone.

As daughters to Reginald Walker, my sister and I had much more leeway than other women in society. Sometimes, I took that leave for granted simply because it was always a privilege I had been bestowed. Now was different.

I managed to sneak past the entranceway with the gaudy fountain my mother insisted my father build for the birds when I was seven. I paused a moment to look at it. For some reason, I sprung a chill staring at the emptiness surrounding it. If I squinted, I could see the silhouette of my mother standing there looking at the birds.

It was one of her favorite places to be before…

I snapped my head to the golden gates and forced myself to head in their direction. A couple of guards rounded the corner of the manor, but no one seemed to have noticed me.

From this point, the quickest way to town was direct: keep on the dirt path. I could always slide into the Forest of Legend if I truly wanted to hide, but immersing myself in a mysterious darkness filled with nightmarish lore was something I wanted to avoid. Seeing the forest made me think of Claire and her mysterious companion. I wondered if she made it home safely and made a note to ask her about it the next time I saw her where we were able to discuss it freely.

Monsters live in the forest, my mother would always say. *Blood Mages who long to take your blood and feast on you until you bed them to end everything. Lycans with teeth as sharp as spears and claws as powerful as cannon fire.*

I used to believe her. As I got older, I realized she was lying. Monsters lived everywhere. Regardless, the forest gave me a bad feeling and I wanted to stay away from it if I could.

The night air stung my cheeks like a slap. Thunder rumbled overhead, but there were still no signs of rainfall. The stars and the moon were blotted out by heavy charcoal clouds so full I was certain water would spurt out at any moment. The darkness helped cover my movements, but my vision was not as sharp as Lizzie's, so my pace was slow and somewhat clumsy.

The closer I got to town, the louder it became. I could hear individual voices—men and women alike—still shouting out prices and items they were trying to sell. There were two distinct types of people on Port Ankura: those with money and those without. It still surprised me to see how far into the night people were forced to work to earn even a pence, perhaps two.

Despite the dark, light spilled out from the various businesses still open.

Candles and fire caused iridescent glows from the windows. I passed Lizzie's artillery and blacksmith business: the lone venue shrouded in black shadows. Lizzie didn't need to make a living so there was no reason for her to be there, and no one dared to steal from the unmanned shop. Everyone knew who my father was and what he would do if Lizzie or I were threatened in any way.

I ignored the men and women still angry over what happened at the Consumption tonight and kept my head down. I couldn't afford to be recognized, even if it would ward off their advances. There were too many people who weren't fans of my father and the collections he enforced, and one way to get to him was through his children.

Glass shattered. Someone broke a window. Flames licked the galley by the ocean, and one man began pouring ale on the wood. I had to hurry while they were still distracted.

It took no more than a minute or two before I crossed the circle and arrived at the brothel.

Blood's Brothel needed no advertising. The building had three levels and was new and well taken care of, unlike many of the other businesses in the circle. I had been here before a few times with my father, when he had discussions with Adrian Blood.

I hoped I didn't encounter Blood tonight. The last thing I needed was my presence here alone getting back to my father. I had no idea if Blood was here or if he was still somewhere within the boundaries of the square, swept up in the riot.

I pushed the door open and was embraced by warmth, thanks to a nearby fire crackling in a hearth.

I tried to see if I could find Marcella, expecting the lobby to be teeming with people. I was surprised to find it nearly empty. There was a barmaid washing a glass and two men sitting on wooden stools at the far end of the room, but no one else.

Tentatively, I stepped forward. Maybe Marcella was hiding somewhere where no one could see her, where no one could recognize her. She might be waiting for me to enter the room before showing herself.

"Can I get you a drink?"

The voice startled me. I pulled my gaze away from an armchair with its back facing me— maybe Marcella was sitting by the fire, trying to keep warm—and focused my attention on the barmaid. There was weariness in her pale blue eyes, and it appeared as though her shift had barely begun.

"Um, no thank you." I took a seat at the other end of the bar hoping to be undisturbed. I didn't like having my back facing the door—I wanted to see who came in and went out—but I didn't want to be near the strange men in the corner either.

The barmaid harrumphed before turning back to her glass.

I drummed my fingers on the bar, trying to lessen how obvious it was I was waiting for someone. Low murmurs caught my attention, and I tilted my head up.

There was a room behind the bar. Most likely a storage room, but for some reason the door was cracked open and I could see a tall man leaning over a chair, his face contorted into a scowl that sent a chill deep into my bones. There was something graceful in his brutality, in his anger, something I didn't expect to see.

Adrian Blood. He was an imposing figure, regal, vicious, and shockingly beautiful. Whenever my father brought me with him, I had to remind myself not to stare. It was easy to be captivated, which was dangerous. The few times he regarded me it was with knowing blue eyes that caused my insides to melt and my muscles to tense.

He unnerved me, and yet I still responded to him. It was both embarrassing and thrilling at the same time.

"...tell me what I need to know." His voice was low and gruff. Soft-spoken yet jagged. If the lobby weren't so empty, I wouldn't have been able to hear him.

"I can't—" The person Blood spoke to seemed to gasp. Whether it was because he could not catch his breath or if it was because he was afraid of the wrath emanating from Blood, I couldn't tell. But there was something in his voice, something that caused me to take notice.

"I suppose I could give you an opportunity to catch your breath."

Adrian stepped back and I straightened. His voice was venomous, his icy blue eyes like diamonds. Although I had seen him a few times before, it still amazed me how tall and solid he was. His shoulders stretched, broad and unmoving, and muscle packed his form. He seemed inordinately strong, though his body was not overtly bulky.

"In the few seconds remaining of your life, it is imperative you choose what you do next wisely," he continued, turning his back on his victim. "I have noticed an important discrepancy in my books. Someone is stealing from me. The amount matters not. Both are equal offenses. It is always on your shift, human. Money disappears when you stand behind my bar, which tells me you are either the responsible party or you know who is. The fact Pepper accuses you speaks volumes. She never lies to me."

"I... I know nothing."

The voice was pathetic, barely there at all. I winced. I began to pick up on Adrian's frustration, laced with a brutal anger unmatched by anything I had ever felt from someone before. More than that, I found myself distracted by what he had called the man in the chair.

Human. He'd said it like an insult.

I turned my attention to the victim. I should mind my own business. I should continue to look for Marcella. But there was something strange about this exchange. The man was not what he appeared to be. I scented danger.

I know nothing. It was a lie.

Adrian paced over to a window and seemed to be staring out at the sea. His jaw was clenched, his elegant fingers curled into tight fists.

The victim was moving in his chair, slipping out of his restraints. He held something shiny in his hand. The chill down my spine intensified as I identified the sharp pointed knife.

The barmaid exited the room then, a case of ale in her arms. She closed the door with her foot, preventing me from seeing what was going to happen. The case filled her arms, and she lifted it as though it was nothing. She seemed unperturbed by what was transpiring in the room if she noticed it at all.

"Wait." The word was out of my mouth before I could stop it. In fact, I was on my feet and moving around the bar. I threw open the door as the victim tossed down his rope. "He's lying. He has a knife—" I clamped a hand over my mouth to keep anything more from spilling out.

Adrian whirled around, not even looking at me, and used his strength to pick up the victim—who had faltered the moment I stepped into the room and spoke—and threw him against the wall. He collapsed into a heap on the floor, his head at an awkward angle. The knife dropped and spun on the floor, in a dark imitation of a spin the bottle game.

His neck had snapped. He was dead. Because of me.

Before I could collect my bearings, Adrian appeared in front of me. "I believe thanks are in order." His eyes pinned me to my place, a cautious curiosity causing them to sparkle oddly. "You saved my life, Ms. Walker. As is customary for my people, it would seem I owe you a debt."

CHAPTER FIVE

Hannah

I didn't need Adrian Blood owing me a debt. He was not the sort of man I wanted to get tangled up with. I took a step back. Which was difficult to do. Nothing physically blocked me from leaving, but his piercing gaze compelled me to stay. I had met him before on numerous occasions when I helped my father with his collection and he never looked at me so intimately before. It was as though I was a book he possessed, finally decided to crack open, and was surprised to see what I was about.

"You are Reginald Walker's daughter." He took a step forward and glanced behind me. I kept my eyes fixed on him, not feeling comfortable enough to let him out of my line of sight.

I nodded once, struck mute. Blood's reputation was he took advantage of the weak and vulnerable. There was a reason he was one of the best businessmen on the island. My father would never admit it out loud, but I believed he felt partially threatened by Blood since the other man knew how to *do* business. Running a brothel on an island known for debauchery was ingenious and my father resented him for it. At least, I assumed this was the reason.

"What, pray tell, are you doing in a scandalous place such as this?" He stepped forward. "Are you here on your father's behalf? Has he added yet another fee on top of the one he added when word spread we might go to war with Underedge and that army of fish?"

I knew I should step back. Even more, I should leave. I risked a glance over my shoulder to see the door was closed. No one was there and I wondered what had caught his attention earlier.

"I doubt your father would be happy knowing you were here after dark by your lonesome." There was a smug smirk on his lips, which seemed to cause his blue eyes to thaw, but only slightly. It added to his haunting beauty.

I regarded him again. Adrian Blood was correct. Father would not be pleased if he found out I was here alone. I had to think of a reasonable lie, one even Adrian Blood would believe.

"I came here to review your books," I managed to get out. My voice still shook despite my best efforts, but at least the words were solid. "There were a couple of discrepancies."

"Hmm." He didn't believe me. I didn't need to possess any sort of magickal ability in order to figure out that much. He lifted his hand to cover his chin. His shoulders hunched forward, but he made no move to come closer. "Why not schedule an appointment with my assistant and review these so-called discrepancies during the day? I didn't think your father worked past five in the evening, much less sent his precious daughter to review the books so late by herself."

I lifted my chin. As much as I wanted to, as much as my insides shook, I refused to cower before him. "I'm sure you realize I'll be taking over for him one day," I said. "I need practice. I do not need an escort everywhere when my father manages Ankura's businesses, including trade, and my uncle governs the island. As for why evening, I understand you choose not to do any business during the day. Why speak to an underling when I could speak directly to you?"

He stared at me for what felt like much longer than was necessary. Finally he smiled, revealing his teeth.

"Do you happen to have your father's copy of his ledger?" he asked. "Because I cannot
see a bag, and I highly doubt it fits into your too-tight bodice."

Despite the fact I wore my jacket, I still shifted with discomfort. The last thing I needed was to let him get under my skin by needling me with things a proper lady should not talk about. It was moments like this one when I wished I were more like Lizzie.

"I do not carry it on my person, no," I admitted. I glanced to the ground beneath my feet. There were a couple of crusted stains, a dull red in color. If I didn't know any better, I would have thought it was blood.

"You were merely excited to come to a brothel all by yourself? Tell me, have you been to a brothel before without a proper escort?"

"Absolutely not." I should have controlled the disgust apparent in my tone. He was never going to believe I came here to discuss business if I was clearly uncomfortable with his business in the first place.

"You sound appalled by the prospect." He crossed his arms over his chest, angling his large body to the side. His eyes remained fixed on me. "Do you take issue with my business?"

"As a business, brothels will always bring in profit, especially in a popular port where seamen and degenerates frequent," I said. This discussion had nothing to do with the books and nothing to do with saving his life. "Which means it's an intelligent decision as a businessman to invest in an idea that will always generate revenue."

"But?" Adrian prodded.

"But," I said, "morally, I find the whole idea repugnant."

He chuckled. "I like you, Hannah Walker," he said, surprising me even further. He pressed his finger to his lips, as though he wanted to prevent his smile from getting any bigger. "You are not afraid to say what you think, are you?"

"It depends on to whom I'm speaking."

"Tell me, are you afraid of me?"

"Do I have reason to be?" A tense silence grew between us. Not because he was angry or upset. If anything, he seemed intrigued by my response.

"You saved my life tonight." He took a step back and turned, arms still crossed over his chest.

"I did," I said.

"Why?" He whipped around, his eyes narrowed. All playfulness had left him. He was intense in his severity.

"Why did I save your life?" What sort of question was that? "I don't understand. Did I do something wrong?"

"What makes you think you've done anything wrong?" he asked.

We were going back and forth almost as though we were in a battle of wits. I wasn't impressed. I placed my hands on my hips and tapped my foot.

"I'm sorry, am I keeping you from an important appointment?" he asked, stepping back from the window to look at me. His eyes were guarded, and it was difficult to read him. I was surprised I was able to discern any sort of emotion on his face. "I thought you were here to see me specifically."

"I am."

"Then why do you seem aggravated by a simple question?"

"I don't understand it," I repeated. "Why would you question me about saving your life? Should I not have done it in the first place?"

"I ask because I'm trying to understand your motives. Nothing in this life is free. Nothing is genuine. What do you want from me?"

"I ask of nothing from you," I said, offended he would say such a thing. "I merely reacted. I saw—"

"Perhaps your feminine intuition detected something was amiss from your seat at the bar," he mused, stepping toward me. Instead of waiting for him to corner me, I began to move around the small room. "You overheard the conversation and grew nosy. The door was cracked open. Pepper hadn't completely closed it. Something she will atone for once I'm through with you."

I stopped my pacing. "Through with me?" I asked.

"I apologize, have I offended you? Do you think I honestly believe you're here to meet with me about money discrepancies?"

"Judging from your near-death experience, I can assure you I am." I was surprised by how strong my voice sounded. "You were interrogating someone to the point you were going to die over it. I'm not sure what further proof you need."

"It surprises me Reginald Walker cares about my money loss," Adrian said, not bothering to mask his bitterness. He walked over to the weapon on the floor, picked it up, and regarded it before placing it in a drawer in one of the side tables.

"You are under my father's protection," I said. This was obvious to me. Surely he had the wherewithal to understand this as well? "If someone trespasses against you, they trespass against him. He would want to right the wrong done to you because it represents a wrong done to him as well."

Adrian started to laugh, a low sound void of any amusement. It sent a chill through my body, and I turned away, fixing my eyes on the window.

"I'm sorry, is something funny?" I asked.

I shouldn't care one way or the other about what he thought of me and whatever amused him. However, I couldn't help it. I missed my chance at meeting with Marcella and wound up saving his life by mere chance. I didn't expect a thank you, and I most certainly did not do it for his gratitude or for him to owe me a debt. It felt as though he was toying with me and I did not have the patience for it, even if he believed he charmed me.

Goodness, this man is so annoying.

"Actually, yes." He stopped his laughing to regard me once again. "If you think your father cares about me and frivolous discrepancies, you are sorely mistaken. I hate to be the bearer of bad news regarding your father, since it's clear the two of you are close, but your father only cares about one thing: profit. If another business doesn't fall under nepotism rising, he will crush my business before I can figure out who is betraying me. I would not be surprised if your father is paying someone to betray me in order to take me down from the inside."

"How dare you," I exclaimed. For a moment, I forgot who I was speaking to. I forgot Adrian Blood was supposed to be intimidating. I forgot I didn't want to draw any more attention to myself than I already had. "Without my father, you, sir, would have no business."

"False, girl." He leaned toward me. He was so close, our breaths joined together. "I would merely have my business in a different location."

"Then why don't you leave?" I demanded. His glare did not deter me from speaking the truth, even though it should have. That was what happened when emotions ruled me, and I did not like it one bit. "If you are so unhappy with the way my father runs the businesses on this island, you are free to leave, Mr. Blood. No one is forcing you to stay."

"Why should I leave when I've done nothing but make a profitable business benefitting both me and your father?" Adrian asked, crossing his arms over his chest.

"If it is making my father a profit, what reason does my father have to sabotage you?" I asked. "You make no sense."

"And you do not see what is directly in front of you. Your father is not the man you think he is. You know this. You refuse to admit it, but you know this."

"I know nothing of the sort."

"Then I misread the type of woman you are."

"What type of woman do you think I am?" I asked.

"An intelligent one."

I didn't want to think Adrian had the ability to flatter me. He seemed like the sort of man who was witty and clever, which I always found was a deadly combination.

My palms moistened with perspiration. I looked outside to the sky, blotted out by the foggy glass of the window. Darkness had consumed the island. A shudder rippled down my spine. Darkness was always the setting in the stories our father used to tell me and my sisters before bed. It was when Blood Mages came out and took advantage of the ignorant or the badly behaved. I still didn't like being alone at night, but meeting with Marcella seemed worth it. Now, I regretted coming here at all. Adrian looked like a pretty picture, but his eyes held secrets—dark secrets I never wanted to discover.

"Hopefully, you will learn who your father really is," he said. Slowly, he paced over to a small shelf and pulled out a logbook. "I have the numbers here if you wish to review them. If you choose not to, your secret is safe with me."

"What secret?" I asked.

"That you were here for yourself," he said. He offered me the book, but I didn't take it. He smirked as he placed it back on the shelf and walked toward me once again. I remained standing where I was, though everything inside of me wanted to run. I almost did when he curled a stray lock behind my ear. "You are a grown woman. You're entitled to be selfish."

"Society disagrees," I said, though I had no idea how I was able to do so considering my mouth had gone dry at his mere touch.

"Fuck society," Adrian said. He let his finger linger on my ear a moment longer and then dropped his hand to his side. "I did not jest when I told you I owed you a favor. You saved my life. I am indebted to you, whether or not I want to be."

"Hmm." I could formulate no response. "I shall be taking my leave."

"That is probably a good idea."

I stepped back, keeping my eyes fixed on him until my hand hit the doorknob and I opened the door. I didn't trust him. I didn't want to turn and leave myself vulnerable and exposed.

"Good evening, Hannah." Adrian bowed his head.

"Good evening," I said before stepping back into the bar.

Only when I hit the back of the bar, nearly bumping into a wench, did I feel safe enough to turn and all but dash out of the brothel. Even then, it felt as though his eyes were on me the entire way home.

I was unnerved by our conversation, by the fact he seemed inclined to owe me anything at all. I feared this put me in a position I didn't want to be in.

I didn't want anything from anyone, especially Adrian Blood.

CHAPTER SIX

Adrian

"Who the hell was she?" Pepper's voice broke through my thoughts, and I forced myself to look away from the exit. I turned to face her, hoping I appeared indifferent. She had a knack for reading me better than anyone I knew. The last thing I wanted was for her to recognize I was intrigued by some girl who could discern truths from falsehoods. My perception was strong and attuned to the magick of others. I did not want Pepper to know of Hannah Walker's gift.

"A chit of a girl who thinks she's rebelling against her difficult life as Reginald Walker's daughter," I said as smoothly as I could muster.

I strode across the lobby to place the chairs on top of the table so the housekeeper could mop. Cleaning was something I never partook in simply because I had better things to do, but I had too much energy burning inside of me and I needed to do something with it. Under normal circumstances, I would have fed on a woman. Not a siren, but a warm-blooded human. I would have peered into her eyes, charmed her into going up to one of my rooms with me, and made her feel so good she begged me to sink my fangs into her flesh. When it was over, I would have made her forget everything.

But not tonight.

"You seem frazzled by her presence," she said.

I placed a chair on top of a small table. Though she said nothing more, I heard a note of insistence. She believed there was more to it and wanted answers.

Hannah's presence had unnerved me. She had saved my life and didn't ask me for anything in return. More than that, she was

Walker's daughter, the one poised to take over his business once he turned old and decrepit as humans were wont to do.

I was counting down the days until I was no longer under his thumb, only doing as he bid me to. If I were not required to follow orders, I would have considered tearing his throat out simply because he had the audacity to charge me exorbitant protection fees. It was no secret the man was corrupt, but after tonight, after meeting Hannah directly instead of seeing her in passing during his collection runs, I believed there was more to her than being her father's shadow. There was an innocence about her, an innocence that drew me in and wanted to get to know her better. How could someone who lived under Walker's roof be so terribly naïve about the sort of man he was?

"She saved my life," I said. I needed to say the words to remind myself it wasn't a figment of my imagination, a wisp from a dream. I might have been too proud to admit a human, of all things, had saved me from another human, but there was more to Hannah than her unfortunate humanity. "Now I owe her a debt."

"A debt?" Pepper picked up a mug and began to inspect it with a careful eye. "How do you think you'll repay her? She does not seem to be the sort who'd let you show her a good time."

"No," I agreed. "She does not." I pushed Hannah from my mind for the moment. "Pepper, I want you to use your ears. The human I killed came to kill me with a knife embellished with silver. Clearly, he was stealing from me, but I doubted he was stupid enough to try to kill me, especially since he knows what I am."

"Have you met the population of Ankura?" she asked. "He *could* be that stupid."

"I want to make sure it's nothing more than that." Perhaps the guilt I felt regarding the siren transport was eating away at my rationality. There was something not right about this situation, and I wanted to ensure the matter was truly settled. "I need you to see if there is anyone who would want to kill me enough to send a human into my establishment with silver. Who would be so bold as to attack me in my own brothel?"

"If that happened," Pepper said.

I gave her a look. I didn't need her arguing with me over whether it was possible something had happened.

"Someone who knew about the Consumption and tried to take advantage of it?" she surmised. She cleaned the inside of the mug and inspected it again. "Someone who knows what you really are?"

"Who knows that besides other Blood Mages and my employees, whom I've insisted say nothing?" I asked. I saw a table with wax staining the surface of the table. I used my fingernail to try to chip it. Someone must have removed the candle to make a mess like this one.

"Walker knows," Pepper pointed out.

"Walker does not want me dead," I told her. My gaze remained on the table. "He wants my money and he *knows* I'll give it to him. No. This is someone else."

"The Pascals?"

"They're tucked away in their wealth on Cardonia," I said. "The king has his nose so far up their asses his face will be stained with shit. Why would they deign to come over here where they aren't worshipped likes gods among men?"

She remained silent, going through three more glasses before putting them away. Each glass found its correct position and was angled in a precise manner. I appreciated her attention to detail. Pepper was one of the older Blood Mages, one of the first I watched the Ice Enchantress create. She knew how to curb her craving for human flesh, even though I was certain she wanted it as much as any Blood Mage.

"I don't like how stupidly courageous they are," she finally said, leaning against the surface of the bar, long strands of hair spilling over her shoulder. "To think he could have killed you in the storage room." She scoffed.

"What I need to figure out is who he was doing this for," I replied. I walked over to the fireplace and grabbed a poker from the tin. I poked the ash a couple of times in contemplation. At any moment, that could be me. Nothingness. Flecks of ash caught in the wind, dispersed across the sea.

"A jealous lover?" Though I could not see her, Pepper's smile filled her tone.

I rolled my eyes at the insinuation. "I try to keep my distance from the attached," I reminded her. "Too messy." I paused and shifted my weight, crossing my arms over my chest and leaning my hips against the table. "There was something about him that seemed calculated. He was nervous, to be sure, but it's more. He came here with a deeper purpose. To kill me. Hence the weapon. But why…" I let my voice trail off.

"Why does it matter *why* it happened?" Pepper asked. She dropped her wash rag into a bucket and looked down at her hands with a sneer. "The only thing that matters is someone tried to kill you and we need to figure out if we killed the threat or if someone else will strike to finish the job."

"If I find out why, I should be able to narrow down who," I said.

"You think the human can help?"

It always surprised me when Pepper knew what I was thinking. It happened rarely but when it did, it left me unsettled. I kept my face as smooth as I could, dropping my shoulders and angling my head to the side.

"I am willing to see if such a thing is possible." I didn't want Pepper to think I was more invested in Hannah than I was. "But I cannot count on humans. You know this."

She scoffed. "They're only good for fucking and feeding." She gave me a sharp glance. "Isn't that right?"

"You know I cannot feed on humans," I said, ignoring her comment. I strode to the next table and picked up the chair. "I'm entitled to a siren's blood as anyone else."

"Tell that to Charles Rochester and his vile beasts," she scoffed and reached for one of the glasses. "I've heard whispers they hunt humans for sport. They're the Lost. Those that get bit and turn into what we are. They weren't created with ice magick."

"His kind aren't within my jurisdiction," I said. I lifted the chair with ease. "I have no concern about them unless it involves exposing us as a whole. If Patrol discovers we aren't a

fairy tale—"

"I thought Walker and Beckett know of our existence," she said, cutting me off.

"As long as their pockets are lined, they retain their power, and their precious daughters remain unharmed. They don't care about us as long as we abide by the rules," I said. The mention of Walker sparked an idea I didn't expect. "Walker might know who tried to kill me."

"It's possible."

My lips curved in a smile. It was a lead. It might lead nowhere, but it was a start.

CHAPTER SEVEN

Hannah

The next morning no sun shined outside my window, only clouds pregnant with rain. One of the maids my father had deemed as a lady-in-waiting—though our family had no relation to royalty or Legacies or anything of the sort—came in and assisted me while I dressed. She helped me pin my hair to my head and powdered my face. I was not particularly fond of makeup, but I did not push her away like Lizzie did. It was easier to let them do what they wanted rather than fight about it. I could always wipe it off.

The moment I headed out of my room Harrold was there. His eyelids were at half-mast, his body as rigid as a wooden plank.

"You have a visitor in the foyer, Miss Hannah," he announced.

My heart skipped a beat and prickles of apprehension swarmed over my neck. Unlike Lizzie, I didn't get many visitors. My father frowned upon me receiving them for some reason he never told me. "I shall meet them in the drawing room," I instructed Harrold. "My father…"

"He is in the study, going over the books, mum." He turned back to the staircase. "I believe we'll be having important guests soon."

"Good." The word came out of my mouth before I could stop it. I hadn't meant to show my relief out loud. However, if my father was currently distracted, I doubted he would care if someone had come to visit me, which gave me more privacy. "Send tea and biscuits into the drawing room, please," I told Harrold. I folded my hands demurely in front of me and began to descend the staircase, trying walk with a confidence I did not currently possess.

"Yes, mum." His voice had a hint of condescension to it, but I ignored it. If he could ignore my slip of the tongue, I could ignore his.

While Harrold went down the hall to cross the foyer to the kitchen, I cut right and hastened to the drawing room. It was the one room in which my sisters and I could welcome our guests. If they were my father's, he would meet them in his study since it gave them more privacy. The staff was prone to gossip, and my father knew this. Unfortunately, there was nothing I could do about it. Whoever it was who'd come to call upon me, I would have to be careful how I received them. There were eyes everywhere and they would tell my father things if it procured them extra coin.

Once in the drawing room, I took my usual seat on the crimson settee. My father had them reupholstered and the fabric was soft, caressing my bare skin as though it was attempting to soothe my racing heart.

Harrold stepped through the door a moment later. "A Mister Richard Dartmoth," he announced before Richard strode in. He looked as if he had not slept. Dark circles lay heavy beneath his eyes.

His appearance piqued my curiosity. What was he doing here? Had we agreed to meet, and I forgot? After what occurred last night, it was a possibility. I wracked my brain, but I found nothing I could recall.

"I shall fetch the tea," Harrold said, but Richard raised his arm to stop him.

"Excuse me, Harrold, but I shall only be a moment or two."

Richard took his seat and I saw something was troubling my friend. The fact Claire was not with him spoke more than words were able to.

"Richard?" I asked the moment Harrold closed the door and gave us much needed privacy. "Is everything all right? Where is Claire?"

I remembered her strolling through the stocks of grass with a stranger. A stranger who was certainly not Richard Dartmoth.

A strange sound came from his mouth, a cross between a sob and a choke. It was something I never expected to hear from him. He had always been cool and strong, ever protective over Claire, eager to start their life together. He was handsome, came from a good family, and accumulated his own wealth by practicing medicine.

"Claire is…" Another sob escaped his throat and tears were fresh in his eyes. "Claire is…"

Harrold interrupted us with a tray of tea and biscuits, despite Richard's statement he wouldn't be here long. Considering I'd told Harrold to fetch the tea before I even received Richard, I was glad to see the butler still respected me enough to listen, despite his subtle flippancy.

I reached out and poured a cup of tea, hoping it would soothe Richard. When I offered it to him, he shook his head, still looking distraught. I put the teacup and the saucer on my lap, holding them like a strange source of comfort. He sucked in a deep breath as he straightened his shoulders.

He looked into my eyes and said, "She's dead, Han."

His voice seemed matter of fact, and I supposed in the medical profession such precision in delivery—especially with bad news—was a good thing. But it felt cold. Almost uncaring, even though I could see the emotion in his eyes, even though I could still hear those noises from moments before. "I can't believe she's dead."

I blinked, slowly setting down my teacup. "I'm sorry," I whispered. "I thought you said Claire was dead."

"I did."

"Ah." My thoughts raced. I wanted to ask about the man but I couldn't formulate the words. Richard was already distraught. I didn't wish to add to it by telling him about Claire being with a strange man last night without a chaperone. "And…it was natural? She was not, um, murdered?"

"Murdered?" His gaze went to my shaking hands as tea began to splatter onto the saucer. "Hannah, are you all right?"

"W-what?" I narrowed my eyes at him and stood. The teacup dropped from my hands, shattering on the wooden floor. Tea stained the hemline of my dress. I began pacing up and down the length of the room. "Of course I am not all right. You told me my friend is dead. How could you expect me to be *all right*?" My stomach twisted tightly but my insides were as thick as a rope. I wanted to vomit.

Everything came rushing in from last night, which felt like an eternity ago. I had forgotten all about Claire and her companion. I forgot about it until Richard walked in the room. I felt guilty.

Horrified. My friend was dead because I didn't stop for her. I retched dryly and took hold of the mantel.

Before I knew what he was doing, Richard jumped to his feet and took my hands in his.

"Let's not get hysterical, Han," he said. His voice was gentle. "Also, I never said murdered. I said she was dead."

"What's the difference?" I asked. "What else could she die from?" My mind went back to the man she was with, and my body seized up. My grip on Richard tightened like he was my lifeline.

"A tragic accident," he said. "A beast, something dreadful. With all the rioting going on, it doesn't surprise me no one heard her scream."

"Actually," I started as I pulled my hands from his and resumed my pacing as guilt wove its darkness through my stomach. I made sure to step around him, avoiding his touch. I wanted something to sink my nails in. I wanted some release for the pain I felt. "I think hysterics is the appropriate way to act, don't you, Richard? Your fiancée was killed, but the way you tell me the news, you're a wooden plank."

This wasn't fair. I had seen the emotion on him. I knew he was feeling great sadness. But I couldn't stop myself from lashing out as the guilt gnawed inside of me, scratching at my innards.

"Are you saying I'm incapable of feeling frivolous emotions?" he asked, his voice raised.

Despite our apparent privacy, I knew raised voices would catch the attention of someone who happened to be passing by the room. I also knew if my father overheard Richard speak to me thusly, he would have him escorted out immediately.

Richard seemed to realize his misstep. He raised his hands, palms facing me, offering a silent apology.

"I am trying to be strong," he said, his voice tight. "You must realize it is not you affected by her death. It is not me, either."

I nodded. That much was true. Claire had both parents and an older sister she did not particularly get along with, but whom she loved. Richard got choked up when he told me, and yet something bothered me about the delivery of his speech.

"More than that," he continued, "I'm used to delivering bad news to a patient's family and I have found the recipients tend to prefer it when said news is delivered by a steady voice. My profession requires me to be emotionless, and it would seem such a thing has transferred over. I do apologize. I would never want you to question my feelings for Claire."

I shook my head. "Of course," I said. I opened my mouth, ready to ask where she was found, and if anyone was found with her. I didn't wish to rub salt in a wound by bringing it up when he was wrapped up in his own grief, but I needed to know, had I called out to Lizzie to stop the carriage, if Claire might still be alive.

Harrold stepped in with a new cup of tea before cleaning up the mess I made with my old one. *See. Ears everywhere.* I reached for the cup as Harrold quickly swept up the shards of glass, the pieces tinkling against each other.

"Of course," I continued after taking a long sip. I took a breath. The questions danced on my tongue, but I swallowed them down. I didn't want to hurt Richard any more than he already was. "I don't know why I even mentioned it. I apologize. Of course, you must be in pain. I hope I did not add to it."

"No, no." He leaned forward. "May I add cream or sugar to your tea?"

Harrold disappeared with the trash, shutting the door gently behind him.

"Yes, both. Thank you." He took my tea from my shaking hands, which I folded in my lap.

His handsome face was calm, but his eyes were filled with something, an emotion I couldn't decipher. When he handed me the tea, I thanked him again and blew on its surface. Steam disappeared over the edge of the cup before I took a small sip. The liquid warmed my throat all the way down to my stomach. I was surprised how cold I had become. Then again, news of death was never something that brought warmth.

"So," I said, trying to figure out the right words, "the investigation…"

"What investigation?" He grabbed a pastry and leaned back against the settee.

"Surely Patrol were called in to investigate? To ensure the death was…tragic rather than purposeful."

"Oh, yes." He heaved a sigh, clearly exhausted. "You know," he dropped his voice, "Patrol doesn't have a reputation for reliability."

"I can put a word in with my father," I offered before taking another sip of tea. "My uncle, even. I'm sure they can encourage Patrol to be more thorough?"

"I appreciate your offer, Han, really, I do. I don't know if that's actually going to do anything in the grand scheme of things." He shrugged before taking a bite of pastry. He chewed with his mouth closed, his head angled to the side thoughtfully. "Patrol have been… I don't want to speak ill of those offering their help, but you know they answer to the king, not our governor."

"It's not really an offer if it's supposed to be their job," I pointed out. I didn't conceal my bitterness. Richard knew how I felt about Patrol. They were men—women were not allowed to join—who had a god complex and wanted an excuse to lord their power over others, especially those deemed beneath "polite" society. "You need not speak politely of them when it's the two of us."

Richard chuckled, nearly choking on his pastry. His eyes lit up, dancing with mirth. It was nice to see him smile, despite his current circumstances.

"Have they said anything?" I asked, placing my teacup and saucer on the table between us. "What happened to her? Who discovered the body?" I leaned forward.

"An anonymous person." Richard dropped his eyes, his smile vanishing. "They never told me who. I did not think it mattered at the time."

"Sometimes, those who choose to remain anonymous are the ones who are behind the crime."

"That's rather morbid," Richard said. "Remember, this was not a crime. Tell me, what makes you say such things?"

"It's the truth," I said. My voice rose an octave higher even though I struggled to keep it down. "Don't you want to find out what happened to her? She was your fiancée. You were going to start a life with her and now that life is gone."

"Don't you think I know that?" He dropped his head, his hands digging into his long, brown tresses. "Please, Hannah, tell me more. First, you insinuate I don't give a damn about the death of my fiancée, and then you pepper me with endless questions and insinuate, once again, I don't seem to care because I can't keep up with them."

I opened my mouth to say something, to apologize or maybe defend myself, when I decided shutting it would probably be best.

"I apologize," Richard said.

I looked into his red-rimmed eyes. "Why are you apologizing?" I asked. "You weren't the one who acted so thoughtlessly."

"My language was unfit for a gentleman," he said. I reached for my tea as he straightened. "The truth of the matter is, I am completely distraught. I have no idea where I am supposed to go from here. I was looking forward to starting a life with Claire. She is—*was*—my best friend and now she's gone. I haven't quite reconciled that."

I dropped my eyes to my tea. The amber liquid moved in a clockwise direction, slow and deliberate. My heartbeat slowed to match its rhythm, pointedly ignoring the swell of guilt pressed heavy on my chest.

"What next?"

He shook his head. "I spoke with Patrol, who mentioned looking at her body, but I doubt any real investigation will come from it. Her body was found a few hours ago so there's not much they can do, at least not right now. I believe they're waiting on a mortician to examine the body in order to determine cause of death."

"Surely a death is enough to set aside proper decorum?" I snapped.

"Oh, Han, I'm so happy to know you," he said, his eyes going over my face. "You have more spirit than most. I suppose that was why Claire enjoyed your company so much. I know that's why I do." He caught my eye again. "I'm sorry. I feel as though I'm losing control of myself."

"There's no need to apologize, Richard," I told him again.

"All I know is her body was discovered in the Forest of Legends," he said. I froze. My skin pricked with goose flesh up and down my body. "I didn't see it myself, but the way they described it…" He let his voice trail off and a shudder ripped across his body. "It seems she was brutalized quite badly. I don't wish to use the same words they said to me in fear of upsetting your delicate sensibilities. Trust me when I tell you it was bad."

I set down the teacup and took a breath for good measure. I opened my eyes and forced a smile on my face.

"Thank you for thinking of me, Richard." I hoped he heard the sarcasm in my tone even if he wouldn't comment on it. I didn't appreciate he'd determined my sex was too fragile to hear what happened to my friend, even if the facts were gory. I wanted to know the truth. Richard nodded once.

"To answer your question," he continued, leaning back in the settee, crossing one leg over the other, "Patrol plans to interview any witnesses at some point today. They've moved her body from the forest to their headquarters."

I was not terribly familiar with forensic science, and yet even I knew moving a body without proper precautions could contaminate any clues that could potentially lead to the murderer.

"They have promised they'll keep the family informed of their investigation, but…" He let his voice trail off again, shifting his eyes away from mine. He picked up his half-eaten pastry and shoved the rest of it in his mouth.

Why was he lying to me - what was he hiding?

I cleared my throat as grief took hold of me.

"I think they're trying to close the case with no real work done," he said.

Richard continued to speak, but I didn't hear. My mind kept going back to Claire being attacked by a beast. As far as I knew, there was no beast on Ankura so brutal, strong, and vicious enough to kill a human being. More so, Richard had not mentioned a second victim. I wondered if Claire's handsome stranger managed to get away or if he led her to her death on purpose.

I knew Richard was lying about something, but I wasn't sure exactly what.

I needed to get to the bottom of this.

And I would, no matter what it took.

CHAPTER EIGHT

Adrian

This morning's news was ominous. A woman drained of blood and left in the Forest of Legend could not be written off as a regular murder. Luckily, the attack was brutal enough it might be disguised as an animal attack, but the truth of the matter was there was not an animal alive that could attack the way a Blood Mage could, especially one not in control of themselves.

Not any woman was murder. This woman worked for me. She helped me transport the sirens to safety and she met the same end as the other before her, Anne, the waterlogged woman Patrol believed Jonathan Nyx had murdered.

When her identity had been confirmed, at first I thought her death was an unfortunate accident. Anne had been a thief who stole away on ships, hopping from island to island. Due to her extensive knowledge of secret hiding places on ships and the quickest direction of transport, she had the exact knowledge I needed.

However, Anne's lifestyle meant she risked her life constantly, even before working for me. The death of these women made me realize both had been targeted. Someone had found out what they were doing for me. It was clear to any Blood Mage one of our kind had killed Claire.

The moment the sun touched the horizon and the darkness overpowered the day, I stepped onto land and headed straight for the brothel. I needed to figure out what had happened. Blood Mages were like human men—they talked when they drank too much, especially to a pretty woman coaxing the information out of them. Perhaps one of the whores or one of the wenches knew something. I needed all the information I could.

By the time I got to the brothel, the lobby was half-filled with men and Blood Mage alike waiting to be taken care of. I spied Pepper behind the bar pouring a pint of ale for a human client while a familiar Blood Mage, Marcus Sawyer, waited for Pepper to give him her attention. He came from the main continent of Cardonia and had been on Ankura for a few months. It was obvious he was halfway in love with her. If I wasn't consumed with the news of the dead girl, I would have found his presence annoying and pathetic. Pepper didn't believe in love, especially considering the life expectancy of Blood Mages.

If only I had Hannah's ability, I would round up every damn Blood Mage I knew and demand to know their whereabouts the night of the Consumption: what they were doing and who they were with. The idea settled in and I considered it a moment longer. I was tempted to use Hannah to tell me what she discerned from the interrogation. Yet there was something inside of me not wanting to expose her to what I was and what others were who lived on this island.

I had to find another way.

I scanned the lobby, unsure who I was looking for. A couple of men straightened, cocking their heads in my direction. A woman brushed my side, murmuring a gentle "Excuse me," before leaving the room. The men were not looking at me. Rather, they were looking at her, waiting for her to notice them.

I smiled and turned from the lobby. I needed to feed first, but once I was finished, I would begin to interview the girls here. They must know something. I would ensure each person who had important information knew telling me would be worth their while.

***

I began with the youngest of the Sirens.

Hessia was beautiful but cold, with hair a shade lighter than wheat and big sea-green eyes that seemed able to penetrate even the hardest of surfaces.

"I'm told you know something about the human who thought he could kill me," I said, stepping into her room, "and whether it has to do with the two slain women."

There was a chill in the air that only came from the stillness before the rain. Her window was open, the curtains fluttering in the gentle breeze.

"I knew of him. He was a sailor," she said fiercely, her eyes burning emerald. "The gossip is someone paid him. Told him exactly what he had to do in order to accomplish your death. Clearly, they want you to stop what you're doing with us."

I stilled. There were only a handful of people who knew how to kill me. Even fewer who knew what I was doing and with whom. Hessia's gaze flashed to the ocean, longing shining through. I shifted with discomfort. Blood Mages were known for shielding their vulnerability, and witnessing a flash of emotion she couldn't control left me unsettled.

"And you did not think to tell me sooner?" I asked carefully, each word clipped.

"I owe you no loyalty," she all but spat before turning her gaze back to me. "What you need to ask yourself is *who* is powerful enough to attempt to kill you so publicly, and whether such an enemy knows what you're doing with my people."

I left her room without another word and headed straight for my personal chambers. Though I slept on my ship during the day as was necessitated by my immortality, I kept my own room in my business so I could feed and be alone.

I stepped through the double doors, making sure they locked behind me. My staff knew not to disturb me under any circumstance when I was here. I passed the couch and my desk, heading for my room with my four-poster bed adorned with blue silk sheets that resembled the color of the darkest part of the ocean.

Hessia's words tickled at my mind. I had many enemies. Though Reginald Walker and I were civil, I would list him as my enemy. I knew not to trust him under any circumstance. But to attempt to kill me? The fact he'd sent a human told me he either knew the man wouldn't be able to kill me or he was incredibly stupid.

The governor didn't approve of me or my business, but as far as I knew, neither of them knew I was going against the secret bargain between Ankura and Underedge as it related to transporting Sirens to Ankura as food for Blood Mages. If they had found out, I doubted much would change, save for the fact Walker would have more of a reason to increase his protection fee as long as he ensured my secret was kept. Beckett, on the other hand, would probably turn me over to Underedge as a way to prove his loyalty to the bargain.

I was surprised neither had yet to approach me about the latest dead girl. Considering I was in charge of the Blood Mages here, any disturbance would rest on my shoulders, and they would want an explanation. If they viewed the body, they must have some suspicion she had been killed by a Blood Mage. Then again, maybe not. Perhaps they were too preoccupied with other things. Or willing to hide the situation under the cover of some made up "beast."

For now, I needed to reach out to Walker and see if he had any information for me. Anything I should know regarding these investigations. At the very least, he would want to increase my collection fee since the threat of exposing Blood Mages was real, and with this latest death, my presence at his home would be welcomed.

I was also looking forward to seeing Hannah Walker again much sooner than anticipated.

CHAPTER NINE

Hannah

The morning of Claire's funeral, my cousins came over to break their fast. My uncle wanted to confer with my father about the progress on working out a peace treaty between Ankura and the Underedge water kingdom, but things did not appear to be going well.

I took my seat, still not dressed in what I would be wearing to celebrate Claire's life, and the food, though savory and rich in both scent and taste, did not tempt me enough to do anything more than pick at it.

While we sat, Lizzie talked of the Consumption, or lack of one. She delighted in stirring up scandalous topics to get a reaction out of others, but I never would have expected her to make the assumption one of us had anything to do with what happened that night.

"Lizzie?" I asked slowly, turning my eyes to her. "What *are* you talking about? How could one of us have helped Jonathan Nyx escape?"

"There is much you don't know about our family's magick," she replied, a serious glimmer to her hazel eyes. "I recognized it, of course."

I was nearly ready to shush Lizzie—her mouth constantly ran wild, and I didn't appreciate she was so willing to divulge our secrets, even to our cousins. I didn't trust them with something as serious as my powers. Not because I did not care for them the way family should, but because I did not want to risk myself. I was uncertain whether Kara had anything to do with milking my magick from me that evening. If she did, it would imply she knew about me. While it could not be helped, I didn't need everyone else knowing it.

Jonathan Nyx had been arrested eighteen times for his magick, and somehow he always managed to elude Consumption.

I did not think I would be so lucky.

"You know something of it?" Jessa asked, her red hair spilling over her shoulder. Jessa reminded me so much of Lizzie—fiery temper, rebellious nature—but she was outfitted in a dress rather than pantaloons and a tunic. Lizzie's masculine clothes ridiculed Father. Some of the town's inhabitants had loose tongues, but she didn't care. As far as I knew, he had no intention of marrying Lizzie off anyway. Deep down, I think he wanted her and Brendan to resume their broken engagement by allowing her to behave in a way that was off-putting to other men.

"You know of our magick?" I asked, looking at Jessa. My cousins all looked somewhere around the room rather than at me or Lizzie. "You do," I said. I turned my attention to Lizzie. "You knew? About them knowing about us, and having magick of their own?" To know my sister was well aware of this and chose not to tell me made me wonder whether there were other things she was not telling me. Lizzie kept her arms crossed over her chest, her face indifferent to my question. "And you did not tell me?"

Her face hardened from raw stubbornness.

"Are you saying you both have something wrong with you?" Everly's penetrating blue eyes shot to me before shifting over to my sister.

"Wrong?" Jessa asked, offended. She shook her head, giving Everly her attention.

"Everly—"

"If you say these abilities are a gift, Jessa—"

"That is *not* what I was going to say," Jessa said. The two seemed familiar enough with each other to cut the other off and not get terribly upset by it. "But to completely dismiss your magick as bothersome is an insult to our mother."

"We aren't even certain our magick stems from her line," Everly said, but her tone implied to think otherwise was folly.

"Maybe if we ask Aunt Thaya," Lizzie suggested.

"Aunt Thaya?" Jessa asked. "You mean the woman who lives in that small village in the middle of the Forest of Legend with other women because she does not wish to abide by the laws of man and would rather follow the laws of the earth? Our mothers did not even speak to her. What sort of information do you think we will find there?"

It sounded suspiciously like a coven, but certainly Thaya was not bold enough to think she could live so openly where it challenged the law and risked their exposure.

I should visit her. She might have seen something that would be useful in solving Claire's death.

"We are getting off topic," Everly said, holding her arms out to her sides as though she wished to keep Jessa and Lizzie's annoyance at bay. "Lizzie, what makes you think one of us would even want to rescue Jonathan Nyx from the Consumption? He is more trouble than he is worth, quite frankly."

"So he should be condemned to die because he uses his magick freely while we choose to hide ours?" Kara asked.

Jessa arched a brow at her sister's passion, and I echoed her sentiment. Kara rarely spoke out of turn, especially when it came to anyone older than her. She pulled at the sleeve of her dress, her mouth curving into a frown.

"I suppose that answers the question then," Everly said. "You freed him, did you not? Another bout of your uncontrollable magick surfaces once again." She snorted. "Why can you not get hold of your ability? Why is it so difficult for you to control yourself?"

"I did not release him," Kara insisted. At Everly's cutting stare, Kara averted her eyes. "You think magick is that easy? I'm *sorry* I can't seem to grasp my abilities. If only we had a teacher to help us with this craft."

Lizzie held up a hand. "Stop fighting," she said, making sure to keep her voice down.

"What you all need to realize is that someone—one of us—freed Jonathan Nyx at the Consumption, putting our entire bloodline at risk. I need to know who did it to ensure it does not happen again."

"You realize there is more magick in Ankura than the five of us?" Jessa asked, her arms crossed casually over her chest, her red hair dropping from her coiffed bun and into her face.

"Clearly, Nyx is a Pyrate Mage. Magick is being sold in the square as we speak. No one is trying to hide it, save for when the Patrol roves around pretending to actually care. It's why Lieutenant Pickard is always barking orders and Henry Davenport is trailing behind him like some poor, drunk puppy." She dropped her gaze to her fingernails, clearly not impressed with the two men in charge of Patrol on Ankura. "I know I could go into the square right now and buy a love potion or a concoction to keep myself looking youthful for the rest of my life."

"They may be a farce," Everly pointed out. "You are aware businessmen take advantage of a woman's desire to look a certain way, to get a man to feel a certain way."

"They do," Lizzie agreed.

"Regardless, *real* magick is being sold in the square," Jessa pointed out through a huffed breath. She did not like opposition to the points she insisted were correct.

"*Regardless*," Lizzie said. "It still puts us at risk because we all have magick. We've all used magick, whether intentional or not." Her gaze lingered on Kara, who could not hold her cousin's stare, tucking hair behind her ear. "We all know the five of us are linked through our mothers, who vanished under mysterious circumstances. No one likes to talk about magick on Ankura or anywhere on Wyntura, but we must if we're going to learn where we come from and what we're truly capable of doing."

"Who shall we talk to about this?" Jessa asked, no longer interested in her nails as her cerulean blue stare locked on to Lizzie's. "Each other? Our mothers are gone. Therefore, there is no one else to speak to about this."

"Ah." Lizzie put one finger up. "This is where I'd like to bring Thaya back into our conversation."

"Thaya?" Everly asked. "You cannot be serious. Mother barely talked to her when she was here."

"Maybe there was a reason for it," Lizzie said. "Maybe Thaya knows what happened to her sisters. Maybe Thaya has magick."

"Then why has she stayed away for so long?" Kara asked. My eyes widened slightly in surprise. Kara rarely spoke up against anyone. "If Thaya is good and wants to assist her nieces, why not come to us and say something?"

"She might not feel it's safe to do so," Lizzie countered, turning her head to face Jessa, who was currently drumming her long fingers against the surface of the table. "I doubt she'd want to risk us. What would it look like if she suddenly came back into our lives after years of not being there at all?"

"Why is she *not* already in our lives?" All four heads turned to look at me, their gazes on my face. My cheeks pinched with the unexpected attention, and I cleared my throat. "I think it's a fair question. Even when our mothers were here with us, she still did not visit. The last time I remember seeing her was during a birthday celebration for Everly, who had turned a year old." My eyes focused on my youngest cousin. "She was there to wish you luck, prosperity, and beauty. She drank cherry wine and danced with a variety of men who sought her out due to her beauty."

I was only two years older than Everly and yet I remembered the day vividly. Perhaps it was because it was one of the last days I saw Mother.

"She has her reasons," Lizzie said, interrupting me from my thoughts. "I'm sure of it."

"You sound as though you know," Jessa said. She stopped drumming her fingers on the table. "Tell me, dear cousin, has our aunt been in contact with you since leaving the family?"

"No." Lizzie's eyes dropped to her lap.

Lie.

I sucked in a breath. Lizzie was lying. But why?

"Then why do you think she knows anything about our mothers?" Jessa continued to pepper Lizzie with questions. Lizzie was going out of her way to ensure she did not look at me.

She must know I had picked up the lie.

"Because the three of you have some sort of abilities, as do the three of us," Lizzie said. "If magick is inherited, it stands to reason our magick comes from our mothers' line. Which means our aunt could possibly possess the same magick we have."

Truth.

At least, Lizzie believed it to be true.

"Even if you're correct," Jessa said, sweeping her hair back, "why has she not reached out to us and discussed this with us directly? Why keep to herself? We are her sisters' daughters. We are family, and we share this genetic trait. If she can help us, and she knows she can help us, why doesn't she help us?"

"Maybe she cannot?" Kara guessed.

"Or she does not know," Lizzie said. "We need to reach out to her."

"How would we go about doing that?" Everly demanded, her gaze darting around the table. "We have not seen her in years. We cannot simply ask Father about her."

"Wait," I said. "Your father does not approve of Thaya's presence either?"

Everly shook her head. "He rarely talks about her, but every now and then I'll hear him grumble about her under his breath when he assumes I'm not listening." Everly's contempt for her father was palpable. Jessa rolled her eyes at her sister.

"Angry words for the favorite one," she pointed out.

"Father only approves of me because I have not disappointed him," Everly replied, her expression flashing a warning. "You painted a scarlet H on your back earlier this year with your illicit affair with Charles Rochester. And Kara looks more like Mother than any of us. He defaulted to me because he had no choice, not because I've earned it in any way."

Jessa held up her hands. "Regardless of everything that's happened," she said, "it's clear we all have magick. Perhaps we've not all known this in some form or another, but it's the truth. One of us freed Jonathan Nyx from the Consumption."

"We don't know that," Everly said.

"What do you mean?" Kara asked. She was pressing her finger into the surface of the table but stopped upon hearing Everly's words.

"As much as Lizzie would like to believe one of us was responsible for Jonathan Nyx's escape, the truth is, we do not know who did it," she said. "Why would one of us release Nyx? Why would it serve us?"

"A life does not need to serve in order to retain the privilege of living," I pointed out, careful not to look at Kara. I also tried to keep my defenses up. Lizzie or my cousins might try to decipher my thoughts, and I did not want them to know my part in this or Kara's.

"Yes, but why would any of us risk ourselves for a Pyrate Mage?" Everly asked, her tone cold and dismissive. "He is a criminal. He would hang even if he did not have magick simply for the crimes he's committed."

"And the good deeds he's done?" Kara asked.

"Good deeds?" Everly scoffed. "He steals from the wealthy and distributes it to the poor. So what? Did you see the way the townspeople reacted when they saw he escaped? When they realized they weren't going to witness him dying by flames? They went mad. Lizzie, your business was damaged in the process."

"What if they weren't angry?" I asked slowly, my mind racing with thoughts. "What if they provided a distraction so he could escape?"

"You believe all the townspeople in Ankura care about Jonathan Nyx so much they would try to free him?" Everly asked.

"More than that, you believe they have the intelligence to organize something as complicated as freeing him from a public Consumption?" Lizzie asked.

Everyone was silent, each turning over the pointed questions.

At that moment, my uncle stepped into the dining room. "Come now, my lovelies," he said. "We must return home before the funeral."

I nodded, snapping myself out of my reverie. I could not shake the thought I was on to something.

I withdrew from the table and headed up to my room to change. I took my time. There was no reason to rush. I was not sure how long I was in my room until a knock startled me.

"Your father wants to know if you are ready," the maid said.

"I will be out shortly." I turned my attention to powdering my face, though I was not sure where to start. Usually, someone else did this for me.

The maid curtsied and left, shutting the door behind her.

I dabbed the brush in the powder before caressing my cheeks with it. Magick rushed through my bloodstream, the tingle causing my muscles to tense.

I looked down at my hands, wishing I could see the magick in its physical form. With my gloves blocking any means of that, I curled up my fingers and dropped them to my lap. I sighed, taking in my appearance.

Another knock on the door made me jump.

"If I have any more bloody interruptions, I will never truly be able to get ready for this thing," I burst out. My shoulders, my neck, my torso, my arms, all burned with magick looking for an outlet. I tensed every inch of my body I could. The last thing I wanted was another bright light beaming out of my home.

The door creaked open. I whirled around, ready to tell the maid I was still readying myself, when I stuttered. There stood my father, dressed in all black, fiddling with the cuff of his coat. I swallowed any retort I might have had for my sister.

“I hear you’re being difficult,” he remarked as he strolled into my room. He seemed to fix whatever was bothering him and dropped his arms to his sides. “As you should be. It is a rather difficult day for you.”

My father had never been cruel, but he had been cold, and there were many times I didn’t think he could begin to understand what I or Lizzie went through as young women in Ankura. The fact he was here, grabbing my brush with one hand and gently tilting my head back, spoke volumes.

“You know, your mother rarely bothered with makeup,” he said as he slowly brushed powder onto my cheeks. “Said it was unnecessary. That her beauty was given to her by the Earth and should be respected as an untarnished gift.” I was not sure how to respond so I said nothing. He moved to my other cheek, as delicate as he had been with the first one. “You remind me of your mother, Hannah,” he said when he finished, putting the brush on the bureau.

“Oh?” I hoped the crack of my voice was indiscernible. “I thought Lizzie had more of Mother’s spirit.”

“Nay, she has mine. I suppose that’s why she and I do not get along, why your uncle and I get together and commiserate because our eldest daughters are our spitting image. You, on the other hand, are everything your mother was and more. This sadness you feel, this anger, these are normal feelings. Like a sea in the throes of a violent storm, this too shall pass, and your waters will grow tame again. Do not be afraid to feel, my dear. Feeling reminds us we are all alive and tells us what we are capable of.” He tapped my nose playfully. “Some might even say we’re capable of magick. But that is between you and me.” He winked.

I peered at him carefully, tilting my head to the side. Did he know? Could he know?

No. He could not possibly… But maybe…

“Well, my dear, it is time we go to this funeral,” he said, patting me on my knee with affection. “They will be missing us.”

"Will Uncle be there?" I asked, more out of curiosity than anything else.

"I don't think so," he said, straightening. He offered me his arm. "He is busy with this Jonathan Nyx mess. Each ship at the harbor has been searched and Patrol insists no ship left here in the last week, which means Nyx is still on the island."

"Unless he can swim the sea," I muttered before I could stop myself.

"Only sirens and mer-men are capable of such magick," my father said, though there was something curious about his tone. "Nyx may be a Pyrate Mage, but he is certainly no merman. You do know that, correct?"

"And Blood Mages?" I asked before I could stop myself. "Are they real?"

My father peered at me, the interest in his eyes mixed with something else. "Blood Mages?" he asked slowly. "Why would you ask about them?"

"I—" I stopped myself from responding. He seemed to know more about me than he let on, and yet I was still unsure. My father had a duty to my uncle. My uncle had a duty to his port and his king. If they discovered I had magick, would they condemn me to death? If they did not and someone found out, would they be the ones condemned? Would I meet the same fate as Jonathan Nyx? "I apologize, Father. I did not mean to speak out of turn."

"No, my dear, I never said you did." He made his way to the door of my bedroom. "You are more than encouraged to ask questions. My concern is who informed you of Blood Mages?"

"No one," I said softly, my mouth dry. "Mother used to recite stories when I was a child as a way to keep me from the Forest of Legends, and I know other parents did the same. I thought they were bedtime stories with a monster that did not exist."

"Your mother told you about Blood Mages?"

I nodded.

"I see." He rubbed his chin. "What did she say about them, exactly?"

I followed him to the door. "She said they were the worst sort of monsters because they were created to hide in plain sight, dripping charm the way their victims dripped blood. She insisted Lizzie and I never interact with them under any circumstance. I thought she was emphasizing her point."

"She was," my father informed me, opening the door. "But she was also telling the truth."

"The truth?"

"Blood Mages are real, Hannah," my father said as we walked down the hall. "They are more dangerous than you can imagine."

CHAPTER TEN

Hannah

My father's bleak words had no time to sink in before we were ushered into a carriage, along with Lizzie, and taken down into town where Claire's body would be laid to rest. The only land available to the people of Ankura for loved ones who had passed on was south of the northernmost harbor. It required one to cross the square in order to access the land, but once we passed it, the grass was green and overrun, the trees tall, their thick, pleated leaves blotting out the sun, and the flowers were wild and bold with the freedom to grow as they wanted. The land here was more rural, and if one continued in the same direction, past the small cemetery, they would be easily immersed within the Forest of Legend.

The square was still being cleaned up after the small Consumption riot. As far as I knew, there had been no arrests made. There were a few injured, but no deaths. I shivered and shoved my gloved hands in my lap. Lizzie shot me a concerned look, but I ignored her, still not ready to forgive her over her lies.

I pulled my stare away from my hands and looked out the carriage. I did not like being so close to the forest. Considering this was where Claire died, it left me unnerved and uncomfortable. I glanced through the branches and leaves, waiting for a monster to emerge and attack us the same way it had attacked Claire. Suddenly it struck me Claire's companion had not been found. In fact, I didn't think anyone realized she had been with someone else.

I needed to tell Lieutenant Pickard.

Once the carriage came to a stop, Harrold opened the door and helped us out. As much as I wanted to disappear in the crowd to look for Brendan, decorum did not allow me such freedom.

The ceremony would be inside the small church. Marble statues of the Five stood in a line behind the pulpit, looking across the small room with forlorn expressions on each of their faces. Even the Moon Mother peered down at me with a carved frown across her perfect face, arm outstretched as though she wanted me to go to her, drop to my knees, and confess my sins.

The blank stare unnerved me, and I was forced to drop my stare. No one knew I had seen Claire that evening. No one besides Lizzie.

The crowd was small and filled with people I knew. They huddled in small groups. Like attracting like. My gaze scanned the familiar faces, hoping to find Pickard. When I was met with no success, I frowned. I would expect him to be here, if only to discover potential suspects. He had given me the impression the attack was not some ravaging animal and Claire was in the wrong place at the wrong time. He seemed to believe, like me, there was more to it.

The twittering of the crowd stopped and everyone seemed to straighten simultaneously. The atmosphere shifted, and I glanced behind me to see my uncle and my three cousins enter the small place of worship. I was surprised to see my uncle after Father mentioned he might not come. They were flanked by two guards who were his personal guards and not Patrol, and their attire was black with an insignia of the Beckett crest stitched into the left breast—a raven with a purple eye surrounded by a gold shield. The eye was supposed to be all-knowing, and the gold was supposed to symbolize wealth and prosperity. It seemed to peer at me from across the room and I shifted my weight, uneasy under another accusing stare.

I wound through the crowd of people, trying not to draw attention to myself. I followed the dark crimson carpet all the way to the altar where I knelt down, carved a line with my chin down to my chest, and then touched the five points of my body that symbolized the Five: forehead for thought, left shoulder for youth, right shoulder for age, heart for love, and lips for spirit. It was something Mother instilled in Lizzie and me, though Lizzie was not as pious. When I finished, I stood then turned around. My uncle was in a huddled discussion with my father and Lizzie was talking to Everly. Jessa was scanning the room and Kara was fiddling with purple beads on her dress that nearly mirrored the design of mine.

Now seemed like the perfect time to speak to her. I made my way to her before Kara realized it.

“Kara,” I said, giving her an easy smile. “So good to see you. I need your assistance with something. Do you mind?”

I knew she would not refuse, even though it was clear by the way her green eyes glanced to the left and to the right she was unhappy about it. She offered me a small nod and stepped through the small gathering of cousins. We proceeded to an empty corner of the church and I gave another cursory look around. I did not see Brendan, or the preacher ready to begin the ceremony. I also wanted to ensure we could speak freely without anyone overhearing.

“I will not speak about the Consumption,” Kara said in a hushed whisper before I even got the opportunity to speak.

“I need to know what happened,” I returned, my eyes flashing. “M-Magick spilled out of me. I didn’t realize I could do that. I did not know my m-magick could, could come out in such a way.”

I did not like saying the word magick, and yet, I managed to stutter it twice. I bit the inside of my bottom lip, as though that might assist me in overcoming my affliction.

“You have magick that can do a lot of things,” Kara said. She tucked a stray strand of hair behind her ear. Her hair was a darker gold than mine, but she had beautiful waves she could not seem to manage. Each time I saw her, there was always some lock of hair in her face, and she was always attempting to push the hair away. “As can mine.”

“Clearly,” I retorted. “What did you do that night? Tell me. Did you manipulate me?”

“What?” Her voice rose and a couple of people turned to look over at the two of us. Kara rubbed her lips together, nostrils flaring. She tucked her chin down, trying to keep her patience. “I would never use my powers to manipulate you, or anyone, for that matter.”

“Well, what do you expect me to think?” I asked. “I felt my energy buzz through me. I can’t explain it.”

“Neither can I,” Kara said. Her voice small and unsure. Gently, she chewed her bottom lip, tugging at her finger. “I… I knew I didn’t want Jonathan Nyx to be Consumed. I couldn’t stop myself from thinking about it. I didn’t realize I was casting something. Maybe your magick heard my desires and the two fused together.”

"But what happened, exactly?" I asked, trying to read her face. She had difficulty hiding her emotions, much like myself. "Nyx was sheathed in iron. Iron is the only known resource able to inhibit all magick."

"That's what they want to believe," Kara pointed out, her voice low. "But I wouldn't be surprised if that was another lie they tell us to keep us afraid of them."

"What do you mean?"

Kara dropped her chin to her chest and started picking at the beads on her dress once more. One of the beads was hanging by a single thread, ready to fall off the gown completely with another tug.

"We don't know anything for certain," she said, looking back up at me. "This power that flows through our bodies is a mystery. We both know that. As a result, we don't know what's a natural inhibitor for it. All we know is we have it and they want to control it. They want us to not exist. The Consumption ritual was created to keep us at bay."

A woman in a black and white dress began to pass out small pamphlets. She reached Kara and me, smiling as she extended her hand to each of us. It was incredibly expensive to re-create even a passage from the Statera Holy Book. However, many places of worship tried to do so at least once a month, as though it was important to them they be regarded as a pioneer in worship. It amazed me that even holy places were in competition with each other.

When she left us, I folded the brittle piece of parchment. "How do you know all of this?" I asked.

Kara sucked in a sharp breath. "I don't, actually," she said. "It was a guess." She shook her head. "I am uncertain as to what happened to Jonathan Nyx. All I know is I did not want him dead. As a Pyrate Mage, he would have been burned at the stake, his soul consumed by the flames."

"They believe he's some sort of demon sent from Hell," I pointed out, fixing the angle on the parchment. "As such, they think fire will send him back." I frowned. "Why are you so concerned with Jonathan Nyx, anyway? Is he some sort of acquaintance of yours?"

Kara shook her head. "No," she murmured. She started fiddling with the bead again, the parchment crumpled in a ball in her fist. She got this faraway look in her eyes like she was remembering something from another time. “I met him once when I was younger, around ten or eleven. I was standing at the docks by myself. I believe Father was inspecting a merchant ship personally and I was to wait on the docks because of some ridiculous superstition about women on boats. Nyx looked like a dream. He was leaning against this wooden leg that held up the dock, his eyes on my father, arms crossed casually over his chest.”

She mimicked what Nyx had done in her memory. “He could not have been older than eight and ten, perhaps even twenty. Eyes rimmed in kohl. Red sash around his boot. He appeared strangely beautiful, though he was not tall nor particularly muscled. His skin was bronzed from the sun. His face was like a masterpiece, completely unmarred by any flaws. I was transfixed.” She swallowed, returning her gaze to my face. Her cheeks were stained pink, as though she was ashamed of herself for thinking this way, especially regarding a criminal such as Jonathan Nyx. “I could feel his magick from where I was. I could feel the warmth, the sparkles the same way the ocean looked under the rays of the sea. In him, I recognized myself and I did not understand that until I saw him with a bag over his head waiting to die. I could not let it happen.”

“So, you used my magick to free him?” I asked in a low whisper. I leaned forward to ensure the others would not overhear me.

“I had no idea what I was doing,” she replied, shaking her head. I did not need to use my ability to know she was telling the truth. “All I knew was I wanted to stop it in some way, even if it cast suspicion on me. I wanted him to be free.”

“We don’t know if it was mine or yours that did the trick,” I told her.

Kara dropped her gaze to her hands, sheathed in silk black gloves, as mine were. “I’m not so sure,” she said. “I can barely control my magick. It seems to respond to how I’m feeling in the moment. I’m surprised my magick did anything at all.” She locked gazes with me again. “Your magick freed him, Hannah. Your magick is more powerful than you realize. You should not be so afraid of it.”

“I am not—”

“You are,” Kara said. “I see it like I see my own magick. I cannot control it. You refuse to familiarize yourself with yours. How can you do anything by shutting it out?” She reached out and squeezed my hand. "I am sorry for your friend. Truly. But you can take matters into your own hands. You could solve this if you really wanted to. Do not be afraid to go after what you want, even if you need magick to do it. If I were able to control mine, I would have freed Nyx myself."

Before I could respond, she gave me a curtsey then disappeared into the crowd. I caught Richard looking at me and he nodded at me. I knew he would want me to sit next to him, and so I would. After one final look for Lieutenant Pickard, I sighed, and made my way to my only friend, Kara's words echoing in my ears.

Her accusation stung. I stared at my hands again, tired of seeing nothing different and yet feeling as though everything was. If it *was* me, if *my* magick caused his escape, I did not regret it. Jonathan Nyx might have been a Pyrate Mage, but he did not deserve to die. It irked me to think my magick could react to Jonathan Nyx and save him without me knowing, but the same could not be said for Claire.

Why didn't I stop? Why did I pass her by?

I could make this right. I could figure out what happened to Claire, but I would need to use my magick to get to the truth.

CHAPTER ELEVEN

Hannah

The first thing I needed to do was figure out what happened on the last day of Claire's life. I wanted to reach out to her parents, but I knew they had to be grieving and wouldn't wish to be disturbed. Instead, I sent a quick correspondence to Richard about requiring his assistance with Father's books. I was much more educated in accounting than Richard could ever hope to be, but men tended to underestimate women. I planned to take advantage of that. Also, I figured Richard would want an excuse to make amends for his behavior a few nights ago. Though we sat together at the funeral, we didn't speak much and there was still tension between us. I wanted to give him the opportunity to get back into my good graces.

He arrived on time in much better spirits than he had been when I'd seen him last. After greeting him in the foyer, I led him down the west hallway and to our library. This was a safe place to work, where I knew we wouldn't be disturbed or overheard the way we might have been in the drawing room.

There were shelves and shelves of books lining the grand room. A settee and couch were in the middle of the room with a small table on either side of the furniture. At the far end of the library was a large desk. Unlike Father's desk, this one was void of papers and unrolled maps, scattered pens, and spilled ink. I had already procured Father's book on Adrian Blood and opened it to the most recent page. I remembered Adrian believed he was losing money. This was the perfect cover to get Richard talking, especially since it was the truth. Hopefully, I would be able to see if I could pull any information from him I didn't know. More than that, I would be able to tell if he lied about anything.

"Go ahead and make yourself comfortable," I said. "I'll have Harrold fetch us some tea and biscuits."

I stepped out of the library, trying to ignore my guilt. Richard was my friend, as was Claire. Was it wrong of me to trick him the way I planned?

Not if this gets you more information on Claire, the voice in my head pointed out. I brushed an errant strand of hair behind my ear and took a breath before moving down the hallway to fetch Harrold. Already, the guilt subsided.

***

It took me a few minutes to return to the library. I wanted to make sure my timing was perfect so Richard felt comfortable before I started asking questions.

Of what he had shared, nothing had stood out to me as strange enough to warrant a check on his true intentions, except for when he initially told me about Claire. The change in his demeanor had become so abrupt—to be so shaken up and then so clinical seemed odd, along with his explanation of why.

There *was* a good chance he was withholding information from me on purpose because he wanted to protect my "feminine sensibilities."

"Harrold will bring us tea soon," I announced when I stepped back into the room. "Have you begun looking at my father's books?"

"Not yet." He smiled though around his eyes he looked exhausted. "You mentioned something about Adrian Blood?"

"Yes." I reached the table and pointed to the book I had already opened. The strong, musky scent of parchment invaded my nostrils as I pointed to the most recent transactions Adrian had reported to my father. "Adrian Blood seems to think one of his employees is stealing from him. He has no proof other than his notes. I wanted to check our books to see if he's being honest reporting his numbers in the first place before Father offers his assistance."

"He doesn't know which employee?" Richard placed both his hands on the desk and leaned into his palms. I stepped to the side before our shoulders could brush, my eyes fixed firmly on the pages.

"As far as I am aware, no," I replied. I couldn't sense Adrian was lying, but that didn't mean he was being truthful. Anyone could manipulate the truth, and I still had a lot to learn about my skills. "I thought you would be the perfect person to assist me."

I pointed to the numbers. "These look the same," I said, "and I expect them to be the same as those he reported to us."

"Does he know the dates of the missing money?"

Drat. That was a good point. Adrian never mentioned dates.

"I believe the past fortnight," I said, clearing my throat. The irony of my own ability was while I could detect lying in others, I was terrible at lying myself. Luckily, Richard seemed to be too immersed in the numbers to notice.

"I'll start looking." He turned back one page, placing his index finger on some of the figures.

I nodded, and gave him a couple of moments to focus on his task before I sauntered back to the old settee. My gaze flickered over the shelves of books my parents collected.

"Any news from Patrol?" I asked casually.

I pretended interest in a thick book with a green spine and ran my finger down it. Dust accumulated on my fingertip, and I rubbed it off with my thumb. When was the last time I had been here, had read anything that would allow me to escape from this world? My mother used to read to me when I was young. Books filled with adventure and romance, books that made my heart pound with anticipation and a little bit of fear. After she disappeared, it was difficult for me to return to the library, so I stopped. Now, though, I realized how much I missed it.

"Huh?" From the corner of my eye, I saw him shake his head. He did not look up, which was a good sign. "No, not as far as I've heard. They might have contacted Claire's family."

"Any word on the body?" I asked. "I know you said it appeared as though she was attacked in the forest by a beast, but have they discovered anything else that changes this outlook?

There was a beat of silence, and for one fearful moment, I thought he figured out my ploy. I risked a glance at him, as he muttered to himself and copied a couple of the figures down on a blank piece of parchment.

"What was that?" Richard offered me a distracted grin. "Patrol are still investigating but I don't think there was a reason for her to be in the forest. Claire is fearless, but she is also clever." He stopped. "I apologize. She *was* clever, *was* fearless." He paused. I reached out and squeezed his hand gently before releasing it. He took a moment before he continued, "There would be no reason for her to be in the forest in the dead of night. I assume she was meeting someone." His tone was hollow. "It's the only thing that makes any sense. Which could mean something nefarious took place."

"I thought you said it couldn't be a deliberate killing," I replied slowly, trying to control the way my words wanted to stumble out too quickly.

"Yes, based on the original nature of her body," he said. "But when I heard her blood formed a stream in the forest rather than the outskirts, like she was within the boundaries and dragged out—" He cut himself off and took in a shallow breath. "I apologize. I've spoken too vividly."

I closed my eyes and listened to his words. For the most part, there was truth to his response. But there was something else, something I couldn't quite put my finger on.

"Hannah?" I snapped my eyes open and faced Richard's concerned gaze. "Are you all right? I'm sorry, I said too much."

"No," I said a little too quickly. "No, I appreciate your candor."

"You know," he said, looking back down at the ledger, "I cannot find anything that would indicate some sort of theft is taking place. Is it possible the recording of the figures itself is incorrect?"

"What do you mean?" I asked, momentarily distracted by his question.

"The numbers might match up, but the total monies collected do not match up to those figures," Richard suggested. "There's a good possibility Adrian Blood has someone he trusts to go through the revenue each night, or each week, and they found a discrepancy. Because everything here seems to be accounted for."

"Huh." I crossed my arms over my chest, stepping away from the stack of books. "Perhaps you're right and he made an error." I pursed my lips and turned away from him. The time for subtlety had passed, and I needed answers. "You said Claire's body was brutalized. Did you see it for yourself?"

This question captured his complete attention. His eyes flashed with sympathy.

"Han," he said. His gaze was firm, but there was a softness in his eyes that caused my stomach to turn. His expression spoke more than his words. "You can't see the body. You know this. They've already removed her from the forest. It would be better if you didn't see it anyway. As strong as I know you are, I don't know how you would react. When I set my eyes on her, I nearly retched. I left the morgue immediately and I have been wracked with guilt ever since."

There were so many things I wanted to respond to. Why did he assume I wanted to view the body? Clearly, he had seen Claire, probably to identify her. I didn't understand why he would leave the morgue so quickly when he had the chance to study the body to see what he could find, see if he could pick up anything that might help the investigation. Clues could have been left on the body. Clues Patrol might not be intelligent enough to deduce unless Pickard was leading the investigation.

"Han?" Richard's voice snapped me out of my thoughts.

I forced a smile. "I can only imagine all you've endured," I said, hoping he wouldn't pick up the way my words were stilted.

"It isn't me," he responded. "We've all felt Claire's loss. We will forever be changed by it."

Again, there was more to his words. I wondered once more if he was hiding something to protect me and bristled. I couldn't detect an outright lie, more a sense of a truth not spoken.

I needed action. A task I could do to keep myself from lingering on ghosts and what-ifs. If Patrol wasn't going to do anything, and were going to write off her death as an unfortunate accident when Richard posited she could have been unlawfully killed, I was not going to wait for Patrol to fail Claire's memory.

Consumed in my thoughts, I didn't notice Richard approaching until he was directly in front of me. Hesitantly, he reached out and placed a hand on my shoulder. It was tense, as though he wasn't quite sure if he was overstepping his bounds. His touch did little to comfort me, but saying so would hurt his feelings, and I felt I had already done enough of that. "I should probably go," he told her. He must have interpreted my shudder as fear. "I have said too much. The last thing I want to do is upset you. Maybe you can address your concerns regarding Mr. Blood's numbers with your father. He will be more familiar than I would with them. I will call on you later this week."

I nodded, not trusting my voice. Silently, we walked from the library and back to the foyer.

"Richard," I said as he retrieved his top hat from our stand and placed it on his head. "You *will* let me know if you hear anything, yes?"

Richard cupped my cheek in his hand, his thumb caressing my skin. His gaze sculpted my face. "Yes, of course," he said.

Harrold opened the door for him. I was surprised to find it raining, despite the warnings the sky had given the past few days. Before I could ask Richard if he needed a carriage, he stepped into the street.

Harrold was about to close the door when a silhouette caught me by surprise. At first, I assumed Richard was returning because he'd forgotten something, or decided he would like a carriage after all.

But the shadow was not Richard.

Adrian Blood stepped in from the rain. Tall, broad, and intimidating, he flashed me an arrogant smirk. I wanted to spin around and retreat to the library to digest my conversation with Richard. Instead, I was rooted to my place in the foyer, the sound of light rain pitter-pattering against the glass of the windows and dropping dully on the wood of the front porch.

"What did I tell you, Hannah?" he asked. "I knew we would be seeing each other soon."

CHAPTER TWELVE

Hannah

"Don't do that," I snipped. His smirk deepened, and he tilted his head cat-like as he took a step toward me.

"Do what?" he asked innocently.

I huffed a sigh. "To you, it's Ms. Walker."

"Oh?" he asked. "You seem to enjoy when I say it. I can tell by your face and the way your heart quickens whenever I say *Hannah*."

I tried to control my traitorous heart, unable to look at him. It shouldn't be possible for him to do such a thing to me. He might try to get under my skin, try to bring a blush to my cheeks, but I hoped I could resist.

"Sir?" Harrold asked in a bored tone. "May I help you?" His face was the picture of disdain. Adrian Blood, one of the most notorious businessmen in Port Ankura, had the nerve to attend our home.

"I am here to see Reginald Walker to discuss important business," Blood said firmly.

I took a moment to scrutinize the man before me. I had only seen him a couple of days ago and he looked exactly the same—striking. Beautiful even. The rain soaked through his tunic, carving out the muscles in his torso. I looked away as my heart stuttered. I wanted to be near him as much as I wanted to be as far away as possible.

Harrold nodded. "Very well, sir." He turned and walked away, no doubt going to retrieve my father.

Adrian turned his icy blue eyes on me. "I nearly ran into a young man coming from your home. Was he calling on you?"

"I don't believe that's any of your business, Mr. Blood," I said, my voice quivering. I dropped my glance, staring down at my clasped hands, and cleared my throat in hopes of making my voice stronger.

"I suppose not," he agreed. "May I come in out of the rain while I wait?" He brushed past me. I watched as he strode over to one of my mother's vases situated on a small stand. His hands were held loosely behind his rigorously straight back even when he was bending over to inspect the vase more thoroughly.

"What are you doing here?" I asked.

He straightened and glanced over his broad shoulder then grinned, flashing his teeth the way a predator might to its prey.

"I'm afraid, Ms. Walker, that is none of your concern." He spun a quick glance around the room then turned back to face me. "May I make an observation? The man who left, he was Richard Dartmoth, yes?"

I narrowed my eyes. "Why?"

"I take it you know him personally?" he asked. "Which means you must be aware his fiancée was—"

"Murdered." The word was tight in my mouth, like a bolt in a ship. "Yes, I am aware."

"Murdered?" He raised his brow. "I had not confirmed that rumor yet myself."

"Richard came to tell me his thoughts, though nothing has been confirmed officially."

"Richard?" His lips curled up as he made his way over to me. "I was unaware the two of you were on a first-name basis."

"Yes, well, you don't know much about me," I pointed out.

Adrian came closer. With each step, he matched the beat of my heart, and his stare never left me. I refused to run. My foolish pride would rather see me devoured than escaping and alive.

"That is true," he acknowledged, "but I find myself curious."

"Well, you know what they say about curiosity."

"Please, indulge me. I'm sure you must be familiar with it, considering you were at my brothel with no chaperone the other night."

My eyes widened and I stepped forward. My hands went up as though I were pleading with him. I flickered my gaze around the room, gently chewing my bottom lip. If even a servant knew I was out at night by myself, I could get into big trouble. If anyone had caught me, my reputation would have been ruined and there was no way I would have been able to take over my father's business.

I pondered that thought. It did not seem as upsetting as I initially believed it to be. Taking over his company was Father's idea, something he expected me to do. He did not trust Lizzie.

"I was correct." He angled his body away to look at a painting of the ocean. It was one my mother commissioned a fortnight before she died. "No one knows about your adventure the other evening, do they? The pretense of being out as a representative for your father was false."

I opened my mouth, ready to deny the claim, when his stare stopped me.

"Do not lie to me, Ms. Walker. I am nearly as skilled as you are at detecting lies, and I would rather not involve your father in my financial matters if you are already reviewing the books. He does not have to know."

I pushed out a sigh. Apparently, this was something Adrian Blood wanted to hold over my head for the foreseeable future.

"What do you want?" I asked, my voice a jagged whisper.

His lips pulled into a deeper smile as he regarded me again, then turned to look at the painting once more. I understood the enchantment it held. I felt it as well. The picture of the horizon at sunset was transfixing. Golds, reds, and purples stained the sky, the sun dipping below the clear, blue sea.

"It's beautiful, isn't it?" I asked. "My mother loved sunsets. She always said sunsets were nature's way of showing us there was beauty even in an ending, and sometimes, there was no stopping the inevitable. Instead, we must welcome our nights—our most difficult, hopeless times—and embrace them as we did the good times."

He turned to look at me, his expression thoughtful.

I lifted my chin. "She also said there were two sides to every coin. Bad came with good, and fear came with certainty. We should not run from those things but embrace them as something we were unable to change."

He inclined his head. "Your mother was a wise woman." He took a deep breath. "I want what you want. I want what you saw at my brothel to remain a secret between us. If anyone finds out I was almost killed by a human and saved by one, my reputation will be tarnished."

"I..." My palms started to perspire. I shoved them behind my back and wiped them on the skirts of my dress, hoping he didn't notice.

"I'd imagine you have told no one about our encounter?." He smiled silkily. "Who could you trust enough to tell? It would require admitting you were at my brothel alone and engaged in conversation with me. And that you saved my life, something a lot of people in this town would not thank you for."

"Is talking to you something I should avoid in the future?" I asked. My eyes widened at my words. They almost sounded...flirtatious, which was the last thing I intended to be with Adrian Blood. I cleared my throat and turned from him, focusing on my mother's vase. "Would it ruin my reputation to exchange words with you?"

"You would be surprised at the effect I have on someone's reputation simply by being in the same room as them," he declared as he moved closer to me. I squared my shoulders, reminding myself not to cower when he got too close. "Tell me, Ms. Walker," he said, his voice hovering above a whisper. The closer he got to me, the more his voice dropped. His breath brushed the column of my throat, causing my flesh to erupt with goose bumps. "Do I frighten you? For some strange reason, you cannot seem to look me in the eye. Considering you've been in my brothel, I can only assume you are much bolder than you would like people to believe. Yet you stand here, avoiding me like some sort of contagious illness. Why is that?"

Where is Harrold? How long does it take for him to retrieve my father?

I did not wish to be around Adrian Blood. He was dangerous, and there was something about him that struck fear in my heart and made it beat with traitorous excitement. Yet, I sensed no harm would come to me when I was around him. Strange, since he had a reputation of being indifferent and ferocious.

"Why were you there that night?" he tried again. One of his hands rested on my hip and he positioned his body on the other side of mine, preventing me from turning from his touch. He had me trapped like a fly in a thickly woven web.

I wanted to look away, but I was captivated by his beauty. His eyes were the clearest blue I had ever seen, nearly resembling the ocean on a sunny day. The rain continued to fall outside, hitting the window the way a lover might when he would throw pebbles in order to acquire his intended's attention.

"Why does it matter so greatly to you?" I asked. "I am insignificant. Another girl who happened to be in your brothel the other night. I am no one to concern yourself with."

He tapped his chin, seemingly confused by what I said. "You are the only person I find myself concerned with," he said, "which is troubling enough. What's worse is you saved my life, which puts me in your debt. A life for a life. Someday, I will save yours."

"I do not require saving, Mr. Blood," I said. *Especially from you.*

He grinned. "Not now," he agreed, "but one day, you might." His eyes darkened. "I'm not the sort who needs saving and yet, if it weren't for you, I would be nothing more than ash. I rarely find myself thinking about mortality and how such a thing affects me. Tell me, if you need no saving, is there something else I can assist you with until you do? Perhaps I can assist you regarding your friend's death?"

I swallowed. He sounded sincere, but I didn't want him to be involved. It would mean a continued relationship and that was the last thing I wanted. I didn't trust him. I didn't trust myself around him. I didn't regret saving his life, but I hadn't realized it would mean this.

"I could gather information on what happened to her," he continued. "I understand Patrol isn't exactly a beacon of hope when it comes to solving crimes. If she was, indeed, murdered."

I hated he was right. I hated that he, of all people, might be my only hope at discovering what actually happened to Claire.

Judging by the cocky smirk on his face, he knew it too.

Before I could respond, my father strolled in, his tunic sleeves rolled to his elbows, the hem slightly untucked. Apparently, this would be an informal business meeting.

I jumped back and nearly caused my mother's vase to crash to the floor. Adrian stepped beside me, brushing my shoulder, as he righted the vase before I could. The aroma of something musky and crisp invaded my senses and I stepped away from him. I needed my distance.

"I see you've met Hannah, though I assure you, she is not normally this clumsy." My father gave me a long look. "I'm training her to take over running this operation, you know."

"I couldn't think of a better person to take your place," Adrian all but purred, his sultry gaze on me.

I bristled. He certainly didn't know me well enough to make such a claim. I looked back at the vase, clenching my jaw tightly together to keep my chin from trembling.

"This way, Mr. Blood," my father said. "We have much to discuss."

CHAPTER THIRTEEN

Adrian

Reginald Walker led me down the chilled west hallway of his manor. Tendrils of icy air pulled me away from Hannah's warmth, which was easy to get lost in. It unnerved me more than I cared to admit, and I was glad to have an excuse to leave her even though a part of me yearned to stay. Such a contradiction of internal turmoil I was not accustomed to, and the complications it caused left me agitated.

I ignored the expensive artwork hanging on the walls, noticing Walker himself looked pointedly ahead rather than at the walls. He headed into the library on the right. Two double doors swept open, and I stepped into one of the largest rooms I had ever been in. The walls were filled with books upon books, a bureau straight ahead and a settee in front of the desk. A small black table was positioned in front of the settee, filled with a stack of yet more books. It looked like someone had been reading here and left without coming back.

Walker headed to the bureau and sat in a dark burgundy chair. He leaned to his left, reaching for something. I stepped closer to the bureau, my eyes going to the window. For such a large room, there was only one window, though the window was as large as one of the walls, and there was a small crook where someone could curl up and read.

There was no way to use the window to slip out, however, unless one decided to break through the glass.

"I do not need to tell you I am not pleased with your interaction with my daughter," Walker said as he pulled up two glasses and set them carefully on the parchment scattered across the surface of the desk.

"She is the woman you intend to take over your collection, is she not?" I asked. My eyes were drawn to him pouring an amber liquid into the glasses. He knew I did not eat or drink human food if I could help it. Everything tasted like ash after feeding on a live human. "Why shouldn't I get to know her better?"

"You keep your place," he snapped, meeting my eyes with a glare. He knew what I was yet he didn't care I could take the look on his face as a personal insult. I had killed for much less. "Hannah is my daughter. What could you possibly have to talk to her about?"

"As I stated," I said, spreading my arms in what I hoped was a placating gesture, "I wanted to get to know the person you intend to take over your duties. I figured it was in my best interest to introduce myself now."

"Refrain from speaking to her again, even when I am present, do you understand me?" He took a long sip of his drink before shaking his head. He slammed the glass down and poured himself another.

"Is there something in particular troubling you?" I asked, taking a step forward. "Something akin to a ravaged body left for dead in the Forest of Legend?"

He snapped his glare at me, his cheeks turning redder than the sunset. "Mind your tongue, man," he ordered. "The walls have ears. Servants talk. Knowing you're here, I'm sure they are listening in as we speak."

"Kill one of them to make an example and I'm certain you won't have this problem," I suggested.

He let out a harrumph and picked up the glass. His hand shook, but he managed to get the brandy down without spilling any. The second glass remained untouched on his desk.

"Why are you here?" he asked when he set down his glass a second time. "Perhaps to claim responsibility for the dead girl?"

I snorted. "Do you think I would leave such a mess?" I asked. I took a seat on the settee and glanced up at the ceiling. It was obvious by his weariness he didn't realize how I had been involved with her. If he knew, I highly doubted he would have let me into his home. "Do you think I would actually risk exposing myself to this world? They burn men and women at the stake, even when magick is not present…"

Walker clenched his fist, keeping his eyes away from me and at the wall perpendicular to where he sat.

“You know what she is,” I said, realization dawning on me. I was surprised I didn’t think of this before. “Your daughter, I mean. That is why she is going to take over your business, is it not? Why you let her attend your collections? Because if there’s a moment when you doubt someone, she will be able to discern the truth.”

Walker pinched the bridge of his nose. Without looking, he reached for the large bottle of alcohol. For a moment, I thought he was going to indulge and drink from the bottle directly, but he curled his fingers and forced his arm back to his side.

“You do not deny it,” I said.

“If you do not claim responsibility for the dead girl, who did it?” Walker demanded.

“Why should I know such a thing?”

“Are you not Adrian Blood?” Walker mocked. “Don’t you know everything?”

I did not deign to respond. I simply looked at him, waiting for whatever he wanted to say.

“The Pascals are coming to Ankura,” he blurted, turning around from me. “They will blame you for this death.”

“I can handle the Pascals,” I replied.

Walker snorted but did not look at me. I bristled.

“They are human,” I said. “Flesh, bone, and blood, like all of you. I could tear into their flesh with my teeth, crush their bones with my hands, and feast on their blood.”

“*What do you want*?” Though he did not raise his voice, he still commanded attention. Anyone else would have flinched.

“I want to know if you tried to have me killed,” I said. My voice was firm but not unhinged the way his was. I placed my ankle on my opposite knee, leaning back into the soft cushion.

Walker blinked once, then turned his attention to the drink, realizing there were two glasses. He picked up the one that was filled and offered it to me. I knew it wasn’t an olive branch, but I stood up and took it anyway before sitting. Instead of drinking it, I placed it on the table in front of me, careful not to set it on any books.

“Kill you?” he asked, pouring himself another glass. “You think I would kill you? Why would I do such a thing?”

In truth, I didn’t know. I paid him good money and I kept the Blood Mages under control. It made no sense for him to kill me even if he did not like me.

“Do you know who might want to?” I asked.

He snorted. This time, he brought his glass to his lips but only took a sip. “Have you spoken to Thaya, my dear sister-in-law?”

The enchantress. I had considered her, but had yet to speak to her.

“Do you think she had anything to do with the girl’s death?”

Walker let out a sigh. “I don’t know,” he admitted, his gaze drawn to his drink. “She’s been pushing me to protect the girls, to get them—” He cut himself off and shook his head. “No matter. Would she go this far to force my hand? I cannot say. Thaya has always been unpredictable, but I highly doubt she would have done such a terrible thing to Hannah. Then again, Thaya’s stubborn.”

“What does Hannah have to do with a dead, brutalized girl found in the forest?” I questioned.

Her father finished his third glass and all but slammed it on the surface of the table. The parchment bristled under the harsh treatment, but Walker didn’t seem to notice or care.

“The dead girl was Hannah’s closest friend.”

CHAPTER FOURTEEN

Adrian

The thought troubled me more than I cared to admit. I did not want to assume Hannah's relationship to the victim had anything to do with her death. But considering the girl died the same night Hannah saved me, I was left with more questions than answers.

After finalizing my business and leaving the Walker Manor—Hannah was nowhere to be seen—I headed to the brothel by way of the Forest of Legend. There, the trees were a darker shade of green, almost black, and even with my sharp eyes and clear vision in the pitch black of night, it was difficult to discern what was tangible and what was my imagination.

Mist seemed to live here, crawling into the dirt, and dancing in the roots of trees. Thistles on the evergreens stood erect like the hairs on a frightened human. The moon was blotted out by a sky resembling spilled ink. I could not make out the stars, even through the small slivers of light between the tops of the tall trees. Everything was still as I made my way to the brothel. No animal scurried through. No leaves floated to the ground. Not even the breeze deigned to travel through the forest, afraid it might stumble upon something as ghastly and as terrifying as what had happened to the girl.

I had hoped to turn my thoughts about the attack and direct them to Hannah, but I could not. I had to focus on the forest.

I didn't want to tempt whatever Blood Mage might be hiding here, waiting for its next victim. Of course, I was more than capable of taking care of myself. The work on the victim was sloppy, *hungry*. The Pascals would blame me for this. Walker was correct. If he was also right and they intended to come to Ankura personally, I needed to prepare.

All thoughts of who wanted to kill me vanished for the moment. I would deal with them later. Though I had taken care of the human at my brothel, I didn't think I had taken care of the problem. He was the pawn, the necessary sacrifice to take me out. Whoever sent him to kill me was certain he would die, and if he did not, it didn't matter because I was dead and that was their intent.

There was an icy cold rooted to this place. Ankura was always cold at night due to its proximity to the sea. But this forest was different. It felt like death reached out and tried to clutch a living person so tightly for their warmth, preventing them from walking through here with ease. For me, it was but a fraction of that, but it still left me unsettled.

I made it to the brothel after we opened. By this time a slice of the moon protruded into the black sky like a thin smile on a mischievous feline. I did not like to admit being perturbed by anything, but the sight of the moon this evening caused me to give it a second glance. I did not trust this moon. I did not trust this night.

When I stepped inside, warmth coated me. It did nothing to thaw the chill that lived in my blood, but tension eased out of my body. Pepper spoke to someone in a hushed voice, their whispers filling the empty room. I knew she was aware I was here. She had given me a subtle inclination of her head as her sole acknowledgment of my presence.

I was more interested in the person she spoke with. He was leaning on the bar, his clothes molded to his lithe figure. I knew he had them custom-made. Everything was the finest quality from his leather boots to his silk shirt. His dark hair was combed back from his face, and despite the casual way he held himself, I noticed the way his shoulders rolled back, his spine straight, revealing the etiquette lessons he had been forced to attend when he was a boy.

I could snap him with my fingers if I wanted to. It would come eventually. I had to wait.

"Diego Pascal," I said. My voice was low but seemed to fill up the room. Diego, to his credit, did not even flinch. He had arrived much sooner than I anticipated, which meant preparations were impossible now. No matter. I would make do. "What, pray tell, are you doing here?"

Diego peeled himself off my bar and straightened. I stood taller than him by half a head, but the height discrepancy didn't seem to deter him. If anything, his lips curled into an amused grin as his eyes traveled up and down my person.

"Adrian Blood," he said with a sneer, his accented voice both soothing and alluring. His quick tongue ensured he never went to bed alone, and he made sure to take advantage of his natural prowess, especially when he was away from court and among people who did not know what a viper he could truly be. "Is that how you address your superior?"

He was baiting me, and I knew it, but I still succumbed nonetheless. Anger seethed through me, not at him but at myself.

"I thought not," he continued, his eyes meeting mine once more. "I see you've kept your business profitable. I'm not surprised. You have a mind for business. It is why I selected you to run things here."

"You dropped me on this spit of land because you can't stomach being here." Each word out of my mouth was sharper and lower with every passing second. My shoulders curved up in order to remind him how much taller I was, how much more powerful. "You need me."

"You need me as well," he said, not balking at my tone. He held my stare with his own like I was an annoyance rather than something to be feared. "Do not forget why you are here, my friend. You are beholden to me. I saved your life, if I remember correctly."

"It is a debt I cannot repay."

"Not in my lifetime, you can't," he agreed. He curled his fingers and looked down at his cuticles, as though they were of more interest than I was. "Tell me, did you encounter a pale-faced sailor with a penchant for silver jewelry?"

I paused. I was suddenly hit with the realization Diego Pascal had a reason to kill me. He never liked me. He was threatened by what I was to him, by what I could do to him if only I could.

"It was you?"

"It was me," he said. A smirk split his face and his gaze flicked up and down my face. He knew I could shred his skin to ribbon and feast on his blood like wine, and he still deigned to challenge me. "I didn't think he would actually accomplish such a thing. I wanted only for him to offer you a warning."

"A warning? A warning of what?"

"A warning I have eyes and ears everywhere," he snarled. His eyes narrowed and his entire demeanor shifted. All of his arrogance morphed into anger, which left a dangerous spark of unpredictability in the air. "I know what you're doing with the mer-folk."

"I'm doing as my king instructs me," I said, deciding to ignore the threat in his voice. As much as I wanted an excuse to tear into him, I knew there was no benefit to me in the long term.

"I take them, I house them, and your Blood Mages feed on them for an affordable price."

"Yet, a waterlogged woman was found in the docks," he pointed out. "Rumor had it she was part of an operation that filtered the sirens from your brothel. You wouldn't happen to know about that, would you?"

"Of course not." I didn't move a muscle. I did not want to give him any hint I knew about the operation I had orchestrated.

"Like you know nothing of this girl in the forest?"

"What *should* I know?"

"Everything," Diego shouted, throwing his arms out. "What good are you to me if you know nothing?"

"I'm the person you have running your smuggling business," I said, each word sharp and low. "I'm the one who knows the deal you entered in with Underedge without anyone's knowledge, save for a select few people."

"You're doing a shit job of it too," he said. "I know you're freeing them. I don't know how, and I have no proof, but I know. I came here to tell you that."

I made sure to give nothing away. I did not blink an eye or flare my nostrils. *I* was in control here.

"I'm also aware Hannah Walker saved your life," he said. "Are the two of you friends?"

I paused, careful of what I revealed on my face. How could he know that? Who had told him?

"I barely know the girl," I replied coolly.

"A pity." Diego began to head out of the lobby. "The girl is a beauty. I would not want her to wind up like the others due to her problematic affiliation with you."

I pressed my lips together, not caring if he saw. I was well aware what he meant.

He was threatening me, and as much as I didn't want to admit it, it worked.

CHAPTER FIFTEEN

Hannah

When my maid woke me from a rather peaceful afternoon nap to inform me someone was calling on me, I waited until I was alone, and then placed my pillow over my face, and let out a muffled scream. I had been looking forward to a day where I could lounge around in a simple dress and not entertain anyone. In fact, I had a book on my nightstand I was hoping to dive into.

Instead, I now had to pull myself out of my bed and wear a somewhat complicated dress. Roseanna helped lace my corset and pull my hair up into an aesthetically pleasing updo, pinning curls to my head and twisting other strands of hair into an elaborate design. It was moments like this when I wished I was more like Lizzie, who did not care about her appearance. Would I could send Roseanna away and receive my guest with wild hair left down and pantaloons instead of a skirt.

But I was not like Lizzie and had to suffer this torture.

"Who is my visitor?" I asked Roseanna as she put the finishing touches of powder on my face and rouge on my lips. I assumed it was Richard, but I realized she never actually told me.

She didn't look up from her task. "He is a stranger to me, mum," she returned, "but he is quite handsome."

It had to be Adrian Blood. Roseanna knew Richard. I didn't think she ever met the brothel owner. There was a chance whatever business he saw Father about last night spilled over to this morning.

My heart fluttered thinking about seeing him again, and I nearly cursed out loud. I refused to be like Everly, swept away by a chiseled face and a façade of charm.

I took my time heading downstairs. If Adrian were calling on me, I didn't want him to think I was eager to see him. In fact, I lingered in my room for longer than necessary to show him I would not be rushed.

However, as I made my way down the staircase leading into the foyer, I knew Adrian Blood was not my visitor. I could only see him from behind, but he was remarkably different. He was shorter than Adrian, but still towered over me, his broad shoulders clad in a navy blue uniform. There was a belt around his waist and matching black leather boots, which came to his knees. He had cropped short chestnut brown hair, and when he turned to face me, his hair fell into his face despite having been combed back.

"Ms. Walker," he said, his hands behind his back. "Hannah." His clear blue gaze scanned me. There was nothing lecherous about his notice. If anything, he was trying to take me in, to study me like I was an ancient text he wanted to decipher.

"Brendan." Relief flowed through my body. If he was here, then that meant he was on

Claire's case. At least, I hoped he was. Despite the history he had with Lizzie, I was grateful for his presence, always steady even through a terrible storm.

I reached the bottom of the stairs and offered him my hand, as society dictated I should. He took it, tilting his head down like he was giving me a little bow, causing even more brown hair to fall in his face. I was surprised by the sudden urge I had to reach up and curl the strands behind his ears.

"You are on Claire's case?" I asked.

He nodded once. "I am."

I was certain my forehead wrinkled in a rather unbecoming way, but I could not bring myself to care.

"Thank the Goddess," I murmured. "I'm glad they have someone who actually knows what they are doing." I made it a point to look around. "I can't see your shadow anywhere. Tell me, is he still sleeping, or did he prefer not to come inside?"

"Henry preferred to wait at the fort," he said, referring to Patrol's headquarters. Fort Crimson lined the western part of the town, blocking it from any natural disasters or attacks from foes. "He sends his regards."

“Does he?” I wiped my hand on the wrinkles of my dress. “Please, refrain from sending mine. He would not know what to do with them if he had them.” I cleared my throat. “Why are you here, Lieutenant? If you are here regarding Claire’s death, why aren’t you out investigating it?”

“I was hoping to ask you some questions about Ms. Turner, if I may?” His gaze moved to the stairs, as though he was waiting for Lizzie to come down them at any second. Not that he would ever admit such a thing, of course. “Is there somewhere more private for us to discuss her case?”

I peered down the hallway. I could take him to the study, but it risked the servants listening in. Was it wrong of me to want to keep Claire’s death and its circumstances as far from gossiping mouths as possible? It was an impossible task, to be sure, but I did not want to feed the hungry, so to speak, even inadvertently.

“The library.” I walked past him and headed down the hallway, clutching my skirts as I

did.

I heard the clip of his boots behind me, and knew he followed. I reached the door and was about to open it when he grasped the doorknob before I did, and turned it.

“You are a lady, after all,” Brendan murmured.

I nodded in a show of appreciation. I wondered if I should have told Harrold to fetch us some tea. Then again, I hoped Brendan’s visit was short, although I was glad to see he was on the case. I knew he would take it more seriously than anyone else in Patrol.

“You were Ms. Turner’s closest friend.”

His deep voice startled me out of my thoughts, and I turned. I hadn’t realized I had walked down the aisle between the stacks of books only to reach the desk where Richard had pored over ledgers the day before.

“That’s correct,” I said. I leaned against the desk as Brendan let the door close gently behind him. I knew it wasn’t exactly proper, but I was tired and curious. Playing the part of the perfect lady when there was a murder to solve and lies to discover was impossible.

“Where were you the night of your friend’s unfortunate demise?” he asked, his tone flat. He stepped down a row of books where I was unable see him any longer.

“Here,” I said. “At home.”

A lie. I was glad he had no magic of his own to detect the untruthfulness of my statement. I crossed my arms over my chest and waited for him to emerge.

"Really?" He seemed surprised. He still didn't return to the aisle, and part of me thought I should follow him down the row, if only to read his expression and try to pick up his lies—if he was lying. "I heard you were out."

I sucked in a quiet breath. "Out?"

"Yes, as in, you were not at home." He stepped from the second row rather than the first,

looking at a bound copy of a novel. From where I stood, I could not tell which one.

"It was the night of the Consumption," I pointed out slowly. "I doubt anyone was."

"After Nyx's escape, you went straight home? You didn't see anything out of the ordinary?"

"Besides a grand escape from the notorious Pyrate Mage?" I asked.

"Don't play cute, Han," he said, dropping his voice. "Out of respect to your oldest sister, I am keeping an open mind, but I need to ask you questions and I need you to answer them honestly." A beat. "Please. Your reputation is better than a girl who slinks around at night without a chaperone when the square is in chaos."

I opened my mouth, ready to tell him about Claire and the stranger, ready to tell him everything, when I stopped myself. His words stung more than I was willing to admit. I thought of Brendan like an older brother—he was supposed to be my older brother—but things changed.

"What is my reputation, pray tell?" I asked, turning from him to the bureau. Two empty glasses rested on the surface next to a bottle of brandy. This must be where Father took Adrian Blood last night to discuss whatever matter they needed to discuss.

"Intelligent, demure." He took a step forward and then another. "Obedient. The people on this island believe you will be running the family business once your father steps down. You do like to accompany him on his collections rounds, do you not?" There was a dark edge to his tone, hinting he did not approve of what we did. I prickled, ready to defend myself and my father, but he pushed forward. "Mr. Dartmoth has nothing but good things to say about you." He set the book down on the nearby desk with a loud *thwack.* "You know Ms. Turner was his fiancée."

"Of course, I know that," I snapped, whirling around to face him again. "She was my closest companion."

"Did you know Mr. Dartmoth had much more amiable things to say about you than he did about her?"

There was an innocence about him now that I could study him up close. In fact, he didn't appear to be more than a few years older than me, and yet wrapped up in a fitted navy blue uniform, every inch of him screamed status and seriousness, and that he took life more seriously than a dying old man.

Every part of him was in place, except for his hair. There was no powdered wig, no combed ponytail. He clearly wanted to retain some semblance of a youth he probably never had the chance to participate in due to the style of his hair, but I could say it fit his face, brought out the edges, and contrasted with his eyes. He was terribly handsome.

"I'm not sure what you mean," I replied honestly.

His gaze dropped from mine to look at my lips, my chin, my neck. He was studying me, looking for a way to decipher whether I was truthful.

"I've interviewed Mr. Dartmoth twice," he continued, "and each time, when I brought up your name, his entire demeanor shifted from mourning and sadness into something much lighter, something territorial and yet proud. His regard for you is high. Higher than it was for the woman he is purported to have loved."

I swallowed. Every word he said was true. At least from what my ability told me.

"Is there a reason you've come to speak to me, Brendan?" I asked. I walked around the desk, placing it between us, as though that would protect me from him. "Are you accusing me of something?"

"You were her dearest friend," Brendan said, walking over to the desk. He did not seem to care whatsoever about this new obstacle between us. In fact, he seemed to be completely indifferent to it. "You claim to be. You were not home when she was murdered."

"You've narrowed down the time of death?"

"You agree you met Ms. Turner the night of her death in the Forest of Legend?"

I blinked once, twice. "No," I said, my tone suggesting the question was absurd, which it was. "Of course not." My mouth went dry. But I had seen her that night, and she was not alone.

"Then where were you?" He put the book down, placed his fingertips on the surface of the desk, and leaned forward. The look on his face was smooth, warm even, but there was an undercurrent of intimidation. "Do you have someone who can corroborate your story?"

I narrowed my eyes. "Are you implying I'm a suspect?" I asked. "What motive would I have for killing my friend?" I threw my arm out. "Brendan, you know me. You know I would never—"

"You are in love with Richard Dartmoth is what I think, Hannah." Brendan stood up straight and shrugged. "You are the one who led her to the forest, and he killed her. I have not yet pieced it all together, but that is the most logical conclusion." He stopped. "I'm sorry, you wouldn't happen to have tea, would you? The island has been rather cold, and I'm still not used to it."

My mouth dropped open. No wonder Lizzie called off their engagement. "You accuse me of murder and then ask for tea?"

"You are a hostess and it is your duty to follow a specific etiquette."

"Not for guests who believe me capable of murder." Magick rushed to my fingers. "You know me, Brendan."

"You are one of the most highly regarded women on this island," he pointed out. "To ignore the close ties you have with not only Ms. Turner but Mr. Dartmouth simply because we've been acquainted would mean I wouldn't be doing my duty to the fallen."

"Your duty," I scoffed. This was exactly why Lizzie had had issues with Brendan. "What of your duty to those you care about? You come here, you accuse me of a crime most foul, and insult me in my own home. How dare you?" My eyes prickled. I should not let him have such an effect on me. I should not lose control in such a manner. I took a deep breath and locked my stare with his. "I think we are done here."

"No." He shook his head and picked up the book, flipping it open. "Only until you tell me where you were that night."

I straightened. "If I am not a suspect, then I shouldn't have to answer at all," I said, glancing down at my cuticles, trying to pretend my heart remained steady against my chest, that my throat was not critically parched.

“I never said you weren’t a suspect.” His gaze found mine, and it struck me by how blue his eyes were. He replaced the book on the desk again. I wondered if he had a difficult time trying to figure out what to do with his hands. “You are. In fact, both you and Mr. Dartmoth are my top contenders. I am not sure which one of you is first, however.” He slowly walked around the desk. “You say you did not kill her. Then where were you that evening?”

I opened my mouth, ready to respond, when a voice cut me off. “She was with me.”

I glanced sideways and nearly collapsed. What was Adrian Blood doing here?

CHAPTER SIXTEEN

Hannah

"Ah, Adrian Blood." Brendan crossed his arms over his broad chest. His eyes narrowed at the man standing at entrance to the stacks. "I wish I could say I'm surprised to see you present. Alas, I am not." He shook his head, dropping his arms to his sides. "You say Ms. Walker was with you the night Ms. Turner was murdered? Care to tell me for what purpose?"

"So, you are confirming she was murdered?" I asked. I probably should have waited for a more appropriate time to ask, but I could not help myself.

Brendan said nothing, keeping his gaze on Adrian. Though he insisted he was not surprised to see the brothel owner, his jaw was tight, and his eyes were narrowed. It was clear he did not much care for Adrian Blood or that I was with Adrian.

"I would love nothing more than to tell you," Adrian said as he swept down the aisle until he was behind the desk. His hand found my shoulder and he gave it an affectionate squeeze, lingering for much longer than was proper. "However, Ms. Walker does not wish to tell anyone yet of our…particular relationship."

It was strange my ability did not detect a lie to Adrian's words. The truth of the matter was I did not want to tell anyone about my acquaintance with him, especially not Lieutenant Brendan Pickard.

I clenched my teeth to keep myself from saying anything improper. Everything inside of me was screaming with frustration. I wanted to rip Adrian's hand off me and douse the exposed skin he happened to touch with cold water. But I couldn't be churlish, knowing he was helping me.

I could not tell Brendan I was at Adrian's brothel in order to meet a witch named Marcella for a potential discussion of the origin of my abilities. He would think I was mad and lock me up. Despite our familiarity, he was duty-bound to his job more than to anything and anyone else. More so, Adrian provided a necessary alibi, an alibi I hadn't thought I'd need, even after learning of what happened to Claire. For now, I would have to go with whatever Adrian had up his sleeve. It was a risk, to be sure, especially considering I could not predict Adrian's thinking.

"I do apologize," the lieutenant said, looking between me and Adrian. "Am I to infer the nature of the relationship between you and Ms. Walker is…romantic?"

"Ms. Walker is right here," Adrian pointed out, giving my shoulder another squeeze.

"Why not ask her yourself?"

I wanted to roll my eyes. I didn't need to look at Adrian to know his lips were probably turned up into one of his smug smirks. He was doing this on purpose. He was using me to amuse himself.

Bastard.

Brendan turned his attention to me though it felt as though he didn't want to. "Well?" he pushed. "Care to tell me the true nature of the relationship you have with Mr. Blood? Were you with him the night Ms. Turner was murdered?"

My mouth dried up. If I said no—which was the truth—I had no alibi I was willing to share. I was unable to tell my sister the true reason I was at the brothel. There was no way I would share this information with Patrol, even if I appreciated Brendan was doing a job most would not take care to do. On the other hand, if I said yes, my reputation would be tainted. On paper, Adrian Blood was a good match—he had his own business, he was handsome, and he was still a bachelor. However, even my father, a man vigilant to exude power and virility no matter whom he worked with, was careful around him.

"Yes," I said with a defiant nod. Let Brendan think what he would. If he truly believed I was capable of murder, he could think the worst of me. I expected more from him. "Yes, I was with Adrian."

Something flashed in Brendan's eyes. I thought it was disappointment. The emotion vanished as quickly as I thought I saw it, and internally I shook my head.

"I asked something else, Ms. Walker," he said, his voice gentle. "Are you and Mr. Blood engaged in a romantic courtship?"

Adrian reached up and began to play with my hair. I ignored a shudder ripping through my body as his fingers combed through the strand. He was not even touching my body and already my stomach was in knots and my breath quickened. I hoped he didn't notice.

I opened my mouth, trying to get the words out, finding them stuck in my throat like the sticky pages of an old book. Adrian's clear gaze pierced mine and I felt myself warm under the intensity. I didn't want him looking at me so openly, especially in front of a man with such power. If he believed Adrian and I were romantically involved, the entire island would learn of it. The lie spreading like the falling leaves in autumn.

"My reputation is important to me, Lieutenant Pickard," I said slowly. I tried to think of the appropriate words to say without giving anything away.

"I'm sure it is," he said, shifting his weight. "All young women must bear the burden of perfect reputations. Unfortunately, once again, that was not what I asked."

"No one knows about us," I continued, feeling Adrian curl another strand around his finger, "and I would hope when you walk out of my home, it stays that way. Not even your friend can know." I hoped he understood I was referring to Henry.

Goddess, if Henry knew about this façade… I didn't want to imagine the scene he might make if he was sober enough to understand.

"Hmm." Brendon pushed his chestnut brown hair from his face and took a step back. Tapping his chin, he began to pace—not up and down but in a circle, as though he were a cat. "How long was she with you?" He shot the question at Adrian like a bullet from a gun.

Adrian didn't miss a beat, even though I was surprised by the question. It seemed too intimate. He seemed to imply a time of death had been established. If I was with Adrian, that meant killing Claire was impossible.

"I will not share such intimate details of my personal life," Adrian said.

I was certain he was enjoying himself more than he should. I loathed him even more for his amusement at my expense. We barely knew each other, and yet he seemed to be interested in me to the point of visiting my residence without calling ahead first. It was turning to dusk—did he not think my family would see him? Did he care? My father would certainly ask questions. Did that mean anything?

"I understand the delicate nature of whatever is between you, but I'd like to put you both on a timeline and see if you match up," Brendan pressed, a smile on his face. It did not reach his eyes, however.

"Match up?"

He dropped his gaze to me. He seemed to soften, but I could not fathom why. Certainly, Adrian was not one many trusted. Then again, he was a prominent businessman and he had many admirers.

"Ms. Turner was murdered at a specific time," Brendan stated. "If you and Mr. Blood were together, as you claim, during the time of death, it would show you did not kill her."

"I already told you I did not," I repeated.

"I do apologize, Ms. Walker, but I am not one who so easily trusts. Even someone as charming as you."

Pain weighed on my chest. Despite our prior relationship, Brendan Pickard was unable to trust me at my word. I let my hair fall in my face, masking the hurt constricting my chest.

Adrian's grip tightened on my shoulder. Pickard had not said anything threatening or insulting. There was no reason for Adrian to be protective—if that was what he was being.

"Then I shall be honest," Adrian said, "but I must have your word you will not speak of my relationship with Ms. Walker. As a man, I'm sure you know the blow would do far greater damage to her reputation, damage she cannot recover from, than it would do to me."

"Quite." Brendan nodded once in acknowledgment.

I knew I needed to tell Pickard I was with Adrian all evening, despite what implications might arise from it. Adrian was trying to assist me, even if he was driving me mad whilst doing so.

“Y-yes,” I finally managed to get out, my eyes dropping to my hands. “I was with Adrian.” Even saying his first name sounded foreign in my mouth. I swallowed, hoping that might help. “I was with him all night.”

Brendan gave me a long stare, suggesting he was uncertain whether he should believe me.

“There,” Adrian said, his tone still nonchalant. “You have her answer. You should go. I saw your partner outside, no doubt smelling of the cheapest ale on Ankura. Perhaps he needs your assistance?”

I furrowed my brow. Henry was here? I thought Brendan said he remained at the fort.

“Yes, well, Henry refuses to come in this place for good reason.” Brendan’s pointed stare caused my heart to stutter. Why was he insinuating I was at fault for the current state of affairs between Henry and me when Henry chose to act this way on his own? I wondered what Henry had told Brendan. It might have been something that caused them to commiserate about being thrown over. “I thank you both for your time and for this information. It’s most useful.”

With that, he stepped back and took his leave. I meant to walk him out, but Adrian stepped in front of me, preventing me from doing so. His arms were crossed over his chest, causing the material of his tunic to stretch across muscles I imagined corded his body, his curious blue gaze set on me.

“Are you so disgusted by me you nearly refuse my help if it means admitting you and I are entangled in an amorous relationship?” he asked. There was something about his tone that implied he was attempting to be unconcerned, but there was a catch in his voice hinting that might not be the case.

“I do not need your help, Mr. Blood,” I told him, trying to ignore the way my body tingled at his close proximity. “I did not kill Claire. I have no reason to lie.”

“You have every reason to lie,” he said. “You are directly related to the governor of the island, and that lieutenant seems intent on trying to dismantle your family.”

“Dismantle my family? Why on earth would he do that?”

“Besides your older sister callously rejecting him, Lieutenant Pickard is not a fan of the Legacies. If someone insists something did not happen, he is intent on proving them wrong. Plus, it is quite clear your friend was murdered, not attacked by a beast in the Forest. He is looking to those closest to her to see if he can sniff out a clue."

"That's all well and good, but as I said, I am innocent. I have nothing to hide."

"Nothing? So that ability you have where you can distinguish between truth and falsehoods is something you would want others to know about you?"

My breath caught in my throat. I didn't think he was threatening me. If anything, he was giving me a warning. I had not considered Brendan finding out about my magick. I didn't want to think about it if he did

Before I could respond, my father stepped into the library. "There you are," he said when he saw me. His eyes narrowed on Adrian. "Mr. Blood. I must say, I'm surprised to see you here…again."

"I was here to see you, sir," Adrian said, "regarding a particular person currently on Ankura."

"Were you?" I detected suspicion in my father's tone, and his furrowed brow and frown indicated he didn't believe Adrian. "So soon after our last meeting? I thought we had discussed everything we needed to discuss. Hmm. I do apologize, then. I must ask you to leave. We have important guests." He shifted his stare so he was looking at me. "Hannah, you must go and get dressed. The Pascals have arrived and we will dine with them presently."

CHAPTER SEVENTEEN

Hannah

The Pascals were more intimidating in person than they were in any stories I had heard. There were three brothers: Diego and Vibora, who were big, strong, and handsome. The third, Sage, was touted as the runt of the litter. He was the youngest, a dwarf, and was cast aside as someone who, although clever, could never be seen to be of any value to the Pascal dynasty.

They stood lined up in the dining hall. I was surprised to see Lizzie already there, eyeing Diego with mistrust. Her lips were curled into a frown and there was a telling wrinkle over the bridge of her nose.

After I quickly dressed yet again, and Father had seen Adrian out, we made our way to the hall where all three men nodded politely at my father.

He waved a hand toward me. "Diego, Vibora, and Sage Pascal, I'd like to introduce you to my youngest daughter, Hannah," he said.

"Another girl," Diego said, his lips curling up in amusement. "I see you are bountiful in opportunities, my friend."

"What, pray tell, do you mean by that?" Lizzie asked, her tone caustic. She did not even deign to look at the eldest Pascal as she replied. Her focus was on the ends of her hair, tossed over her shoulder so they surrounded her in messy waves.

"Only that the man in possession of daughters is more powerful than the man who possesses sons," Diego said.

"How do you figure that?" She straightened, dropping her hair from her fingers.

"He can choose which family to align his own with under the auspice of marriage," he explained simply. "For example, because your father is in possession of two daughters, he could attempt to send one of you to court in order to attract the attention of the Crown Prince. If your father proved successful, he would be able to lift his status higher than it already is, and he has another daughter he could do the same with."

His dark gaze flicked over to me as I slid into my chair. Though he was handsome and soft-spoken, there was something about him that left me unsettled. However, his words were true.

"Why are you here?" Lizzie asked bluntly.

"Elizabeth," my father muttered under his breath. His fingers curled into fists at his sides. "Behave."

"It is a simple question, Father," Lizzie replied, though her eyes continued to hold Diego's.

Vibora chortled as he brought his goblet of wine to his lips. "Seems like daughters prove to be a handful," he stated to no one in particular.

"And Walker only has two," Diego said, shifting his eyes back over to my father, who still stood by the entrance we'd walked through. "Your brother-in-law has three daughters, correct? Ankura's beloved governor?"

My father nodded.

"Then he truly is the most powerful man on the island."

"Yet you are here," my father said. He stood next to his usual place at the head of the table. Harrold was there to sweep out his chair so my father could sit without bothering to pull out the chair himself. "Not that I am ungrateful for the opportunity for us to get to know each other better, my lords."

"We are not lords," Vibora said, looking between Diego and my father. There seemed to be tension between them.

"He knows," Diego said, not taking his eyes off my father. "He's…being respectful."

"He's reminding us that despite the wealth our family has, we don't have the power we desire," a taut voice said beside me.

I looked over, surprised by the heavily sarcastic tone. I was unused to such bluntness. Sage Pascal, fingers clutching his goblet of wine, didn't seem to care how he sounded.

“Power seems to be as elusive as true love, is it not, brother?” Sage questioned, his eyes narrowed on his older brother. He brought the goblet to his mouth, taking a long sip. I thought perhaps it was to prevent himself from saying more.

Diego glared at Sage, not bothering to hide his frustration. There was no lie in Sage’s words. In fact, no one had lied so far.

“I have come to express my interest in aligning my family with yours,” Diego declared, looking at my father.

The kitchen staff began to bring trays of hot food to the table. Spiced pig, sweet fruit chopped up and mixed together, as well as crisp, freshly baked rolls were all placed on the long table. Without waiting, Lizzie reached out and snatched a roll for herself. She began to peel pieces off and plop them into her mouth. My father glared at her from across the table.

“When you say align,” my father said slowly, “what do you mean?”

“Marriage, of course,” Diego said as though it was obvious. “I would like you to set up a meeting with the governor. I find it fitting to select a daughter of his because he is the only man more highly ranked than you.”

I let out a breath I hadn’t realized I was holding. Relief overwhelmed me. Diego Pascal was *not* interested in selecting Lizzie or me. One of my poor cousins was now going to be placed on the chopping block and I was glad for it, but felt guilty at the same time.

“I shall reach out to my brother-in-law, if you wish,” my father offered. “May I ask what prompted your visit, or is a romantic journey in search of a wife the only reason you’ve braved passage through the Valley of Bones to get to Ankura?”

“We have the best seamen available,” Diego said, wiping the corner of his lips with his napkin. He had barely touched his food. “I am not worried about a small passage of ocean water.”

Lizzie’s lips curved into a frown, her fingers picking at the tablecloth. She was surprisingly quiet through this discussion.

“You know, I heard a fascinating snippet of information when we docked,” Sage Pascal said, holding up his fork as he spoke. “A girl was savagely murdered, her body left in the Forest of Legend. Is that true?”

“What gruesome supper conversation, Sage,” Diego admonished, his gaze slowly shifting over to his brother. His lips twisted in disgust. There was a darkness permeating his already dark eyes and I shuddered. I would never want him to look at me that way for any reason. "Perhaps we should talk about things you're more familiar with, such as flowers or books."

"Well, brother, on that point, we should discuss things you're familiar with, like Blood

Mages and whores," Sage bit back.

I coughed, placing my hand over my chest as though it might assuage the amusement formed there. I rather liked Sage's caustic tongue.

"Ah, but let's not forget, Sage, you have your own knowledge of whores," Diego said. "While we're here, we should look for a wife for you as well. I'm certain Blood's Brothel has someone desperate enough to get away from that blood bath she would agree to marry a dwarf."

"I'm not a dwarf everywhere," Sage said through gritted teeth.

Vibora chortled again so hard he nearly choked on his spiced lamb. Lizzie's lips curved up, her hazel eyes sparkling with amusement as she finally lifted her eyes to look at Sage.

"I did not welcome you into my home to speak such vulgarities in front of my daughters," my father said disgustedly.

I reached for my wineglass and brought it to my lips, but I did not drink. Wine dulled my senses and I wanted to be sharp. The Pascals had more power than everyone in Cardonia and were part of the elite class known as the Legacies. To sit with them for dinner was both confusing and intimidating.

"I apologize," Diego said smoothly, a friendly smile sliding onto his face. The malice he had for his brother was gone in an instant now his attention was on my father. "On behalf of myself and my brother. It was a long journey. My brothers and I are hungry and unsettled. I believe a good night's sleep should do the trick."

"Perhaps a trinket or two infused with some sort of spell might work as well," Sage put in.

My father cleared his throat. Witchery was something one never spoke of, let alone jested about on Ankura. Inexplicable things happened here at times, as though magick touched the island, but those who occupied this place loathed anything to do with it. In fact, there was an infamous trial of a Summer Witch who was burned at the stake, back in the month of Mawrth in the year two hundred and one. She was an example to everyone else who possessed any hint of supernatural abilities that such powers were the work of evil and would be sent down to the Hellmouth to be punished in fire.

I shuddered thinking about it and dropped my hands to my lap, clutching my skirts. I had gotten quite good at controlling my ability, or so I thought. Yet, recklessly, I saved a man's life using magick, revealing what I could do. I shook my head, clenching my teeth together at my idiocy. I had to be more careful, or I could have exposed myself even more. I needed to figure out if Adrian Blood was going to do anything about what he knew. The majority of people here had strong prejudices against any sort of magick, even little trinkets old crones sold to make a few shillings in order to feed themselves. Adrian might turn me in at any moment.

But given his willingness to provide me with an alibi, I doubted he had any intention of sharing my secret. I had this odd assurance deep in my bones Adrian Blood would not do such a thing.

"You and your family are always welcome in my home, provided you observe proper decorum when it comes to my daughters," my father said. "For now, I'm certain you all must be hungry and weary. Fill your bellies with wine and food, and sleep for as long as you need to. I shall reach out to our governor in the morning after we break our fast in order to set up a meeting."

Diego lifted his goblet in my father's direction. "I can drink to that," he said.

When supper concluded, my sister and I were allowed to leave while the men reconvened in my father's study. I could smell the heavy scent of rolled tobacco in the air and I heaved a sigh. I hated the smell. It was difficult to remove the scent long after the tobacco had been used.

Instead, I found myself heading to the library. I should have been getting undressed and sliding into bed, but my mind buzzed with so much activity it was difficult for me to find calm. I decided a book would soothe my overstimulated senses.

Upon stepping inside, I found Sage Pascal sitting on our couch, a book already in his lap. He looked up at me with spectacles on his face, and then turned back to his book.

"Why am I not surprised to find you here?" he asked, closing the book gently and setting

it aside.

"Why am I surprised to find you here?" I returned.

"I'm not welcome in studies and other places where visceral masculinity is required," Sage said, hopping off the couch. "My brothers, while well-meaning, can be heartless. Personally, I believe it's because my mother adopted me before she died and they did not like the ugly addition to their family." He placed his hands behind his back. "Tell me, your friend Claire, she was not mixed up in the occult, was she?"

"Why is her murder so fascinating?" I demanded. I curled my fingers into fists at my sides, hoping the folds of my skirt hid them from view.

"Because of the nature of her death," he explained, as though it was obvious. "I mean no offense, my lady, but I heard the rumors the moment we stepped on Ankura. Beasts savaged her body, feasted on her blood, much like a Blood Mage might. I'm curious to see if they are true."

"You think a Blood Mage did this to her?" I didn't want to laugh because he seemed so serious, but the corners of my lips twitched up despite my best efforts. "Surely you are old enough to know they aren't real. Blood Mages are stories parents tell their daughters to keep them from roaming around at night with unsavory characters. They do not exist."

"Surely you are old enough to know things are not always what they seem," Sage replied. "Ankura has always been touched by magick—all three port islands have been. You know this. Deep down, you know you do. But with beauty comes darkness. Blood Mages may be stories, but those stories may be based on fact, and I intend to find out if that's true. I assume you're doing the same, considering Patrol has a notorious reputation for doing everything but their job?"

My mouth went dry as he spoke. It was difficult to disagree with him.

He nodded even though I said nothing.

"As I thought. Then, my friend, if you are trying to discover the truth, might I suggest being open to the possibility she was, in fact, mauled by some sort of monster? I guess we'll never know unless we view the body ourselves, hmm?"

I nodded once, my eyes on my book. Sage Pascal was correct. I needed to view the body to understand what had happened to Claire.

But I didn’t know how I was going to accomplish it.

CHAPTER EIGHTEEN

Hannah

I waited at least an hour before changing out of my nightdress and into something more practical and warming. Judging by the bleak sky, I expected the night to be as bitter as the previous one. Once I was dressed and had on comfortable, sturdy boots, I pulled my hair up, out of my face, and headed for the window. I unlatched it, opening it up, and though there wasn't a wind to slap my face, the cold had the same affect.

I needed to see Adrian. I needed to see if he had found any tangible information on Claire's murder. After our meeting earlier that evening, I hoped he might look into it, if only so we did not have to keep up the ridiculous pretense of being lovers. I wasn't certain if Adrian would share such information, and rumors here spread as quickly as illness. The last thing I needed was my reputation ruined, especially since Lizzie's was already in shambles.

"Where are you off to?"

Her voice surprised me, my heart jumping against my chest like it wanted to carve a hole and leap from my interior to get away. I actually had to place a hand over my chest as a way to settle myself. "Lizzie," I managed to get out, turning around and facing my sister. *Speak of the devil.*

"You're going out again, I take it?" She shot a pointed look at my faded blue evening dress, more practical than stylish. "Was supper not stimulating enough for you?"

"I, I have—"

She held up a hand to stop me from trying to offer an explanation we both knew was a lie. "You do not have to explain yourself, dear sister," she said, taking a seat on the edge of my bed. "If anyone knows a thing or two about sneaking out and finding adventure, it is me. Ensure you don't let your adventure ruin any prospects you may have."

I knew she was talking about her courtship with Brendan, and my lips dropped into a frown. She still never told me what happened. Everyone, including Brendan, believed she was having an affair with an unsavory man, but Lizzie was loyal to a fault, and I knew she loved Brendan. However, when she broke it off, there were times she still snuck out, so I was left unsettled and confused. I wished she would trust me, but I needed to trust she would tell me when she was ready.

I swallowed and nodded. "I won't."

Her lips flicked up into a smile that did not reach her eyes. "Good. The last thing I would want is for my sister to follow in my footsteps. Not when she has the whole world at her feet."

I pulled Lizzie into an unexpected hug, but before she could hug me back, I released her and headed out of my room.

I managed to get out without anyone noticing. The sky was black with gray clouds floating like ships lost on a peaceful sea. I sank deeper into the warmth of my coat and cut across the large field before stepping onto the dirt trail, which would take me into town.

The air smelled of burnt meat and stale ale. My gut twisted and my nostrils dilated as feces and urine competed with the spices of food being cooked in hearths. Town was different at night. It wore a mask, concealing itself from prying eyes during the day. Once daylight succumbed to the moon and stars, however, the town was free to be itself.

Not even Patrol went out of their way to do their jobs and enforce the law, not when women with painted faces and tight corsets flashed their bright, cheaply made dresses, enticing Patrol to forget who they were. Men crammed into taverns like fish, trying to lose their sorrows and their stress in overpriced ale while children waited for scraps of leftover food or begged for coins. Some went so far as to steal it and, if they were stupid enough to get caught, the consequences were harsh and unsanctioned.

I hated walking through town, especially at night, but after what happened to Claire, there was no way I was going to cut through the Forest of Legend. I didn't like the thought of being alone where no one could hear me scream for help, especially since there was a good chance the legendary Blood Mages roamed the Forest of Legend at night before being forced to return to their ships before the sun cracked the sky like a whip.

My father's words flitted through my mind about the reality of Blood Mages, and I shifted under my large coat. I wasn't prepared to tempt fate. That was what probably happened to Claire. She got into trouble and no one knew. She never had a chance.

I let out a shaky breath and tried to look as inconspicuous as possible. A couple of men hollered after me, but otherwise ignored me.

I blocked out the lies being shouted across the square, how the items being sold were reduced in price for a limited time, how women were attracted to ugly men, how children were in desperate need of help. Communication in town was always wrapped with believable lies. It was practically a requirement to manipulate the world around them in order to best suit their needs.

Blocking out the lies when there were so many from different people pinched at my head. I practically skipped into the brothel when I saw it two stores down from Lizzie's shop.

I made my way to the tavern area as I had done the last time I was here. It was much more crowded at this hour, and there were two people behind the bar serving drinks as quickly as they could.

I paused a moment, taking everything in. Adrian would have towered over everyone, but I did not see him. A woman brushed up beside me in a skintight corset and skirts that flared around her generous hips.

"Marcus Sawyer," she called into the crowd. "Your donor is waiting for you."

A handsome man with short brown hair and blue eyes passed me, not even bothering to look my way. I let out a sigh of relief. It didn't seem I was consequential enough to turn heads, which was fine. As in the square, I did not inspire much notice, and that was ideal for my purposes.

I made my way to the bar as more names were called out and more people filtered through the small space. For some strange reason, I was not overwhelmed with mental noise here. I still picked up lies, but they were minimal compared to the square. I felt comfortable here, relaxed, as though no one would dare harm me.

When I reached the bar, Pepper was handing mugs of red ale to waiting customers. I wondered how alcohol could be a deep, crimson color, and if it was alcohol at all. She caught my eye and gave me a friendly smile. I tried to smile back and hoped it came out that way. Although it felt like I was grimacing instead.

Pepper reminded me of Lizzie, thanks to her rebellious personality. She wore a tight corset on top, but pantaloons and boots. It was a strange combination of clothing that worked for her. She wore her curly red hair down and it fell over her shoulders and bounced whenever she moved.

"Are you looking for Blood?" she asked me. "Adrian, I mean."

I nodded.

"He's on his ship," she said. "At the docks. Large ship called the *Freya*."

"Thank you."

I slipped off the stool and headed out of the brothel. I felt oddly disappointed Adrian was not present, but I was curious about his ship.

Instead of crossing the square, I took a dirt path winding around the businesses, which spilled out by the water. The Forest of Legend danced on the edge of the trail, and there was such stillness it made breathing difficult. I tried to collect my bearings and focus on what was in front of me, to ensure my mind did not paint images in my head, causing my body to sense things not there.

As I walked, all I could hear were Claire's screams even though I knew it was nothing more than the wind. Leaves rustled overhead and I quickened my pace. I was unfamiliar with what sort of creatures lived in the forest, and Mother had always warned us away from the area. Lizzie, always braver than me, was willing to visit the forest, but only during the day. Even her bravery had limitations.

By the time my feet stepped on the sand, I let out a breath of relief. I was safe, free from the reach of the forest. For now.

My eyes scanned the ships bobbing up and down in the gentle ocean. The *Freya*. I walked slowly. The sand made it all the more difficult to go as fast as I would have liked, and without meaning to, I began to kick up the sand, so it sprayed my skirts and got into my shoes.

I passed small rowboats gently bumping into each other, crowded together like fish. I passed two sailboats with enough space for one or two men. There were ships farther in the water, too grand to safely dock at the port. The rowboats probably belonged to the men who crewed those ships and had anchored here for the evening.

But no ship that clearly belonged to Adrian Blood.

I let out a sigh, turning around. I wondered if he was back at the brothel while I was out here, chasing a ghost ship.

I studied the horizon once more. The darkness consumed everything it touched. Even the ocean appeared black. If Adrian's ship was out there, I didn't see it.

Until I caught a glimpse as the clouds slid past the moon. The glow of the moon lit up a small ship close enough to the land I could walk the length of the wooden dock and step onto it without appropriating a rowboat, something I had no intention of doing.

I stepped onto the dock, which creaked loudly under my weight. Thunder clapped overhead and I jumped, letting out a squeak. I nearly lost my balance and collapsed into the water.

The last thing I needed right now was to lose my head.

I felt a small prickle at the back of my neck, like a fingernail caressing my nerves. A shudder slithered down my neck and my shoulders hunched forward. I sucked in a breath, trying to steady my racing heart.

Another ripple of thunder clapped overhead and I jumped once more, squeezing my eyes shut and tensing every muscle in my body. A drop of something wet hit the tip of my nose and I popped open one eye.

Another drop hit my shoulder, and then my arm, and then the docks.

I rushed down the rest of the dock and had to lift one arm over my forehead in hopes it would help block my face from the onslaught. My hair clung to my skin, and my dress was plastered to my body.

By the time I reached the ship, my skin was all goosebumps. I wrapped my arms around my body, hoping to preserve heat. I tried to look at the deck of his ship, hoping for some hint he was present, that my isolation here on the old western docks in the rain was a figment of my imagination.

Thunder clapped overhead. The rain ricocheted off the deck. I lifted my foot, ready to step onboard, when something grabbed my shoulder.

CHAPTER NINETEEN

Adrian

After my encounter with Diego Pascal, I needed to discover who was behind the murder of that girl, Claire—Hannah's close friend. Clearly, Diego blamed me, and as much as I wanted to argue with him, he proved correct. As the eldest created Blood Mage on Ankura, I was responsible for what happened concerning those lower than me in the hierarchy. I thought I had everything under control. I provided food for the Blood Mages at my brothel for reasonable prices. The brothel was discreet and no one could uncover who was human and who was something else entirely. I knew the others did not prefer mer-folk to humans. The blood was cold and tasted of fish. We were lucky to be out in the open, free from the cages of silver we used to be kept in.

It had been years ago, but I still remembered to this day. I would never allow myself to be caged again. Pascal might think he had control over me, and in a way, he did. He controlled my business because he gave me the funds to start the brothel, and he gave me my freedom and my rank, but this meant I answered to him under every circumstance. I thought it was something I could live with. Now, I was not so sure. Pascal could take everything from me, and I refused to let that happen.

I had already interviewed the women who worked for me. I needed to talk to Charles Rochester. He would know if any of his Lost Boys had done something drastic. Rochester had the unfortunate distinction of being a Pyrate Mage turned Blood Mage. He had magick I would never be able to possess, but he also was animalistic in his craving for blood because he was bitten himself. *Blood fed blood.* I knew that better than anyone else. I had learned to temper my cravings over the centuries. Rochester had not had that time. He had been forced by the Pascals to be responsible for others like him, bitten rather than created.

I thought it was in my best interest to talk to someone else who might know what happened. Thaya Beckett lived in the Forest of Legend. Nothing happened here she wasn't privy to, which meant she had to have known about the dead girl before the body was discovered. I'd have to return to the forest. Under normal circumstances, I didn't mind the forest. When I wanted a challenge, I hunted a deer and fed from it. Ever since Claire's death, ever since my own attempted murder, I was unnerved by being within its grasp if I could help it.

But there was no seeing Thaya anywhere else.

If I could get this over with, it was one less thing I'd have to worry about.

I headed for the forest, trying to forget the way I felt the last time I crossed through. I had no idea where Thaya and her coven of enchantresses were stationed. They kept their location hidden, especially from Blood Mages. I knew they were aware I was here.

"Bold of you to enter my forest without my permission," a musical voice said from behind me.

My lips curled up into a stiff smile. For someone as stealthy as I prided myself to be, that she could sneak up on me without me noticing left me more unsettled than I cared to admit.

"We have something to discuss," I said, turning around nonchalantly.

Thaya Beckett was a beauty in her own right, but paled compared to her sister, Hannah's mother. Her stringy blonde hair was left undone and I spied bits of twig and leaves tangled in her locks. Her golden-brown gaze locked on my frame, and I wondered if she had the ability to cast some sort of spell to keep me in my place.

"I already know the Pascals are here on Ankura," she said, gesturing with her arm in the direction of the docks, blocked by the thick, heavy forest. "The island's entire ambience shifted. There are more shadows present." Her gaze flicked over to me. "More than usual, I should say."

"Do you know who killed the girl?" I decided it was better to be direct than to dance around why I was here. I didn't wish to spend more time with the enchantress than I had to.

"If I did, I would be speaking with him and not you," she said snippily.

"Him?"

She rolled her eyes. "I expect a man to be messier," she said. "They're much more animalistic, having difficulty controlling their instincts than a woman. A woman would clean up her mess whereas a man expects to be taken care of, as though his mother is going to live forever and continue doing that. As though women were put on this earth to either be wife or mother, always beholden to a man and never herself or her own desires."

I rolled my eyes. "Save your preaching for the more delicate." I was in no mood to listen to her complain about something that was never going to change. "I came here for answers."

"You think I would be willing to give them to you?" She snorted.

"I'm sure you don't want Patrol combing through the forest and discovering all the rituals you and your coven perform," I said. "Jonathon Nyx might have escaped his Consumption, but I highly doubt you will have the same good fortune."

"I make my own good fortune, Adrian Blood," she said, the corner of her lips curling up into a smirk. "I don't need help from a Blood Mage, especially one who needed my niece to save his life."

I drew a deep breath. The only people who knew about that were Hannah, me, and Pepper. Beyond that, no one knew. I hinted I was aware of Hannah's abilities to her father, but Walker didn't know *how* I knew, and he hadn't bothered to ask.

"Oh yes, I'm well aware of everything you've done, everything you're involved in," she said. There was a sparkle to her eyes but not in a way that dazzled. Rather, they cast spells by looking upon someone. "You're responsible for the death of that poor girl in the water and for the one here in the forest. Both were working for you, were they not?"

She already knew the answer. I wasn't going to hook myself up to her line. She could make whatever assumptions she wanted.

"I did not kill either girl," I said. "I intend to figure out who did."

"I would appreciate it if you did not," she said, looking down at the grass. She bent down and pulled a wildflower without straining as she ripped it from its roots. "I rather like the idea of

Nyx being blamed for it. Patrol are actually looking for him."

"You would want one of your own to experience Consumption?" I asked, not bothering to hide the surprise in my voice. Magick was rare enough as it was, and I expected the magickal community to look after each other the way I looked after Blood Mages.

"Jonathan Nyx is not one of my own," she said, each word sharp and jagged. "He will never be."

"So, you know nothing?"

"Nothing I'm willing to share." She cocked her head to the side. "I know what you're doing with the sirens. I must say, I respect you for doing that. No person should be forced into a life of servitude." Her smile crawled onto her face. "Someone knows what you're doing and is trying to stop you, Adrian Blood, but it isn't me or my enchantresses."

"How do I know that's true?" I asked, though I must admit I did believe her.

"Because if I wanted you dead, I would have killed you the moment you stepped into my forest," she said. She nodded toward the trees. "Now, get out before I do Ankura a favor and kill you here and now."

"I do not take threats lightly, *witch*," I said with a sneer. "I would not underestimate me if I were you."

"Do not underestimate *me*, Blood Mage," she snapped back. "I loathe you and your existence, but we are on the same side in regard to the sirens. For that, I shall let you live. But cross me, and you will be nothing but ash."

"And you will be nothing but ribbon."

I turned and made my way to my ship.

CHAPTER TWENTY

Hannah

"Hannah Walker," a familiar voice said from behind me. Adrian's tone was low but curious. He stepped in front of me, dropping his hand from my shoulder. "What are you doing here?"

I put my hand to my panicked heart, trying to calm it down. When I opened my mouth to respond, the onslaught of rain and a particularly loud bolt of thunder cut me off.

I must appear like some pathetic animal. My hair matted to my face, and completely drenched.

He, on the other hand, was stoic and beautiful, and I could not help but stare at him, my mouth hanging slightly agape as I did.

His wet hair fell into his face, the blond tresses now a golden brown. There was a glow to his skin, one that made him appear otherworldly. Whether that meant he was an angel sent from Everend or a demon sent from Hellmouth, he certainly did not look like he was from this realm.

His clothes clung to his body as did mine, but his revealed how much muscle he had. I shifted my eyes, uncomfortable with how much was exposed through his white tunic. I had never seen a man's form before outside of a book or a painting, save for the other time I saw Adrian in the rain.

I felt a tug in my pelvis, drawing me to him even though my first instinct was to get away as fast as I possibly could. His shoulders carried more power in the rain, and his torso was solid as a stone, as if nothing could penetrate it. There were lines and ridges across his body, red blemishes under his collarbone and on his chest. My fingers itched to touch the discolorations, and I wondered if he had been wounded at some point. It was a silly thought. Of course, someone like Adrian Blood has been wounded.

"Are you quite finished gawking at me?" he asked. "Ms. Walker, you have a look on your face that seems to imply you've never seen a man before."

I cleared my throat. I didn't like the amused sparkle in his eye or his teasing tone. "Can we get out of the rain?" I asked haughtily.

His smirk only deepened, and his eyes raked over me like a confident feline assessing its prey. "Of course." He stepped back and gestured to his ship. "I assume Pepper told you where to find me?"

I nodded, not trusting my voice as he took my hand and placed it in the crook of his arm. I told myself he was only touching me because he wanted to ensure my safety, especially in this heavy rain, but it was no use. I felt my cheeks fill with color and I was grateful for the shadows or else I was certain Adrian would notice my blush.

We stepped off the dock and onto the *Freya*'s deck. The ship itself was rather large for one man, which made me wonder if he had a crew somewhere on Ankura. I knew he had a reputation before I began to assist my father with his collections some six months ago, upon turning ten-and-seven. Which meant Adrian Blood had been on the island for a long time. I wondered if he ever left Ankura and, if so, who ran his business in his absence.

He led me across the slick deck, and I gripped his arm tighter, hoping I didn't slip and drag him down with me. My boots were sopping with rainwater, the material sucking at my feet. We reached the end of the ship where there was a small opening in the floor with wooden steps descending below. Adrian slowly began to maneuver down the stairs and I pulled in a deep breath as I followed, praying I didn't stumble there as well.

When we finally reached the bottom, the muscles in my body relaxed and the tinkering noise from the rain sounded soothing rather than intimidating. The way it hit the wood was musical and consistent.

I could fall asleep to that sound.

The hallway was narrow, even with Adrian stepping in front of me so he could lead the way. I had no time to stop and study the other doorways and where they might lead as he brought me to the end of the hall. Two doors filled the wall and Adrian released me so he could press his hands on the golden knobs and open them.

"What is this?" I asked, following him inside.

My eyes caught sight of a bookshelf filled with books, a desk painstakingly organized and neat, two small trunks at the foot of the bed, which appeared to be nailed down, and a large window to the outside. Warmth washed over me, easing the cold away from my skin. I was still wet, but the chill had subsided.

"This is my bedroom," he remarked, heading over to the trunks at the foot of the bed with a feline grace it was difficult to look away from. Each step he took, even as he walked away from me, was poignant and powerful. He commanded the room.

My heart quickened, my eyes darted around, and I took a step back. Realization settled. I was in Adrian Blood's bedroom all by myself, and the only way out was behind me.

I took another step back, keeping my eyes focused on him the whole time.

He opened the trunks and began to rifle through its contents. Silence filled the room as I took another step back, the door hitting my back.

Adrian turned. My eyes darted to his hands, noticing clothing in them. I shivered. I longed to get out of my wet clothes, but doing so would mean my skin would be touched by something that had also touched Adrian's. I hesitated.

"Stubborn fool," he said, taking a step toward me. "Does your pride know no bounds?"

"This is not pride, but propriety," I shot back. "It would be unseemly if I wore your clothes."

"Would you rather be unseemly or caught with a cold, or worse?" He dropped the clothes by my feet. "Tell me, how would you explain that to your father when he expects you to be the good girl he thinks you are?"

As much as I hated to admit it, Adrian was right. If I caught a cold, or worse, I would have no way of explaining myself.

"Fine. Would you mind turning around?" I slid off my coat then reached behind me and removed my dress. It easily came undone, leaving me in nothing but a corset and petticoats. I sucked in a breath and shot Adrian a glare. "Well?"

"You may need assistance with your corset," he pointed out. "The rain has a tendency to tangle things together."

I reached behind me to pull the lace from my corset to prove him wrong before insisting he refrain from looking at me, but found the rain *had* made it more difficult to unknot. I clenched my teeth together to keep myself from grunting and yanked. It refused to budge. I felt my face turn red, but I locked my jaw. I would not ask him for any sort of assistance.

"Like I said, stubborn fool," he muttered. "*Hugstari.*"

His hands ghosted over my skin, moving my fingers off the lace so my arm fell slowly down to my side. I should have pushed him away. I should have turned and walked out of the door.

With nimble, strong fingers, he undid the knot and began to tug the lace out of the corset. A gentle coolness swept across my chest, and I sucked in my stomach, crossing my arms over my torso in hopes they might assist with keeping me warm. My spine straightened as the corset had opened in the back, leaving me entirely exposed.

Without warning, his fingertip brushed my spine and my eyes snapped open as I let out a

hiss. I glanced behind me, glaring. "Don't touch me," I snarled.

He took a step back. "You have nothing to fear from me," he said. "If I wanted to consume you, I would have already."

I shuddered. I had no doubt he would have.

"Why are you here?" He stepped to his desk, dragging his fingers along the surface. I imagined him doing the same to me.

I forced myself to look away and all but stomped over to the wall opposite the one with the bookshelf. I was tempted to sit on the edge of the bed, but the last thing I wanted to do was insinuate I wanted something more intimate than the relationship we had already. My back remained rigid, clutching the clothes he had given me to my chest.

"You should put those on, my lady," he said. "Wouldn't want you to catch that cold we discussed."

My cheeks burned.

"Do you know the Pascals?" I asked. I slowly released the material of clothing on the edge of the bed and began to unbundle it.

"Why would you ask such a thing?" He sat at his desk, looking at one of the parchments he left on the surface. His shoulders were relaxed, his gaze scanning the document.

"I need to change so please refrain from looking at me while I do so," I said. My voice shook, and I looked up at the ceiling in exasperation. How could I come across as confident when I was unable to utter a command with conviction?

Adrian's stare snapped up into mine and the corners of his lips quirked. The icy blue color glittered in amusement.

"Is that what troubles you?" He stood, dropping the parchment to the table dismissively. "You must be aware I am more familiar with the female body than most. I do own a brothel."

"Yes, well, regardless of your familiarity with the female form, I still ask you turn around and give me privacy."

"As you wish," he said, tilting his head down in a nod of acquiescence.

With as much speed as I could muster, I managed to strip the underdress off my still-damp form. I took a breath and yanked the pantaloons up my legs before doing the same with his tunic. My hair was certainly a mess, but I didn't pay it any mind until I ensured the loose tunic was wrapped around me sufficiently so none of my body would be exposed to him. Once I was satisfied everything was tucked away and securely in position, I cleared my throat.

"You may turn," I said. "Thank you. You have not answered my question regarding the Pascals."

He dropped his gaze to my body, studying me. My cheeks flamed at his piercing gaze on and I tensed.

"Why do you ask about them?" he enquired.

"My father is hosting them," I said, rolling one of my sleeves so it bundled at the wrist.

Adrian paled. "At your home?"

"Where else would my father host them?" I asked. "He already gave them rooms." I frowned, seeing Adrian's perfect face marred by the furrow in his brow. "You seem taken aback. What troubles you?"

"All of it." If he had had the parchment in his hand, he would have turned it to dust with the sudden fire in his eyes. "The Pascals should not be here. I didn't think they were staying. I didn't think—" He cut himself off. "This puts me in more danger than I have ever been in before."

CHAPTER TWENTY-ONE

Hannah

"How do the Pascals put you in danger?" I was more comfortable talking about what seemed like a safe topic, one where my magick cooled instead of burning my skin, and made me yearn to touch his flesh. My magick's reaction to a person had never happened before and I was unsure of what to make of it. I tucked it away, deciding to come back to it later.

Adrian glanced over at me, a light wrinkle between his brows.

"What were you thinking about then?" I asked. My mouth went dry and I looked down at my tunic—*his* tunic—and fiddled with the hemline I thought I had tucked into the pantaloons. The drops of water seeped into the wooden floor near the pile of clothes I had stripped off.

"Do you not already know?" He stepped toward me. His parchment forgotten. "You, who can read thoughts and are touched by magick—by evil." His lips twitched at the last part of the sentence.

"I cannot read thoughts, I can merely—" I cut myself off, pressing my lips together. There was no need to tell him. It was none of his business.

His lips turned up into a grin and I cleared my throat, stepping away from his bed and my clothes. I went to the small window showing a view of the ocean. It was so dark outside I was unable to distinguish the sky from the sea.

"I know," he said, his voice low. "If you could read thoughts, I doubt you would be here alone with me."

"Will you never say what you mean?"

"Don't I?" He stepped forward. "Call me a liar."

"Why do you hate the Pascals?" I asked, searching his eyes for a hint at the truth.

A darkness touched Adrian's expression, one which reminded me of the darkness outside. His, however, was infinitely colder than anything outside.

"I never said I hated them," he said slowly. "I merely said I was in danger due to their presence."

"Why do you think that?"

"I know it. Use your ability. Tell me if I'm lying."

A rush of air filled my chest, the way it did when my head cracked the surface of the water after a lengthy swim underwater. "I would prefer not to."

He leaned on the edge of his desk. "You do not take advantage of the gift you have?"

"You think it's a gift?" I scoffed, reaching up to rub my throat. His eyes followed my gesture with such intensity blood rushed up my neck to my cheeks.

"If I had the ability to distinguish truth from lies, it would be akin to reading someone's mind," Adrian said as though it were obvious. His gaze remained on my neck. "Yet you cower from such a thing."

"You think it is something I should be thankful for? Why would you wish to know when someone is lying to you?"

"You have the ability to know who to trust," he said as though it was obvious. "Should your life ever be threatened, you'll be able to prepare for it."

"Why would anyone wish to kill me?"

"Now I've claimed you as mine, I'm certain a list will begin to form."

I blinked once, then twice. "I'm sorry," I said. "Could you please repeat yourself? You said you claimed me? What do you mean?"

"You sound surprised. You were there when Lieutenant Pickard was interrogating you regarding your whereabouts the night your friend died. I told him we were in the throes of an amorous connection."

"Yes, I remember *that*," I said, leaning down to inspect my boots. "How could I forget how easily you tarnished my reputation in a few easy sentences?" Another thought struck me. "But I know Brendan, and he would never say anything. He's not even supposed to be investigating Claire's death. Word is Patrol wants to write this off as accidental, say an animal is responsible."

"You think it isn't?"

"Actually, I had a rather interesting discussion with Sage Pascal," I said. He'd told me he had no affection for the Pascals. I doubted he'd credit anything Sage said.

"Sage Pascal?"

"Yes, Sage Pascal." I narrowed my eyes. "You are a master manipulator, aren't you?" I crossed my arms over my chest and stepped toward him. It felt freeing and slightly uncomfortable to move in his attire, but I realized why Lizzie preferred such clothing over dresses and corsets. Movement was less restricted. "I have asked you twice about the Pascals and you have used your silver tongue to talk about something else to keep you from addressing my question."

Adrian's lips quirked up as he towered over me. It was only then I remembered how tall and broad he was and how unprepared I was to fight him should he threaten me. I sucked in a breath and glared back. I refused to cower before him and leave quietly, disappearing into the cold, rainy night. He would give me answers. I would see to it.

"There are plenty of things I would love to do to you with my wicked tongue, but manipulating you is not one of them," he said, his voice low and silky.

I tried to figure out the best way to respond. If Lizzie were here, she would know exactly what to say to put him in his place. His eyes would light up and there would be a glimmer of respect in them because she knew how to play the game men and women seemed destined to play with each other, both craving to be the one with power. I, on the other hand, preferred not to be seen at all. There was power in being underestimated due to my sex and my perceived intellect. I should feel more confident around Adrian Blood since he knew I could distinguish his pretty words for the emptiness they truly held, and yet I felt no lie in his statements. Whatever he meant by them, he was sincere.

"Stop it," I told him, my words stumbling out of my mouth.

He raised his hands up as though to placate me. "Stop what?"

"Stop flirting with me," I continued. "I know you mean what you say, but I don't want to hear it."

"Shall I call you beautiful then?" He tilted his head to the side. "Are those the words you'd prefer to hear?"

"I'd prefer to hear none of it, save for the information I've already requested," I said. It was easier to hold my position the more I spoke with him. He didn't seem perturbed when I found a footing in my voice, either, as I expected. "The Pascals—"

"Fine," he said, turning dismissively. He began to fiddle with the sleeve of his tunic. "The Pascals are the richest people in Cardonia."

"Everyone knows that," I snapped. It seemed he waited for me to carry on. I cleared my throat, interlacing my fingers and resting them in front of me, not responding.

Eventually he said, "Yes, well, what you may not know is how they maintain their power." He took a seat at his desk, his shoulders back, posture perfect. "They create things, invest in things. Things that will help them accumulate their wealth, and to increase their power over the continent."

"Power? I thought the king was the most powerful man in Cardonia. It is his title that grants him such powers, as the Union of the Five decreed it so."

"Three little men and two women hiding in their high towers stop the thousands and thousands of people that make up the four islands of Cardonia from actively participating in creating laws that shape their daily lives. It seems slightly unfair, don't you think?" Adrian asked. "Men can be bought and paid for, whether it be with gold, women, and sometimes men. Regardless of the means, all men want something, which means they are easily corruptible. The Pascals have the most of everything, which means they can use their power and influence to sway those men in whatever way they want, even the king himself."

"The king of Cardonia can be bought?" I asked.

"Even powerful men need money," Adrian said. "As powerful as the king is, he is nowhere near as wealthy as the Pascals."

"What could he want that he does not already have?" I asked.

"Have you not heard there is a war brewing between Cardonia and the Underedge?"

"The kingdom of the sea? I thought that was a silly bedtime story."

"You think everything is a bedtime story," Adrian pointed out. "The king wants his prince to marry the siren princess, but the Underedge refuses. War is brewing. There can be no war without money, and the king is already in debt."

I swallowed. I stepped to him, shaking my head. "You think the king needs the Pascals and their money in order to fund a war?" I asked. "How do you know these things?"

"How, indeed?" He rubbed the surface of his desk, a small grin on his lips. "Running a brothel has its benefits."

"I'm sure it does," I quipped before I could stop myself.

"Hannah Walker, are you being saucy with me?" His smile widened. "I like it."

"I care not." I brushed my hair over my shoulder. "That does not explain why you are afraid of the Pascals."

"Who said I am afraid of them?"

"You said you feared for your life."

"I said it was a risk to my life they are here. Under no circumstance did I say I feared them."

"Why are you *concerned* for your life, then?" I fiddled with the other sleeve of his tunic, trying to roll it up to my wrist. "Considering you possess a swell of women you could give them for a night or two, I am surprised you cannot arrange some sort of exchange."

Adrian's nostrils flared, his attention dropping to the surface of his desk. He swatted away what could be dust, but I saw nothing there. "What makes you think I possess my women?" he asked in a low voice. "Those who work for me do so willingly."

"I am unaware of anyone who would want to be beholden to a man, exchanging their body for any sort of compensation."

"You sit on a throne of privilege," Adrian pointed out. "How could you know anything about anything? You have been sheltered your entire life, and yet you think you know how life works. You will be sorely disappointed, princess. Your narrow vision of the shoulds and should-nots of life in Ankura, in Cardonia, are nothing more than fantasy. Let me be the first to tell you nightmares are real, but they are not like you might expect."

I let his words settle in. Could he be right? Did I truly not understand the way this society worked?

"You say they are residing in your home for the duration of their stay?" he asked, slowly standing again.

In our discourse, I saw Adrian Blood could not sit still. Whether standing and sitting, walking to me and away from me, something was making him ill at ease. Something was under his skin. But what?

"Yes," I said. "Why?"

"I'd like to ask for your assistance," he said. He walked around the desk and leaned against it, curling his fingers on the edges as though he wanted to nail himself to the wood. "I know I am already indebted to you, but I need information on the Pascals."

"Information?" I echoed.

He did not seem to hear me. "I will provide you with more assistance in the murder of your friend."

"You already owe me that," I said. "I want something else."

"My, my, Ms. Walker, I did not expect negotiations would go this smoothly with you," he said. "What can I offer you? I am completely at your disposal."

"I want you to tell me all you can about Blood Mages," I said, catching his gaze. "I will be able to tell if you're lying to me. I have no qualms about using my powers to find out the truth."

"I have no doubt," he said. "What is your sudden interest in them?"

I debated whether I wanted to tell him about my conversation with my father the day of Claire's funeral. Context might help him, but it was something I didn't necessarily trust

anyone with, especially Adrian Blood.

"That is not your business," I said quickly. I turned from him so he could not read my face. *Calm yourself, Hannah.* He did not possess the ability to read my thoughts or decipher my words. "Do we have an accord?"

A beat went by. I was forced to shift so I could look at him again.

He smiled at me, a smile that slid down my spine and buried itself deep in my core. It was not something I considered pleasant, but it was something I craved more of.

"Yes." He stuck out his hand and I shook it. I ignored the jolt when I touched his cool skin. "You should go home, Ms. Walker. We would not want you catching a cold in the rain. I shall walk you home myself."

There was no room for argument in his tone, and to be honest, the prospect of fighting with him sounded much more exhausting than I cared for. As such, I let this man do as he

wanted and chaperone me home.

CHAPTER TWENTY-TWO

Adrian

Walking Hannah home was not something I had expected to do or care about. Rain still poured down in sheets, filling the moving ocean as the waves crashed into each other. For a moment, I wondered if Underedge knew what I was doing, and if the news angered them. I refused to worry about it now, not when I still had to figure out who was trying to kill me and who had already killed two of my human associates.

"I did not think you would care enough to walk me home," Hannah said, cutting through my thoughts. We stepped from the dock to the slope leading back to the town square.

"Do not mistake my chivalry for caring," I said. "You are someone I need to keep alive, at least until I have fulfilled my debt." *And to figure out who knows what I'm doing with the sirens.*

I could not be sure, but something akin to disappointment flashed across her face. Her eyes focused ahead rather than at me, and something tightened in my chest, though I was unable to put it into words.

The sky was full of clouds, trapping the chill on the island. Even I found myself desiring the cackle of the flames to chase away the cold. The low murmurs coming from the square softened the more we headed toward her home. Now the only sound filling the silence was the swaying trees, the whispering grass, and the waves meeting the shore.

"It appears a change of clothing was not necessary, considering this rain does not seem to be letting up any time soon," I said, needing to break the tension. I was ultra-aware of her presence, of her curves outlined beneath the clothing she wore.

It must have something to do with the way she moved in my clothing, and the fact she had undressed in my chamber. No one besides Pepper knew where my ship was, and it had surprised me she would tell Hannah where it was. Regardless, I hadn't expected the way my clothes would cling to Hannah's body, and I found myself staring at her for much longer than I anticipated.

Hannah was beautiful in an earthy sort of way. High cheekbones, curly hair swept up in intricate designs, and I'd noticed the way her clothing was tailored to her body. Yet it was more than the physical that drew me. There was an air about her, a spring to her step. One of innocence and naïveté. She saw sunshine even in the darkness. A dangerous thing, to be sure. The world was filled with darkness at all times. Light interrupted it, certainly, but light was temporary. Light faded. She needed to learn the truth or else she would be sorely disappointed.

She reached up to bat damp hair from her face and I followed the movement from the corner of my eye. With her hair up, with the rain matting it together, it gave me a better view of her throat. From where I stood, I saw the way her pulse danced against her flesh. *Here is a target prepared only for me, to sink my fangs in.*

A gust of wind slapped my cheek and I pulled my eyes away, focusing in front of me.

The last thing I needed was to be tempted by Walker's daughter, especially the one he respected the most. I fed on humans from time to time, but always the willing and wanting. Hannah would never want me, especially if she found out what I really was.

I shifted my shoulders, trying to ease away the discomfort developing between the blades at the thought. The rest of our journey passed in silence.

We came upon the closed gates to her home a short while later. She held the rails of the gate at the wider space where the two gates met with a chain, and then turned to look at me. For a moment, she did nothing but stare into my face. It left me more unsettled than I cared to admit.

"Thank you," she said finally.

I reached out for her face and cupped her cheek in my hand. It was cold to touch. Walker's voice screamed through my head, telling me to leave his daughter alone, and yet I felt myself tethered to her, unable to escape from her clutches.

She didn't lean into my touch, but she didn't shrink from it either.

"Take care," I said over the rain.

Hannah nodded and I dropped my hand, taking a step back.

She slipped through the opening in the gates and didn't look back as I watched to see she had reached the manor without getting caught.

I wished I was able to ensure her safety within the vicinity of her home, but with the presence of Diego Pascal and his brothers, I could not.

She was safer with me, a monster, than she was in her own home.

CHAPTER TWENTY-THREE

Hannah

I was surprised by Adrian's insistence on walking me home, and shaken he was adamant about obtaining information about the Pascals. There was something he was keeping from me.

When I returned to my room, I took a deep breath. I knew I should get Adrian's clothes off as quickly as I could and toss them into the fire, but I couldn't. Not yet. They were warm and soft against my skin, even if they were soaking wet. I leaned against my door and closed my eyes, allowing myself a moment to appreciate the feeling. There was something else, something that smelled like him—salt, but something fresh, something clean.

Adrian Blood was no doubt a pyrate. There was no Cardonia flag legitimizing him as a business owner attached to his ship. Any merchant who did not want to be attacked by the Navy flew a flag with Cardonia's emblem—the head of a Snow Wolf baring its teeth against a dark purple background.

Pyrates were criminals and tended to have magickal tendencies. It was one of the reasons so many were victims of Consumption. I knew Adrian was something else, but what , I couldn't say. Part of me didn't want to know. If I did, I wasn't sure if I would be comfortable working with him to solve the mystery behind Claire's murder, and to help figure out why he believed the Pascals threatened his life in some way.

I released my breath and pushed away from the door, crossing my arms to grasp the hem of the shirt in my hands. I lifted it off my frame and headed toward the fireplace in my room where there were still embers crackling, though the flames had already died down.

I wondered how long I'd been gone. I forced myself to remove Adrian's clothes and instead of throwing them in the hearth, I hung them in my wardrobe to dry. After, I slipped on a nightgown and crawled into bed, closed my eyes, and waited for sleep to take me.

Unfortunately, it didn't. I stared at the ceiling, watching as shadows played in the darkness until the storm finally subsided and dawn began to break.

***

Despite having barely slept, I didn't wish to get out of bed. Adrian's questions regarding the Pascals and the uncharacteristic passion I had seen emanating from him when he found out they were on the island kept me up all night. Upsetting someone like Adrian was something I assumed was impossible. The Pascals were notoriously wealthy, but Adrian didn't seem to care much about money. While his books indicated he made a steady profit running his brothel, it was nowhere near as much as the Pascals.

By the time I forced myself out of bed, my maid had left. I pulled on a dress and fixed my hair so the frizziness from the previous evening's downpour was tamed and my hair was pulled away from my face.

I made my way down the stairs to the dining room, where I was surprised to see not only my father, Lizzie, and the Pascals, but my cousins and uncle there as well.

"Hannah," my father bellowed, standing up and gesturing at me with his arm. "So good to see you. Please, come. Sit. I'm sure you're hungry."

At that moment, my stomach rumbled. I ignored the stares sent my way as I crossed the room and took the only remaining seat, which happened to be next to my sister. The scent of freshly made bread and fried eggs tickled my nose and I realized how hungry I was. Cutlery scraped against plates and Sage stood on his chair to reach for another roll, something his brother, Vibora, found amusing.

"What?" my uncle said, turning his head so he could look over his daughter Everly and past Lizzie to fix his gaze on me. "No hug from my favorite niece?"

"Ha, ha, Uncle," Lizzie said, though her voice was strained and her eyes were on her food as she stabbed at some of the egg with her fork. "You make that joke each time you say it, and amazingly, it gets more and more amusing each time. Tell me, what's your secret?"

"Elizabeth," my father said, his voice firm. He put down the goblet and gave her a warning look, which she pretended not to notice.

"It is quite all right, Reginald," my uncle said, holding up a hand. "I am glad to see everyone so soon after the funeral under better circumstances. Has there been any word among the businesses in the square since Nyx managed to elude us once again?"

"None that I've heard."

"Nyx?" Sage asked from where he sat. "As in, Jonathan Nyx, the Pyrate Mage?"

"Who else would it be?" my cousin Everly asked, her tone flat, her blue eyes narrowed at her full plate. Though she picked at her food, none of it seemed to make it in her mouth.

"You must forgive my daughter," the governor said, his eyes sharp and narrowed at Everly. "She tends to forget her place."

That was a lie. Everly knew her place, but she didn't like it. Beauty was both a gift and a curse, and she reaped both, depending on what the situation called for. Currently, if I had to guess, she was not particularly fond of being paraded in front of strange though wealthy men she had no interest in. She was only sixteen, the youngest of the Beckett sisters, but the most beautiful. Though any of them would make a worthy wife, Everly managed to stand out, even amongst her sisters.

"No one has seen or heard from Nyx since he escaped Consumption," Lizzie said.

"Nyx escaped Consumption?" Sage asked. He dropped his fork and turned his attention to my sister.

"Are you going to repeat everything we say?" Everly asked.

"Indulge me, Ms. Everly," Sage said. A dry smile twisted his lips up. "I do not have the fortune of living in a grand home and experiencing peace and solitude. I am not as privy when it comes to current events as I want to be."

"You might not have that particular fortune, but you have every other one," she retorted.

"Everly," her father said, a warning clearly lacing his tone once again.

"I do not have the fortune of indulging my desire to say everything I feel without penalty," Sage retorted.

My mouth dropped open. Even Lizzie smirked, despite her best efforts not to. Jessa dropped her eyes to her food, a thread of red hair falling into her face, while Kara shoved a large piece of meat into her mouth. It was clear my cousins were trying to hide their amusement.

"We shall find Nyx and make him suffer if it's the last thing we do." My uncle hit the surface of the table, causing his silverware to clatter together. His face turned red as he grabbed his goblet and took a hearty drink.

I cast a glance down at my hands, still feeling magick crackling within my joints. I fancied I was a lightning goddess with the power to turn a black sky gold and cast the fire of life on anything dry and dead. I swallowed and looked up, only to see Sage's narrowed eyes peering at me. There was something about his expression, something I didn't trust. I had a feeling he could see through the walls I'd built around myself. His fingers caressed the stem of the goblet, seemingly deep in thought.

"Would our plan for Nyx make you happy, sir?" Diego Pascal asked as he set his goblet down, his gaze fixed on my uncle.

"I-I suppose," my uncle responded.

"I shall get Nyx to you, then," he said with as much certainty as one might have if they said the ocean was blue or the sun was gold.

My uncle and my father exchanged familiar glances, the type formed after years and years of close acquaintance. Both men chuckled and my uncle took another gulp of wine. "Will you now?" he said when he finished. "I know your family comes from great wealth, Pascal, but in my experience, wealth tends not to translate to action."

Diego Pascal's face grew dark. His jaw clenched. Vibora's gaze darted from his brother to my uncle and back. Sage seemed reluctant to take his stare off me despite the distraction.

"Money buys much more than you realize, sir," Diego snapped.

"Yet you have no crown upon your head." My uncle set his goblet down and picked up a smoked rib. He turned it, eyeing the amount of meat skeptically. "Unfortunately, you cannot create a daughter for the king, can you, my friend? Otherwise, you'd be betrothed to a Legacy, something you've always wanted, is that not so?"

"I do not need a crown to prove my power," Diego said. His accent got coarser as his patience began to wane.

"Perhaps not. But it would be nice, yes?" My uncle toyed with his wineglass. "You need not be here, dining with two of the most powerful men on Ankura, to seek permission for anything. You could go after whatever it is you want."

"If I retrieve Jonathan Nyx's head, will you give me your permission to marry one of your daughters?"

Everyone dropped their utensils in unison. Lizzie sputtered, Jessa's eyebrows shot up her forehead, and Kara's gaze fell to her lap. Everly was the only one of us who wore a cool mask of indifference. At least, I assumed she wore a mask. The majority of the time, it was difficult to decipher what she was feeling.

I shouldn't be surprised by Diego's forwardness. He'd said this was his intention all along. But to speak so casually of it in front of all of us was treading the line between propriety and willful arrogance.

"You…want to marry one of *my* daughters?" My uncle seemed to be trying to figure out if Diego Pascal knew what he was asking, if he had actually considered the implications of it.

"I do." He nodded

"Why would you want to do that?" My uncle cast a glance at the women sitting to his left, across from Lizzie, Vibora, and me. "My eldest has a scandal tied to her name. She cannot marry anyone at her station, let alone above it. My middle child is moody, withdrawn, and does not know her own mind, while my youngest child is most beautiful, but she follows rather than leads and is too idealistic in matters of the heart."

"Idealistic?" Diego's eyes swept to Everly. It was no surprise he would be interested in her. He probably believed she was mild-mannered and subservient the way she was beautiful.

"She believes she can marry for love."

"I see nothing wrong with that." He seemed to soften as he continued to regard Everly. Despite a slight pinkening of her cheeks, she had no other reaction. She carefully touched her food with her fork. "Perhaps we can make that happen," he murmured.

"I order you not to discuss marriage with my daughter, Pascal," my uncle commanded, no hint of mirth in his gravelly tone. "However, I am curious about your notion about getting Jonathan Nyx." He turned back to my father. "Reginald, shall we withdraw to the library?"

"I think so."

The men, including the Pascals, stood and headed down the hall, leaving me and my cousins to our own devices.

"All right," Lizzie said, crossing her arms over her chest. She glanced around, ensuring we were alone, before turning her attention back to us. "Who wants to start?"

Jessa turned to Lizzie. "Start what?"

"Start the discussion on how we save Everly from marrying a Pascal."

CHAPTER TWENTY-FOUR

Hannah

After my cousins and uncle took their leave, I read for a few hours in the library before finally withdrawing to my room. I was buzzing with energy, too wide awake to even think about sleeping.

I needed to do *something.* I needed to figure out something to place my energy in before my magick bubbled out of me and I revealed my true nature in front of the Pascals.

I closed my eyes and concentrated on my magick. It was there, warm and tingling like a friend who had come to call to say hello. It stemmed from my mother, which meant even though she was gone, she was within me.

A door creaked open and distinctly masculine voices filled the hall. I froze, shoving my hands behind my back, holding my breath. The footsteps got louder. I could make out the accents and realized it was the Pascals. I was not certain if it was all three of them or if it was merely two, but they seemed to be going somewhere.

Where could they be going at this hour? I blocked out the temptation to decipher their words, to see if they were lying to each other about anything.

As I did, Adrian's voice filled my ears with darkness and silk and the desire to extract more information from the family. There was a chance I could search their rooms quickly. If they left to experience the nightlife in Ankura, I had the time to perform such a search. I wished Adrian had given me more information as to what I might expect to find.

When their voices disappeared, I padded over to my door, keeping my weight on the balls of my feet. I tried not to make a sound, but could not be sure I hadn't. I opened the door a crack and peered out. I took a step outside, then another. Without thinking, I began to follow the two of them as quietly as I could.

"Miss?" I let out a muffled shriek, not expecting to see one of my maids staring curiously at me. "Oy, I'm sorry, miss, I—"

I didn't have it in me to shush her outright, and yet I stuck up my index finger and continued to gesture at her. The last thing I needed was her disturbing anyone who might see me enter Diego Pascal's room and assume the worst. My room was on the opposite side of the house, in the west wing. There was no reason for me to be here.

She ceased talking and waited for me to gather my bearings. When I finally calmed my heart, I straightened. She was carrying a stack of neatly folded clothing and her hair was starting to come undone after a rather long day.

"Yes?" I finally asked in a whisper. I almost felt sorry for her. I knew she was probably exhausted and wanted to turn into bed. However, annoyance bubbled up my chest. Why was she here? What could she possibly need?

"I do apologize, miss," she said, and though she recognized I wanted her to lower her voice, it wasn't by much. "I only wanted to know if you needed me to send Roseanna to your room to help you change into your shift?"

"Oh." I ran my fingers through the bit of hair that had fallen from my pins. "Of course you did. I…I apologize for my brash tone." I shook my head. "I can take care of myself tonight, Abigail, though I do thank you for your assistance."

She curtsied and headed off, disappearing down the hall. I shook my head at myself. Why did I assume something nefarious? Certainly, she would probably gossip about me being in the east hallway this late in the evening, but there was nothing malicious about her, at least from what I perceived.

I took a breath and steadied my nerves before crossing to the other side of the house. When I reached Diego's door, I wiped my hands on my dress. Part of me thought it was best to halt my plans. If Adrian needed the Pascals investigated, I was certain he could take advantage using his own resources. I was not a thing he could take advantage of simply because I had access to the brothers.

I could not help my curiosity, though. I needed to find out what the Pascals had that would make someone like Adrian Blood afraid.

I moved back to the door. All good sense left me as I peered to my left, then to my right. When I saw the hallway was clear, I took the golden doorknob in my hand and attempted to open the door.

It was locked.

Drat.

I pushed out a breath. My senses tingled. My magick warmed my hands. Because the door was locked didn't mean all hope was lost. I reached up and slid a pin from my hair. A lock fell, caressing the back of my neck. I shivered, my shoulders hunching up to my ears. I took the pin and carefully slid it into the small keyhole. I wasn't certain if Diego was in his room or if he had disappeared with his brother down the grand staircase. There was always the chance he had retired for the evening. If that was the case, I was sure I would be able to come up with some sort of explanation as to why I was coming into his room without knocking and without a chaperone.

Thank goodness Lizzie had taught me how to pick locks when we were younger. She was always doing things like that, things that should've gotten her in trouble but didn't, partly because Mother allowed exploration and education in all subjects, and partly because Father was too preoccupied with his own work to understand what we were doing.

When I heard the telltale click of the lock coming undone, I held my breath and waited. It sounded like a bell echoing down the hall. I was sure someone was going to catch me. I knew I should leave, but I didn't. Instead, I paused, waiting. My knees screamed at the pressure I was putting on them kneeling, but I remained as still as I could be.

No one reacted to the sound. So far, so good.

I swallowed and slowly stood. My skirts ruffled and I pressed one hand over my mouth, hoping to conceal any frustrated grunts at my skirts or sharp intake of air as I stood. I replaced the pin and scanned my surroundings again. Everything was still.

You could always turn around and no one would know you were here. Unless Lizzie tries to read your thoughts, no one would learn your intentions tonight.

Adrian wants answers.

My magick warmed around me. I *wanted* to do this for Adrian.

I forced myself to turn the doorknob and step into the room. I didn't want to think about this new desire to help Adrian.

I closed the door silently behind me. I pressed my back against it, trying to make out what I could from my position. With luck, I could find something without disturbing his room and alerting Diego Pascal someone had been here.

Unfortunately, darkness bled in, causing shadows to enter the chamber and dance across the furniture. I swallowed, trying to do something active instead of standing and gawking. I had been inside a man's bedroom before. Not any man's: Adrian Blood's. I shouldn't be incapable of action simply because I was in a room that belonged to the opposite sex.

But there was more to it than that. I knew it. This was Diego Pascal's room, and in here Adrian believed I would find information. But I didn't know what.

A squeak in the hall caused me to jump. My head snapped to the door. I froze, waiting. I didn't think my best bet would be to attempt to hide. Not when I had nowhere to go. I wouldn't be unable to fit underneath a bed the way I used to when I was a child.

Another moment passed. No other noise came at me. Slowly, I let out a sigh of relief.

When I was sure I was still alone, I stepped forward. There was a small bureau positioned on the opposite side of the room. It was the most logical place for me to check to see what might be hiding in there.

The problem was, I was unsure as to what I was looking for. Was he supposed to have telling documents regarding nefarious plans? Was he supposed to have a particular weapon?

I sat on the chair and slowly slid the first drawer out. It squeaked, the sound ripping into the silence like a shot. I tried to slow it, cursing the drawer all the same. I didn't realize everything made such noise.

I couldn't find anything in it apart from a couple of blank sheets of parchment.

I slid the drawer back and moved on to the drawer on the right. This drawer was quieter and inside were small, inscribed pieces of parchment.

It was difficult to read the words on the parchment in the darkness. I wished I had enough forethought to bring a candle with me. I brought the parchment close to my face, my eyes squinting as I tried to make sense of what I saw. Nothing was of particular interest, save for some numbers next to initials.

Carefully, I folded the parchment and stuck it in my bosom. I knew there was a chance this could be nothing. I was likely committing theft for no reason. Regardless, I didn't want to leave this room without something I could give to Adrian. He had yet to help me solve Claire's murder and I was beginning to lose my patience. If I gave him this, it might motivate him to help. Perhaps he could track down the man I'd seen with Claire before she died.

Maybe I should go visit Nessa Waverly. She had a knack for finding people and solving crimes Patrol could not. I would be willing to pay her for answers. Should I tell Brendan what I saw that night? Every time I thought about it, my heart ached and swelled with guilt.

You must do this. For Claire. Pride has no place in death.

I knew the voice in my head was right. I had to do something, and sitting around waiting for Adrian to help was getting me nowhere. I'd give him the parchment in the hope it would spur his assistance, but I wouldn't wait around for him. I still had Sage Pascal to worry about. He was investigating the crime as well, though I didn't know why. I didn't trust him, and I was more inclined to believe Adrian's assessment of the Pascal brothers even if I had no expectation he'd actually be of assistance.

The doorknob squeaked. Though the shadows were dark and ominous, I could see the dull glint of gold as it moved to the left, then to the right.

Someone was sliding in a key, trying to get inside.

There was nowhere for me to hide. I wasn't able to crawl underneath the bed and I couldn't step into the wardrobe and hide there.

I was caught, and there was nowhere for me to go.

CHAPTER TWENTY-FIVE

Hannah

My heart thudded against my chest, beating against the parchment between my breasts, and my throat clogged with what felt like sand. I couldn't breathe. I was pinned to the spot as the dark, assessing stare of Diego Pascal tracked across my face.

"Pray tell, what in the blazes are you doing in my room?" He stood in the doorway, outlined against the light in the passage.

I shifted awkwardly. Clearly, I was snooping about his room for no reason. If I were a maid, I might have an excuse, but since I was a Walker, I needed to think of something else.

"Well?" His words slithered around my body in a deceptively soft caress. "Have you no answer?"

"I…" What would Lizzie do in such a situation? "You want to marry one of my cousins, and I thought maybe I could help you."

He crossed his arms over his chest. "How would we accomplish such a thing by you in my room snooping through my belongings?" he said with a sneer.

I had no explanation, nothing that would make sense, so I dug myself a deeper hole. "*I* want to marry you," I said before I could stop myself.

He blinked in surprise. "You," he said, his tone flat. "You wish to marry *me*?"

"I…"

"You're a liar," he said. Finally, he stepped through the threshold, his eyes narrowed. He noticed the open bureau drawer, and then the ink I had knocked over in my haste. "You don't want to marry me. I can assure you, you have much better prospects than me as a husband."

I swallowed, stepping back as he casually walked into the room. I wished I knew him well enough to know what to expect from him. All I could hear was Adrian's words echoing through my mind like a clock's bell going off again and again like an alarm.

They are dangerous. They are dangerous.

Silly me, I had almost laughed at him. Diego Pascal seemed charming, kind. Shrewd when it came to business, cunning when it came to decision-making, but he had always been respectful in front of me and Lizzie. Now I realized how easy it was for him to hide himself from anyone he chose. His pretty face was a mask, perhaps hiding a vicious monster underneath.

"And *I* would not want you as a wife," he continued. He walked forward until I had nowhere left to go. My back hit the wall and I was pinned to it, unable to get away.

It was then I had a startling revelation: there was nothing truly intimidating about Diego Pascal. Though he was the oldest, Vibora was more powerfully built, with sweeping broad shoulders and muscles packed onto his body. He also stood at least half a head taller than Diego. Sage was more intelligent and craftier, being able to have conversations on the latest piece of literature as well as an updated piece of policy from the main continent. Diego was probably the best looking of the three in the traditional sense, but that was it, and in a family where power was everything, looks fell to the wayside.

"You are insipid and timid," he continued, interrupting my inopportune observations. "You do your father's bidding without question. You are not as pretty as your sister or your cousins, though not quite a weed. I don't like my women damsels. I like them warriors. Warriors are always destined to lose, you see. I like my women begging for mercy because it gives me a sense of purpose. I get to grant them that. It's where my power comes from. Not dominating the weak but taming the strong. You are the former."

"You think one of my cousins is the latter?" I asked. I wanted to keep him talking in the hopes one of the servants would interrupt us. Even if it might tarnish my reputation, I would rather be thought a harlot than whatever Diego might have in store. "Someone you can tame?"

"I'm unsure," Diego admitted, tilting his head to the side. Dark brown locks fell into his face like thorns from a vine. "But I will enjoy finding out. I've already seen much more spirit from your sister and cousins than from you." He reached for my face and I drew back farther, trying to create space between us. My heart beat like that of a frightened bird.

I did not want to fear this man in my own home, and yet I could not help it.

"Why are you here in my room breaking proper decorum? I'm not sure what to make of you. You have thrown me."

"Is that a good thing?" I had no idea what I was saying. I didn't know if flirtation was clever or idiotic. I knew if he was talking, he wasn't threatening or harming me.

"As I said, I'm not sure."

I felt tears gathering and I tried to rid myself of them without them rolling down my cheek and revealing my fear. I was sure he would enjoy it.

"I apologize for being so forward." I swallowed, trying to moisten my throat so my voice avoided cracking. "I shall not bother you again."

I stood straight, rolled my shoulders back, and tried to walk around him, but he was unmoving. He stepped in, blocking me where I was. His eyes narrowed on my face, watching every part of me. I had no idea what he expected to find, and no idea what he wanted from me. I had been caught. I apologized. What more could I do to right my wrong?

"On the contrary," Diego said. "I want to see more of you." His eyes dropped to my body, scrutinizing my shapeless dress then back to my face. Though I knew I was not wearing anything particularly revealing, my neck crawled with a discomforted flush.

"You raise an interesting proposition, Ms. Walker. I assumed I would bind myself to one of your cousins because their father is governor of this spit of land. But I find myself more intrigued by the idea of you or your sister because I came to realize your father has more power than your uncle. The governor may rule Ankura, but your father is the one who runs the business district, does he not? Making collections, offering protection?" He asked the question, but judging by the way he lifted his brows, he already knew the answer. "Your father smiles charmingly, but slices throats with the lights out. I see the business he deals in. I see the unsavory characters he works with. Adrian Blood. Charles Rochester. Jonathan Nyx. Criminals, Pyrate Mages, Blood Mages."

"Blood Mages?" I asked before I could stop myself.

"Oh, you haven't heard?" His lips curled back to reveal a delighted smile that clashed with the darkness of his inky eyes. "Blood Mages are real. In fact, I wouldn't be surprised if what happened to your dear friend was a Blood Mage. She was found in the forest, was she not? Alone? Bloodied, body brutalized? Sounds like a Blood Mage."

"Or a beast," I forced myself to say. I hated to admit my voice was weaker than I wanted it to be.

"Poor thing." He cupped my cheek in his palm and his thumb caressed my bottom lip. I wanted to shudder, to forcibly remove him and bathe myself in the hottest water Roseanna could boil to get the memory of him off me. "Wrapped up in your fantasy about what's real and what's not."

Magick flared under my skin, reminding me I could use it to protect myself. It would also reveal what I was, and I didn't want Diego Pascal knowing I had magick. He might turn me into Patrol, or he might have something more nefarious under his pristine sleeve. I didn't trust him.

But it didn't mean I couldn't use my ability in other ways.

"Why are you here, Mr. Pascal? In our home?" I asked, tilting my head to the side, subtly removing my face from his palm. I sounded more confident than I felt, but I pretended to be Lizzie. I pretended I was stronger. "I doubt you are here because of your wish to marry a woman you can tame."

My magick hummed, waiting for the answer. He searched my eyes for a long moment, expecting something. Finally, he dropped his hand. "Nothing more than what I've stated," he said. He reached for something around his waist.

Lie. He was lying. There was another reason he was here.

"Do you know Adrian Blood?" I didn't understand where my boldness was coming from, and I didn't want to question it now, even if it meant silence could save my life. Diego Pascal was a high-born first son to a dynasty, the wealthiest family in all of Cardonia. The only person who had more power than he did was the king. Maybe. I didn't think he would harm me, especially in my own home.

"Adrian Blood?" His hand stopped at his hip, clearly thrown by my question. "Do *you* know him?"

"Of course I do," I said. "He's one of my father's clients."

Diego Pascal chuckled. "He is paying your father for protection?" He seemed surprised by this, as well as amused.

"Why is that amusing?"

"Because Adrian Blood does not need protection from a human," he said.

"Human?" Suddenly, I was transported back when I first saw Adrian that night. He, too, referred to the man who threatened his life as a human in a derogatory way, seeming to imply Adrian was something else.

But what?

As far as I knew, Adrian was a man. An arrogant man, a powerful man, a businessman, but a man nonetheless.

"You poor, stupid fool," Diego said, his teeth a slash of white in the darkness. "Do you find yourself attached to him? I have heard rumors the two of you are engaged in a relationship of sorts. Tell me, what does your father say about that?"

"How could you know—"

"What you need to understand, my dear, is I have eyes everywhere," he said. He brought up his hand, and in it he held a small blade, thin and so clean it reflected on the dull rays of the moon spilling into his window. I sucked in a breath. "I am watching you when you breathe, when you sleep, when you think no one is around. I am taking in everything you have to offer and I will find the secrets you don't want anyone to know. You and your family will belong to me. You will be beholden to me. Do you understand?"

Before I could respond, he pressed the blade against my cheek. It pierced the skin though I felt nothing. If anything, a shiver of pleasure coursed through my bloodstream and dried out my mouth. Not because Diego Pascal was administering the pain, but at the pain itself, which struck me as strange since I hadn't realized pain and pleasure were two sides of the same shilling.

"You are a pretty enough thing, Hannah Walker," he said slowly. "I would hate for anything to happen to you. You might wind up meeting the same fate as your friend." He stepped back, replacing his blade at his hip. He reached in his coat and pulled out a dark blue handkerchief with the letters *D.P.* stitched in black silk and handed it to me. “For your cheek.”

I stared at the handkerchief stupidly. I remained where I was, unmoving, surrounded by a heavy blanket of silence.

Before he said anything else, the muted silence faded and I was suddenly back in control. My magick burned through me, begging to be released, begging for vengeance for even the smallest of cuts. I curled my fingers into tight balls to prevent the magick from coming out. The last thing I needed was Diego Pascal knowing my secret.

But that did not mean I had to play his game.

I took the handkerchief and threw it at him, using a hint of magick so it smacked his face with more force than it should have.

I reached up and with my bare fingers, wiped the blood from my face, as I made my way out of the room. He must be connected to Claire’s death in some way, and I would figure out how, no matter the risk.

CHAPTER TWENTY-SIX

Hannah

Would it be dramatic to thank The Five I woke up the next morning, still alive, still breathing? The moment my eyes cracked open, my hands touched my chest, feeling the beat of my heart reminding me I was still present.

Adrian was right. The Pascals were dangerous.

I didn't have information for him other than the piece of parchment I still had, but maybe I could coax more out of him. I couldn't tell my father what happened.

Throughout the day, I tried to think of any excuse to avoid common areas: the library, the foyer, the dining room. I didn't want Diego to look at my face and see the thin cut on my cheek and smirk like the two of us shared an intimate secret no one else would understand. I refused to share anything with him.

I even considered going to Lizzie's armory and blacksmith shop. When I suggested this, Lizzie deemed it unfitting as they were still repairing it from the night of the Consumption. Lizzie's business was one of the few ravaged by stones and fire, and though the majority of her merchandise was still intact, there was still a broken window and a burned door needing repair.

"Why the sudden interest in weapons?" Lizzie asked as she pinned her hair back from her face. Somehow, she was able to speak around the pins in her mouth, refusing to allow a lady-in -waiting to assist her. "Tell me, is this about your mysterious dalliance with your unnamed suitor?"

"Suitor?" I asked, placing a hand over my heart.

"What else am I supposed to believe?" Lizzie asked. "You haven't told me otherwise. I made an assumption considering how secretive you've been, and the only thing you might have been tight-lipped about is a man Father doesn't approve of." She placed her hands on her hips, pinning me in place with her stare. "Well? Am I right?"

I opened my mouth, ready to refute her claim. Granted, Adrian had told Brendan we had an amorous relationship, but I didn't want to lie to Lizzie if it was possible.

Unfortunately, I was not so sure I could tell her the truth and expect her discretion. Being in a relationship with a man Father did not approve of was much different than being in a relationship with Adrian Blood.

"Yes," I said slowly. "Yes, that's it. I… I cannot tell you anything about it because it's too early."

Lizzie flicked her wrist at my words nonchalantly, waving my explanation away. "No need to explain anything, my dear sister," she said with a grin. "I was young once. I understand."

"You're only two years my senior," I pointed out.

"Regardless," she said. "Does he treat you well? Does he love you?"

I started laughing. It was not my intention to belittle a genuine question since she cared about my well-being, but I did it anyway. Adrian Blood loving someone other than himself? The thought was comical.

"Love has not entered into our courtship," I said, still giggling.

Lizzie smiled. "You do not seem too bothered by the notion he doesn't love you," she pointed out. "I would have assumed you'd be more upset."

"I'm not," I assured her. "I am having fun. I know at some point Father will need me to marry someone in order to make some sort of agreement with another powerful family. I understand my duty. I refuse to wait around for it. Especially after Claire."

Lizzie nodded, her eyes glimmering with understanding. "You know, I hear the prince is looking for a bride," she pointed out. "What do you say to being a princess?"

"I would no doubt find it rather boring, if I'm being honest."

Lizzie laughed, and I joined her.

"I never apologized for what happened at the funeral." Lizzie's eyes were cast downward as they normally were whenever she wanted to apologize for something.

I sighed, looking away. I didn't want to talk about the funeral or our fight. I wanted to go to Adrian and discuss the Pascals.

"Lizzie, I feel as though the past fortnight has been like any other," I said. "Nyx escaped because something happened and we don't know what." *Lie.* I waited for her to use her ability on me again, waited for her to break the sanctity we had created between us as she had done before.

But it didn't come. I continued, still careful with my words. "Claire is dead. The Pascals are here for an indeterminate amount of time." I heaved a sigh to add extra emphasis. "There is no need to apologize. I feel we've both been through a lot, more than anyone should have to suffer through."

"Actually, Han, I wanted to speak to you about something in regards to our abilities," she said, moving her gaze from the floor to look up at me. For a moment, she seemed hopeful. "Perhaps when I come home we can discuss it?"

"Of course," I said. "You seem busier than usual."

"The possible war with Underedge has forced me to increase my production," she said, shrugging on a light jacket. "Even though the future is uncertain, we need to prepare."

Words eluded me. I knew from my collection rounds with Father the protection fee had increased because of the threat, but besides that, there was nothing else indicating tension in town.

I slipped out the doors around the time Lizzie left for her business, hoping the servants would assume I was accompanying my sister. True, I'd be going to town with Lizzie, but from there, I'd be heading to the fort while she went east, into the square.

"Shall I say hello to the lieutenant for you?" I asked as the ink-black fort came into view.

"You can tell him many things," she replied as she walked the other way, "but hello is not one of them."

My lips curved up and I shook my head at Lizzie's back. I wished my sister would tire of her anger at Brendon, and I wished he were less prideful and tell her he was sorry for his behavior. They were good for each other, and that was difficult to say for Lizzie.

Not that she would admit it.

I turned on the heel of my boot and picked up my skirts. Dust filled the air due to the horses nearby, both trying to get their fill from a trough of dirty water and bumping into each other clumsily.

The square was quieter during the daytime. Though, once the sun descended, anything was possible. This was why Father and I tried to do our rounds before nightfall, but Adrian Blood dictated his collection be done at night.

I glanced up at the sky, letting out a breath. Though it was not yet noon, the sun warmed me.

The door to Brendan's office was open. I stepped out of the blistering sun. I appreciated the cool shade the stones provided, insulating whoever was inside the office and protecting them from the heat. I reached up and rubbed the back of my bare neck, wiping off slick perspiration. I wiped the sweat on my skirts before glancing around and realizing there was a chance I had embarrassed myself. However, there was no one here.

I saw a small desk with scattered parchments and pens, spilled ink, and stains on the cherry oak. I stepped toward it and glanced at the parchment. An arrest record. A map of some continent I had never seen before, with ink blocking out the majority of it. I touched the ink with my index finger and rubbed it against my thumb. It was fresh, which meant whoever had been here must still be nearby.

"Hello?" My greeting echoed off the stone.

The room was rather small with a variety of personal articles confiscated by Patrol from the criminals they arrested. A lot of cutlasses and daggers, a belt that held individual bullets for muskets. A compass, a couple of tricorn hats. A lone red scarf looked familiar. In fact, I could not be certain, but it reminded me of the bandana Jonathan Nyx wore around his boot.

Bile rose in my mouth as the scent of urine and fecal matter hit my noise. There was also blood and vomit mixed in as well. The fort housed a small prison for pyrates and criminals. I couldn't hear if the cells were occupied, but the scent lingered. My stomach turned, and I wanted to empty its contents on the floor then rush out of the room so I could breathe in fresh air. How anyone could bear to be in here for longer than a moment, let alone hours each day, I couldn't fathom.

I swallowed deeply and stood up straight. I stepped away from the desk, passing a ring filled with at least thirty different keys. I wondered if they unlocked the businesses lining the square. I was almost positive, if they did, the business owners were not aware Patrol had them. Lizzie refused to trust Patrol with access to her business, except, Brendan and Henry Davenport if she had to, and he was sober.

"Well, well, look what the waves swept ashore," a familiar voice remarked from behind me, causing my shoulders to drop.

"Oh, not a Walker," another voice said, this one low, grating, and heavily slurred.

I turned around, surprised to find Brendan and Henry sauntering into the small office like a couple of street cats who had eaten well. Their gazes flicked over me.

"My sister sends her regards," I said to Brendan.

Henry rolled his gray-blue eyes. "Here we go," he muttered, walking past me to sit at his

desk. At least, I assumed it was his desk. It would make sense why the ink had spilled.

"How do you stand it in here?" I asked, crossing my arms over my chest.

"What do you mean?" Brendan asked, glancing around.

I gestured with my arm. "The smell. Are you telling me you don't notice it?"

"It's the sort of thing one gets used to," Brendan said with a shrug. He eased over to the desk and picked up the map. A frown marred his chiseled face and he gave Henry a look of aggravation. "This you?"

Henry shrugged, reaching into his uniform pocket and pulling out a silver flask. He uncorked it and brought it to his lips. Brendan's frown stiffened.

"You know you cannot drink on the job," he said, his voice dropping though I could hear him distinctly. "It is a dishonor to the uniform."

"This uniform and honor do not belong in the same sentence," Henry muttered, but he put the cork back and replaced the flask inside his uniform. His gaze found mine. "What are you doing here by yourself? Don't proper girls like you need an escort?"

I ignored him. "I need to speak to you about the Pascals," I said to Brendan. "I take it you are aware of their presence?"

Brendan flared his nostrils. "I am."

"I also take it you are aware they are staying at our manor," I stated.

Brendan's gaze went from the map over to me. There was something in his eyes, something that seemed pensive, but also troubling. I was not quite sure how to explain it, but it was something substantial for Brendan to react thusly.

"Why?" he asked, his tone careful. "There's no lodging available at the Ripper Inn?"

Henry chortled, leaning back on the chair so it rested on the two back legs. His feet were crossed at the ankle, resting on the surface of his desk, fingers cupping the back of his head.

"The Pascals at the Ripper?" he asked. "That's a laugh."

"What is it you want, Hannah?" Brendan asked through a sigh. I had barely been in his presence for a few minutes and he was already tired of me.

"Has Sage Pascal been here to try to see Claire's body?" I asked.

Henry's weight came crashing down and he placed both hands on the surface of his desk, looking up at me with his eyes wide and his mouth open.

Brendan narrowed his blue eyes. "How could you possibly know such a thing?"

"He mentioned he was going to conduct his own investigation," I said. "May I ask you a favor? I know he is a Pascal, but I insist you not allow him to see her body. Under no circumstances, no matter how much currency he tries to bribe you with—"

"Brendan Picard cannot be bought," Henry said. His tone was serious, though it was something Patrol muttered about their commanding officer when he was not around. They did not like men who stood for something because it made them recognize how easily persuaded they were.

"I said attempt," I snapped at him. I never got along with Henry, even when Lizzie was engaged to Brendan. The man was constantly feeling sorry for himself, drowning away in one of his vices because of an engagement gone wrong. It was pathetic and I refused to tolerate such behavior.

"Why would Sage Pascal be interested in the body of a dead woman he didn't even know?" Brendan asked. Every time he appeared pensive, he reminded me of a puppy that simply waited to be told what to do in order to make his owner happy.

"I…I do not know," I said. I knew he suspected her death a murder, but I was unsure as to why he thought such a thing. "I'm only concerned

he is not granted access to the body."

"What makes you think I would grant him access?" Brendan demanded.

"Because he's a Pascal," I said. "Even though he is…different, he still wields the power and affluence his brothers do."

"What part of 'he can't be bought' don't you understand?" Henry asked, leaning to the left and looking at me accusingly.

"What part of 'do not drink on the job' don't *you* understand?" I retorted.

Brendan pursed his lips together and seemed to be fighting a smile.

"I feel better addressing my concerns with you, Lieutenant," I said. "I'm unsure as to why they are here, but I'm certain it's not because of Diego Pascal's desire to marry one of us."

"Excuse me?" All amusement vanished from Brendan's chiseled face. "He's proposing marriage?"

I shifted my weight. "Why do you sound so surprised?" I asked. "Why else would he be visiting? The main continent does not take Ankura or the other two port islands seriously."

"I'm surprised he would look beyond the main continent for a wife at all," Henry muttered.

"Did he say to whom he was proposing?" Brendan asked.

"It was not stated," I said. "Though if he asked Father's permission whether he intended to marry Lizzie, I highly doubt my sister would approve."

"The fact your father gives you such freedom—" Henry began.

"You must be careful around the Pascals, Hannah," Brendan said, cutting Henry off. His blue eyes darkened, locking his gaze with my own. "You mustn't marry any of them. You must not let Lizzie or any of your cousins do so either. If the Pascals are here, something is afoot." He brought his fingertips to his chin. "The fact Sage Pascal wants to conduct some sort of investigation makes me wary."

"You think their presence is related to Claire's death?" I surmised.

"I am not ruling anything out at present," he said, going over to his desk.

I followed him. "What do you know?" I asked. "Have you come up with anything?"

"What's it to you?" Henry asked.

I sneered at him. "Something has to get done," I said. "You must have found something implicating someone in her murder besides me." Suddenly, I recalled the real reason why I was here in the first place. "There was a man."

"A man?" Brendan asked.

"A man?" Henry asked after Brendan, his tone flat.

"With Claire that night," I said, ignoring Henry's dry stare. "I saw them skirting the edge of the forest. I…" I swallowed, the words caught in my throat. "I should have stopped that night. I should have told Lizzie to pull the carriage over."

"Lizzie was driving a carriage?" Brendan asked.

"Of course she was." Henry did not sound surprised.

"I saw Claire," I continued. "I saw her and I did nothing. She was with a man. I didn't recognize him. Average height, average size. Other than that, I could not say. Was she found with anyone?"

"Great description," Henry interjected.

"No." Brendan shook his head. "It was her in the forest. You say there was a man with her." He turned his attention to Henry. "That might explain the skin under the fingernails."

Henry nodded, his face somber.

"The fingernails? What fingernails? What skin?"

A glance passed between them, the sort of glance that only occurred when someone knew another for many years and could read lines on their faces and the silence hanging in the air.

"You must tell me," I insisted.

"We don't have to tell you anything," Henry said.

"Is there anything else about this man?" Brendan asked, searching my face. "Anything you can tell me?"

"You think he's responsible?" I asked. My heart thudded. Of course he was. Who else could it be?

"I cannot say," he said. "But if you have anything else, I will investigate further."

"I have told you everything I know," I said.

"What about his teeth?" Henry asked.

Brendan shot him a look.

"What *about* his teeth?" I asked.

"Were they shaped in a peculiar way?" All hint of drunkenness was gone. If the subject were lighter, I might have remarked he sounded sober.

"I…" I let my voice trail off, trying to remember. "I do not know. I don't think I saw them. Why?"

Another look.

I slammed my palm on the surface of the desk, snarling. "Why?" I asked. My magick slipped out of my control, causing the parchments and the ink to spill out again. Luckily, I didn't think they realized magick caused the mess. "*Why*?"

"Leave the investigation to us, Hannah," Brendan said slowly, placing one hand on my elbow and gently leading me out of the room. "It's too dangerous for you to involve yourself, especially with the Pascals sniffing about."

I wanted to contradict him. I wanted to argue. But I bit my bottom lip and let him lead me out. When I stepped outside, I had to squint. The sunshine was brighter than I anticipated and the air was gratefully fresher. I inhaled deeply and turned to the horizon.

For another young woman of my station, it could be dangerous, but I had magick, and I was done running from it. Now was the time for me to use it if I was going to get to the truth of Claire's case.

I refused to be afraid any longer.

CHAPTER TWENTY-SEVEN

Adrian

Charles Rochester lived in the Devil's Mouth, a cave on the eastern part of Ankura. It got its name because of the jagged rocks making up the caves, which opened over a deep part of the oceans where obsidian sliced through the surface of the water like teeth. It was a dangerous trek, and the majority of the population of Ankura tended to refrain from going there for any reason. This allowed the Lost to be more isolated, away from temptation, away from humanity.

The trek was more difficult than it appeared. I had to cross through the northern part of the Forest of Legend, which spilled into the Black Beach. A dirt path curved and narrowed all the way up to the Devil's Mouth. It meant getting dirtier than I cared for, and posed a possible strain on my body.

By the time I reached the mouth of the cave, my tunic was torn in the right sleeve and the tips of my boots were crusted with mud.

Without warning, someone came up behind me. I was faster than my attacker, and when he tried to lunge at me, I grabbed his wrist and threw him over my shoulder. He crashed to the ground. I snarled, my fangs protruding from my mouth. It was the only warning I was willing to give.

"All right," a familiar low, scratchy voice rang out from across the awning. "That's enough."

A silhouette formed from the mouth and Charles Rochester emerged from the shadows. The man walked like he was captain of a ship, strutting on granite, hands on his hips. His height was average, but he was stocky and filled his tattered clothing with muscle. A rusted cutlass hung at his hip though he didn't actually need the weapon. He could kill with one blow if he wanted to.

My attacker remained prone. I assumed he waited for permission from Rochester before he moved.

"Adrian Blood." He nodded at me once, his slate-blue gaze focused on me. Suspicion

clouded his face, his lips pulling into a thin line. He glanced at my hands and then over my shoulder before his gaze rested on me once more. "What the fuck are you doing here?" He motioned at the still man on the ground. "Go," he commanded.

The man got up slowly and scurried away into the darkness.

"I need to talk to you," I said. "I know you've isolated yourself in this cave of monsters and misfits, but I was wondering if you had heard of the dead girl found in the Forest of Legend. She came from a family, one of gauche affluence."

He stilled, his eyes narrowed. I kept my face perfectly neutral, but his reaction intrigued me. Judging from the glimmer of concern in his eyes, he was familiar with a girl from an affluent family and actually seemed to care about her well-being. I might be able to use that to my advantage later on.

"You know her?" I asked.

"I said nothing," he snapped. "Is there a name attached to this dead girl?"

"Claire," I replied. "Claire Turner."

"Turner?" His shoulders sagged forward a fraction and I knew Charles was relieved. Whomever he cared for, it was certainly not Claire. I tucked the information away and stepped forward. Two of the Lost appeared from inside the cave, ready to spring into action. "You want me to call them off? I won't. Not until I know you're not a threat."

"I should have expected suspicion," I said. "Were you not a privateer when you were alive? Did you not frequent this island a few years ago? Were you not a legend here? The people loved you until you disappeared. Now, they assume you're dead, like every other hero." Charles bared his teeth like a rabid wolf. "What do you want, Blood?" he asked. "I doubt you want to remind me about my life before I was turned into this by one of your Mages."

"I want to know one of your uncontrollable animals didn't kill an innocent girl," I demanded. I was tired of games, tired of waiting around for answers.

"Innocent?" Charles's shoulders rolled back and he crossed his arms over his chest. "Claire Turner, you say?" He began to pace. "I've heard of her. Not as innocent as you might think. She liked to skip out on her poor fiancé from time to time. But more than that, she was doing naughty things to the sirens you feed your Mages. Freeing them when she thought no one was looking. I assumed she was trying to do this without your knowledge, but now I realize doing something without you knowing on Ankura isn't possible, is it?"

"You know about the sirens." I tried not to let my surprise show. Everyone seemed to know, everyone save the humans.

"How could I not when you're dumping them off the Black Shore? Some of my Lost

Boys fed on a couple." I growled at the thought. "Well, we wouldn't have to, would we, if we had access to your brothel like the others," Charles said, his fangs extending. "If we could feed—"

"It cannot happen," I snapped. "They are not aware of your kind."

"Tell me, why should we continue to keep your secret?" he asked, looking away, voice strained. "Why not expose everything?"

"They'll kill you and you know it," I returned. "You are an abomination, an unfortunate accident. Tell me what I want to know so I can protect you."

"Protection? From you?" he scoffed. "I like my odds on my own, thank you very much."

He crossed his arms over his chest. "But I do like the idea of Adrian Blood owing me a debt. What say you? Will you grant me a favor in exchange for information?"

"I don't have time for this," I repeated. "When you've come to your senses, you know where to find me."

I turned and almost made it to the edge of the cliff when Charles called me back.

"Talk to the girl," he called. "The one who follows you around like a goddamn puppy.

She knows more than she lets on, Blood. And when you realize I'm right, I expect that favor."

I flared my nostrils. I refused to acknowledge his words, despite their leaving me more than a little disturbed.

CHAPTER TWENTY-EIGHT

Hannah

I need to see Adrian. Perhaps there was some way I could sneak into the mortuary and see Claire's body. My stomach twisted at the thought. I didn't want to see the damage done to my friend, but I knew I needed to. If I couldn't confront what she was faced with, I was unable to do her death justice. I was certain, she would do the same for me.

I returned home, trying to figure out a way to pass the time. I considered picking up a book to read, but couldn't bring myself to open one. I didn't want any of the Pascals interrupting me. Especially Diego. I was afraid to step foot in the east hallway, so I kept to my rooms, taking a long bath and then a nap afterward.

Diego was a monster and not one I knew how to handle. Blood Mages needed to be stabbed with iron in the heart or have their head sliced off. Pyrate Mages needed to be vanquished based on their familiar element. Everyone knew Jonathan Nyx was a summer mage, which meant his familiar was fire. It was why Patrol intended to burn him. But Diego Pascal had no magick, at least none I knew of. If he had a weakness, I was unable to guess it.

I had Roseanna bring me my dinner, and when Father asked me to attend supper that night, I feigned illness. No one bothered me all evening, giving me the perfect opportunity to change into a dull gray dress, a large black overcoat, and worn brown boots. I pulled up the collar of my hood, hoping it might mask my face.

After a moment of consideration, I decided to change. Instead of a dress, I went into my wardrobe and pulled the clothes Adrian had lent me that night in the rain. I should have burned the evidence I had them, but I couldn't bear to destroy them.

Fool.

His voice flitted around in my head like a moth I had trapped when I was younger. My mother had released it, telling me if it liked us well enough, the moth would come back. It never did.

I changed out of my dress and pulled on Adrian's clothes so no one would recognize me. They wrapped my frame in a gentle embrace and I brought the material of the tunic to my face and inhaled. There was a subtle hint of smoke and salt. I released a breath, squaring my shoulders. I tried to ignore I felt more comfortable in his clothes than I did my own.

When I was ready, I placed the parchment I took from Diego Pascal's bureau into my pocket and snuck out of my bedroom through my balcony. The last time I'd stepped onto the nearby tree and shimmied down the trunk, I'd been twelve and much lighter. I couldn't tell if the branch would carry my weight without snapping. The wind tickled my hair, whispering in the leaves. I wondered if it was warning me to stay home and not visit Adrian.

I managed to climb down and land on my feet without much difficulty. My feet tingled, but I didn't know if that was due to how hard I landed or my magick protecting me from the fall. There was still a lot I needed to understand about my ability, especially after that day in the square.

I couldn't dwell here long. No doubt, I'd be caught by my father's guards if I lingered. After a cursory glance around, I saw no one.

A chill swept under the folds of the warm coat. Fog from the ocean was rolling in so thick it appeared to be snow, swallowing up unsuspecting victims in its wake. I should stay where I was.

But I *needed* to see Adrian.

I moved fast. I knew the route to the brothel better than I knew the one to Lizzie's business. I kept away from the forest. The fog had already touched the area and I could see ribbons of it threading through the woods.

I dodged children still out in the street, even though the moon was up. A whore cradled a young child to her, who seemed upset about not being able to explore the rest of the night like the rest of the little ones.

I slid into the brothel, which bustled with clients. I beelined for the bar and took my seat. I watched a tall, broad man with a smirk and penetrating blue eyes enter the room, no doubt looking for his next prey. His teeth were gold and his neck had long scratches on them, probably from a recent conquest.

I saw mostly men drinking ale and keeping to themselves. A few had women present, some forward enough to bounce on their knees, drawing attention to their breasts and the line of their neck. Others were at the bar, waiting for their turn with one of the women. I saw a couple of women sitting as well. I didn't recognize anyone from my social circles, but if they were here, they would attempt to disguise themselves. One woman in particular wore a fake moustache, her face was completely void of powder and rouge: her hair hidden by a hat. Her female form was easily detected in her manly attire. I wondered if she was disguising herself in order to hide her identity or if it was part of some sort of game she played. Her gaze drifted to mine and my heart stuttered.

Instead of looking away bashfully, she held my gaze and her lips turned up.

I blushed and placed my hands on the flat surface of the bar. I caught sight of the storage room where I'd seen Adrian interrogate the man he thought was taking his money. The door was closed, unfortunately, and I was left staring at the wall in front of me.

"You look upset." Pepper's voice startled me out of my thoughts. "Looking for anyone in particular? A witch, perhaps?"

I swallowed. There was a knowing glint in her brown eyes, and her chin jutted out with confidence as she lifted up a used glass and began to dry it with a dirty washrag.

"No, of course not."

Pepper turned her head down, her eyes focused on the glass. "Not you. The proverbial good girl, hmm?"

I remained silent. I couldn't tell if she meant to insult me. Whatever it was, I didn't take offense or the bait, shifting in my seat while tucking stray hair behind my ear.

"If you're looking to see Adrian, I'm sorry to inform you, you came at a bad time."

"Oh?" I turned back to her.

"He's feeding," she said.

"Feeding?" I wrung my hair over my shoulder, trying to make sense of her terminology. "He's eating a later supper, you mean?"

The smirk on her face turned into a wide grin, though she didn't look at me.

"Whatever you want to call it," she said with a shrug. She placed the rag on the counter and picked it up so she could look at it in the candlelight. Her eyes narrowed when she saw a blemish. "He's indisposed."

"Shall I wait?" I asked.

Pepper brought the glass back to her other hand and swiped at the blemish. A determined wrinkle formed over nose. "You can do as you please," she said, "though I wouldn't suggest it. Adrian refuses to see anyone after a feeding. He needs some time to recover."

"Recover?" I shook my head, trying to understand. "From a meal?"

"My sweet birdie," Pepper said, her painted lips widening, reminded me of the jesters the king kept in his court, forced to make the Legacy laugh when he was in a dreary mood. "You know nothing about the world outside your little perch."

"I don't see what this has to do with Adrian."

Pepper leaned in close so close I could feel the cool air emitting from her nose as she blew out a breath. "You smell like him. I don't understand what he sees in you." Her voice was low so only the two of us could hear. Her fingers trailed my bottom lip. "Pretty, certainly, but too pure for my preference. Naïve. Hopeful." She shook her head. "Your looks are wasted on you, I'm afraid." She dropped her hand and picked up the glass and inspected it once again. "I would leave, little bird. Adrian will not emerge and I highly doubt you want others to recognize you in a place such as this. It would ruin your sterling reputation."

She turned to put the glass away. I should have been angry at her dismissal, but I couldn't find the energy for it. Instead, I stayed in my seat and waited. If anything, maybe I would finally catch a glimpse of Marcella and get her advice on what happened with Jonathan Nyx as well as the magick, which seemed to touch me and my cousins.

After some time, when neither of them emerged, I stood on shaking legs. I'd been here a few times by myself, but there was something in the air, something sinister. A danger lurked overhead, and no one seemed to feel it but me.

I made my way through the crowd, careful to avoid wenches holding ales and a man with a red bandana wrapped around his face so only his eyes showed. For a moment, I thought it was Jonathan Nyx, blatantly disregarding the risk to his life by frequenting a popular haunt on the island. I blinked and the crowd had swallowed him up.

When I finally left, I could breathe again. I reached in my coat pocket and pulled out the neatly folded parchment, the one I stole from Diego Pascal's room. Holding it in my hands filled me with relief. I quickly replaced it and headed home, ignoring my frustration with Adrian's absence, and a prickle of an emotion I didn't recognize, something that made me loathe whomever he was dining with.

CHAPTER TWENTY-NINE

Hannah

Before I reached the familiar iron gates of my home, I stopped. I didn't need Adrian to sneak into the mortuary. I could do it myself. Claire's body was in the heart of Fort Crimson, outside the square. Because the fort wrapped around the small square and extended out to the Forest of Legend, the majority of the square was blockaded in the event of an attack or a natural disaster. However, Patrol headquarters, the prison, and the mortuary were located in the fort because there was no other space on the tiny island of Ankura to put them. I had to be careful. I knew Patrol would be out and about, especially at night.

I reached up and patted the back of my head, ensuring my pins were there. I'd been using them more and more, and they came in handy. They were like my tools: a key that got me into every locked door.

"This could be your chance, Han." Though I spoke the words, it felt as though Claire was speaking to me.

Before I left, I caught sight of Diego Pascal in his room, standing by the window staring down at me. He positioned himself so I could see him, the light from the room shining on his face. His dark stare felt like it was burning my flesh. He frowned as he narrowed his eyes. My heartbeat quickened and my blood ran cold. I held his stare, despite the fear bubbling inside of me. After a moment, I turned and headed for the village.

The village was surprisingly quiet. There were still a few men outside, drunk and meandering around, a few women lifting their skirts and showing off their ankles. I didn't like the square being empty. There was a good chance I would be seen. I lifted the collar of my coat and tucked my chin down, hoping to hide my face and mask my sex. I was grateful I'd decided to wear Adrian's clothes. If I resembled a man, maybe no one would bother me.

After cutting across the square and heading to the fort, my tension eased. A couple of men in their red uniforms spilled out of the office I was in hours ago, but I didn't see Brendan or Henry. A good thing since either of them would have recognized me.

I could see more fog rolling in. The waves crashed gently on the shore. There was no sign of disturbance. So far, dealings with Underedge seemed to be going all right. At least, I imagined so. If they were not, the hotheaded Mer King would have sent his army to attack us. I hoped we were adequately prepared. My father needed to reach out to our king and demand soldiers—Navy and Army. I wasn't sure if the king would respond as the war was only with our port town and not the entire continent.

"…still can't find the bloody bastard."

"How could he disappear with iron 'round his wrists?"

"You think he had anything to do with that Turner girl?"

I looked over to the left of the square where two Patrol members stood, smoking and holding unauthorized mugs of ale.

A pause. "Not Nyx's style," the second man said. "Wouldn't kill 'em much as he would kiss 'em." He dropped his mug to the ground, and his fellow office did the same. "We'd best be getting back to work."

I held my breath, pressing my lips together so tightly I was sure my teeth would cut the inside. I wanted to press my hand over my mouth to keep any sound from coming out, but I didn't want to move and risk having them catch me.

After their voices faded away, I waited another beat before I relaxed. When I was certain I was alone, I made my way across the road until I was pressed against the fort. My heart skipped a beat as my magick swirled inside of me, waiting to be used. If only I knew how to use it to disguise myself completely.

I followed the edge of the fort until I reached a small door hidden in the black stone. I wasn't surprised to find it locked and quickly removed a pin from my hair to unlock it.

"I did not expect to see Hannah Walker breaking into the mortuary late at night," a voice said from behind me. "But then again, I wasn't expecting to find Hannah Walker late at night at all."

My pulse raced in panic at hearing Adrian's voice. I hadn't heard him coming. He was the last person I expected to run into, especially considering Pepper's declaration he was indisposed and would be for the remainder of the evening.

I turned my attention back to the lock and tried to focus. "What are you doing here?" I continued to move the pin in the keyhole, attempting to find the latch. It was difficult to do now I had someone watching me.

"Pepper told me you were looking for me," he said.

"I thought you were busy." There was no way this lock was this impenetrable.

"I was." There was a smirk in his tone. I refused to look to see if I was right. Any sort of smile on Adrian's face would be distracting. "I'm not now. You almost seem jealous, Ms. Walker."

"Jealous?" I stopped what I was doing to look at him. I needed him to see my face to understand how ridiculous he sounded. "I think not." I turned back to the lock.

"Not to worry, my dear," he said. "Your secret is safe with me." He knelt down beside me and I nearly stumbled, seeing how close he was. "May I assist you?" Before I could respond, he took the lock in his hand and broke it off.

My mouth dropped. "How did you…?" My voice trailed off as I slowly stood. My knees screamed in pain from kneeling on the hard stone, but I didn't let on. I replaced my pin, my hands going to Adrian's.

"The lock was rusted," he explained.

Lie.

I opened my mouth to demand the truth when Adrian fixed a penetrating stare on my face. Before I knew what he was doing, he cupped my cheek and slowly traced the cut Diego Pascal had given me the night I stole the parchment from his desk. Adrian's blue eyes narrowed and his jaw popped with tension.

"Who did this to you?" he demanded. His voice was soft, quiet, and lethal. I swallowed the lump in my throat. His touch was gentle, reassuring, and his caress lit my body on fire. "Tell me."

"Diego Pascal," I said, my voice barely above a whisper.

His nostrils flared. "This was after I sent you to find me information?" he asked.

I sunk my fingers in the thin material of the pantaloons I was wearing. For some strange reason, I found it difficult to tell Adrian the truth. I didn't want him to be concerned about me. I didn't want to assume there was a chance he could be concerned about me at all.

His fingers caressed the wound. My eyes fluttered closed, and before I could stop myself, I leaned into his touch. His hand was cool but soft. The tension in my body eased as he touched me.

He pulled away from me abruptly, dropping his hand to his side. I opened my eyes in surprise and watched as he stalked closer to the door of the mortuary. Every muscle in his body was filled with tension. He flexed his fingers before curling them into tight balls he left hanging at his hips. When he reached the door, he took the handle in his hand and practically ripped the door off its hinges. I was surprised it hadn't fallen off.

The square was shrouded in darkness and the voices from the marketplace floated over to us. For the most part, though, the night was silent. The waves of the nearby ocean smoothly came to the shore and the stars twinkled over us. I was never a fan of the dark because of the monsters it hid. But now, I understood its importance, its benefits.

I followed Adrian through the door, hastening my steps to keep up with him. The last thing I wanted was someone catching me lingering outside.

We walked into the room, inky black filling the confined space. The pungent smell hit me immediately. It smelled like rotting flesh that had spent too much time in the sun. My stomach twisted and I wanted to gag.

Adrian didn't seem to notice my struggle and I didn't wish to call attention to it. He seemed to possess the ability to move through the area without concern.

When we spilled out of the hallway, we stepped into a room with three tables. Two were empty. One held a body. The stench overwhelmed and suffocated me. I had to turn my head as my shoulders rose up to my ears. I was ready to throw up and I didn't care if I did it in front of Adrian.

"Brendan mentioned skin," I managed to get out. "Under her fingernails."

Though I was unable to see Claire up close, her body was far from being the way I envisioned it. Her skin was sliding off the bones, and her air fell out in clumps. Blood stained her open cuts, clumping up.

I placed my hand over my mouth. I wasn't sure if it was an unconscious reaction to seeing the desecration of a woman I considered my closest friend, or to keep myself from vomiting. Clearly, she had suffered before life escaped her body. If what Brendan and Henry said was correct, she fought hard before dying.

I hesitated, frozen where I stood. I wanted to walk over to her. I wanted to know who could do such a terrible, vile thing to a human being, and I believed looking at what happened would help me understand.

But I was scared. I didn't want to see the horror I could have prevented. I didn't want to be confronted with my selfish mistake. I was too ashamed.

My magick burned inside of me, reacting to my thoughts, trying to protect me.

Do not be her. Walk over there. Look at your friend. Learn from her. Solve this for her. You won't get anywhere hiding in the shadows. Step into the light, even if you are afraid.

I forced myself to walk over to Claire's body. She was worse than I could ever imagine. Surprisingly enough, seeing her helped temper the scent and I didn't have the desire to throw up anymore. I reached for her hands and then stopped myself. I didn't want to touch her, even if I could see flesh under her nails.

"She fought back," I said, pointing to her hands while being careful not to touch her. "Skin there. Do you see it? Underneath her fingertips."

Adrian opened his mouth to respond when the door to the mortuary creaked open.

"I know you're in there," a voice shouted. "You broke the lock. But that's not going to do you any good. You're trapped inside."

CHAPTER THIRTY

Hannah

Without warning, Adrian crossed to me, stepping around the slab Claire's body rested on. He didn't stop until one hand cupped the back of my head while the other held my hip. Then he claimed my lips.

I could barely breathe as his lips touched mine. I'd never been kissed, save for a sloppy kiss at fifteen when Henry had been drunk and thought himself in love with me. It was wet and clumsy and put me off kissing. Until now.

I expected Adrian's kiss to be passionate, even hungry. Instead, his lips were soft and coaxing, not demanding. The kiss made me light-headed, and my knees buckled slightly. I had to lean into him to keep from stumbling and losing my balance. His hand tightened on my waist.

My stomach tumbled, causing it to feel the same way my head did. His other hand came up to cup my cheek, his long fingers extended into my hair.

It was difficult to be upset at the kiss, difficult to be frustrated when it made me feel…special. Cared for. Of course, the notion Adrian Blood could care for me was absolutely ridiculous. However, it didn't deter me from enjoying being in his arms.

When he finally pulled away, it took me a moment to catch my breath and open my eyes. After I did, I could not look away from him. He didn't seem as affected by the kiss as I was, neither gasping for air nor clutching his chest to calm his beating heart. He was, however, looking at me strangely. I could not describe it even if I wanted to.

"Ms. Walker," a familiar voice said.

I closed my eyes. Out of everyone who could have caught me, why did it need to be

Henry Davenport?

I turned to face him, certain my cheeks were as red as the sash Jonathan Nyx wore around his boot. I cleared my expression of emotion as much as I could.

"Henry," I replied.

Adrian shifted behind me, the material of his clothes moving against my back.

"That's Lead Davenport," Henry corrected sharply.

"A promotion," I said.

"You sound surprised." Henry's gaze locked with mine.

I didn't want to insult him. I didn't want to be petty, especially not after what Adrian and I had discovered from the body. And not with the history I shared with Henry.

"I'm glad for you," I said, hoping kindness was the correct response.

His lips twisted into a combination of a frown and a scowl.

"Lieutenant Pickard mentioned your relationship with Mr. Blood," he said. He began to circle Adrian and me, his gray eyes fierce and angry. There was something else. A longing for something that would never be his, and a bitterness revealing he had yet to accept it. "I'm glad for you as well, though Adrian Blood is not the sort of man who inspires loyalty, Hannah."

Adrian tensed behind me, and I reached back and took his hand in mine without thinking.

I squeezed it once. I was emboldened and his hand felt nice against mine. I wanted him to know, regardless of what Henry said, Adrian needed to hold his animosity back so Henry would not smell it. Henry had a knack for getting underneath a person's skin, of saying things to hurt with intention. I remembered when he tied a man to a chair based on the presumption the man was stealing from him. If Henry outright insulted him, I was unsure as to how Adrian would react.

"I am perfectly capable of making decisions on my own," I said. I released Adrian's hand.

"Clearly," Henry said bitterly, his eyes narrowed at my hand now that it was free. "I only want what's best for you, and Adrian Blood is as sordid as he is dangerous. Have you not heard the rumors about him? How he uses women as nothing more than a means to an end?"

"I am an equal opportunist in that regard," Adrian said. "I use men as I use women."

"What are you doing here, Henry?" I asked. "I didn't think you were on Patrol at this time of night."

"I wanted to see if there was anything I could pick up on the body," he admitted. His eyes shifted over to Adrian. "Hannah, why are you here with him? I don't want you hurt." His gray eyes burned into mine. "Adrian Blood has left broken hearts, among other things, in his wake." *Truth.*

I swallowed. I shouldn't care what Henry told me. Most of the time, he was drunk and didn't understand what he was saying. Whatever his intentions, they left tiny little cuts as they landed on my skin.

"My relationship with Adrian is none of your concern," I told him, my voice shaking as I did so.

"What are you doing here?" Henry asked, forcing his gaze away from me and onto Adrian.

I clenched my teeth to keep my anger and my magick from spilling out. Henry must be bitter because I chose not to follow him into the dark trenches his drink led him to, whereas he assumed I followed Adrian here to see the brutalized body of my best friend.

"Surely you must know I've come to see Claire," I said as though it were obvious. "Brendan accused me and Richard of having some sort of affair and I plan to prove myself innocent of the crime. I wanted to see if there was any evidence that might help. Upon seeing the body, surely you know I'm unable to wreak havoc in a way that would leave her looking like that."

Henry shrugged. "We do not know what to think," he admitted, walking over to where

Claire's body lay. His nose wrinkled, probably from the smell. "You know how Brendan can be. He peppers things with as many theories as he can and waits to see what sticks. He meant no insult."

"He was in my home when he said those vile things," I pointed out. "Richard has not been over to see me since. He might actually believe what Brendan said."

"He might not like you're affiliated with a man who has ties to the seedy underworld of Ankura," Henry pointed out, shifting his attention back to Adrian. "You know, Mr. Blood, I find it rather odd you decided to befriend Hannah at the same time her father has demanded an increase in his collections. There wouldn't be any sort of connection between the two, would there?"

"Hannah bound herself to me," he pointed out. His voice was as smooth as the waves rolling to the shore. "I did not seek her out. You see how lovely she is. From the rumors I've heard, Mr. Davenport, I'm aware you two dabbled in your own love affair that, unfortunately for you, did not work out. I, on the other hand, appreciate her and do not plan to let her slip through my fingers so easily."

I didn't like Adrian giving his opinion of my failed relationship with Henry with such familiarity.

I almost wished Brendan had caught me rather than Henry. There was too much history between Henry and me, too much we had not touched upon, even though he courted me for a few weeks at most.

It'd been the previous year, when I was six-and-ten and he had turned twenty and joined the Crimson Navy. He did not drink then, but he and Brendan were close. They had been close since they were children who both grew up on the streets of Ankura and wanted a better life for themselves.

Brendan met Lizzie because Henry had sought me out when Lizzie and I were scouting buildings for her blacksmith shop. I remember it so clearly, the way Henry would look at me with such intensity my stomach would turn, and every hair on my body would make me feel so aware of myself it was difficult to remember I was surrounded by people.

When Henry didn't receive the promotion he wanted, he retreated into himself, having regarded his value as a man in the work he did. He started drinking and turning into a sullen person I didn't want to be around any longer, and I stopped seeing him.

Henry made a guttural sound I couldn't decipher. I'd almost forgotten about what Adrian said until he placed a hand on my hip, giving it a gentle squeeze, as though he was marking his territory. As much as I wanted to pull away from him, I resisted. If Henry saw me with someone else, it might encourage him to stop looking at me with such sad eyes.

"Hannah is rebelling against society," Henry said, his tone light. "She's sneaking into mortuaries and has engaged in a ruinous relationship. She's mourning the loss of her friend. When she comes to her senses, she will realize what vile filth you really are and peel herself away from you."

"I'm right here," I said, glaring at the two of them. "As much as you both like to think you know me, you don't. Instead of making assumptions about my feelings about Claire's death and how I'm handling my emotions, you can ask me." I shifted my gaze to Henry. "I think we are finished here, Henry. I've seen what I came to see. Adrian and I will be leaving."

"You've done a lot more here than look at things," he pointed out, taking a step closer to me. "If you needed somewhere private, you should show him the place by the old docks where you and I would go when we wanted our own privacy."

Adrian growled. Any sort of charm he'd held on to vanished. His nostrils flared, his body tensed, and his jaw popped. I'd seen Adrian angry before, but I hadn't seen him menacing. As much as Henry's words insulted my honor—especially since we hadn't done anything inappropriate during our time at the docks—he didn't deserve Adrian's wrath. I placed a hand on Adrian's forearm, hoping it would calm him. There was no need to give Henry such attention. It was exactly what he wanted.

Adrian didn't even look at my hand, but the tension in him eased slightly.

Henry, however, watched every move I made. "You surprise me in your selection of men, Hannah," he said.

I didn't want to hear this. Not now. Not from him.

I wrinkled my nose. Now we were away from Claire, I could smell the vile hint of alcohol as it hit my face. "You need to go home, Henry," I murmured. I tried to keep the sympathy from my voice, knowing it would make him angry. He was a proud man, and it was one of the reasons we didn't fit well together. I tried to reach for him so I could take his hand and give him a gentle squeeze in order to emphasize my point.

"Don't touch me," he said, dodging my hand, his eyes narrowed. "You don't get to tell me what to do. Not after…" He let his voice trail off and I was glad he did. I didn't want Adrian to know Henry and I used to have a relationship that pushed the boundaries of social acquaintances. "Did you find what you were looking for, Hannah? Or did you think the mortuary where the rotting corpse of your friend still rests was the perfect location for a midnight rendezvous with your new lover?"

Anger bubbled up inside me, stealing bits and pieces of my breath. I narrowed my eyes, ready to attack. It was such a familiar feeling I hadn't felt since being with him, it was easy to slip back into the role.

"We were leaving," Adrian said, slipping his hand into mine.

I opened my mouth, ready to argue with him, to tell him I didn't want to leave, not after Henry's display, but Adrian led me out.

We walked away from the fort all the way to my home in utter silence. Each time I opened my mouth to demand Adrian give an explanation, I faltered. My magick pushed and pulled in my body like the jerky movements of sails in the wind. It was probably a good thing I didn't get the chance to react to Henry. My magick might have spilled out without any urging.

When we reached the iron gates, Adrian took my hand and stopped me. "You must stay away from Claire's case until I look into it more," he said, his tone adamant. "Do you understand?"

"Why?" I asked.

"Because I insist on it," he snapped. His gaze searched my face and he towered over me. For a moment, I was certain he would kiss me again and my stomach flipped at the thought. "Don't do anything reckless, do you understand? There's more to this than you realize."

"You saw something on the body," I guessed. "What did you see?"

He turned and left without saying anything more. I wanted to call him back, but I knew it would only draw attention to us. Instead, I headed inside, slipping through the front door with no one seeing me. I was about to climb the stairs when Harrold stopped me.

"You have a note," he said, handing me a piece of parchment. There was a floral, musky scent to it I didn't recognize.

Meet me in the Forest of Legend tomorrow night. We have much to discuss. -M

CHAPTER THIRTY-ONE

Adrian

After I left Hannah safely at her home, I considered interrogating Pepper about what Charles Rochester was implying in regards to our discussion and who might want to kill me. He referred to her as a shadow, but I knew exactly who he meant. But dawn was starting to break, and I had to return to my ship. Once there, I found myself consumed by thoughts of Hannah Walker.

I stared at the wall in my chamber, my feet resting on my bureau. The waves rocked my ship slowly, so much calmer than the storm a few nights prior. I wished it was enough to lull me to sleep, but it wasn't. She was seared into my mind.

I shouldn't have kissed her. And yet, I could still feel the rush of blood inside of her as I met her lips, the way her heartbeat doubled with anticipation.

She wanted this too. What was more startling was my reaction: I had no heart of any sort, but when I kissed her, I could have sworn…

That was not possible. I would not even entertain it.

I took my feet off the bureau, stood, and stretched my arms. I turned my thoughts to Claire. There was skin underneath her fingernails, indicating a struggle. She fought back. A Blood Mage might have healed by now, but it was worth looking into.

***

When darkness descended, I threw on my coat and stepped off my ship. Each time I touched land, it gave me a spark, a thrill. I was alive, despite the fact I shouldn't be, and while I couldn't roam during the day, I was lucky to be able to roam at all.

The brothel was still closed, and I pulled open the doors to step inside. Before I could turn to the lobby and confront Pepper, the siren I'd interviewed before, the one with the startling eyes, caught my attention. She pressed her lips together and inclined her head to the staircase.

I followed her up the stairs, careful to keep my footsteps light. If she didn't want Pepper overhearing her information, I would respect that.

When we reached her room, I closed the door behind us and waited. She was by the large window, her back to me, one hand on the glass. Though her face was hidden from view, I could picture longing in those eyes. She had a view of the ocean from her room. I hoped she saw it as a small gift rather than a curse, being so close to home and yet unable to reach it.

"I don't have time to wait," I told her.

"You'll have time for this," she snapped, looking at me over her shoulder.

Without warning, I used my speed and rushed to her. I leaned forward so my face was a hair away from hers. She didn't flinch, she didn't recoil at my glare. She stood her ground, though I noticed her hands shake, and her knees nearly gave out. Stubborn fool.

"You will not speak to me this way," I said, each word clipped and careful. "If you have information, give it. If not, keep your mouth shut."

"When will I be transferred?" she asked without wavering, searching my eyes. "You've been promising me the last week."

"Much has changed since the Consumption," I said. "You know this. What do you expect from me?"

"I expect you to keep your word, Blood Mage," she said.

"Two people are dead. Two people who would have freed you already. Does that mean nothing to you?"

"Do you honestly expect it to?"

I didn't. Their deaths meant something to me because if people started to piece together what the dead had been doing, they would figure out I was involved as well.

"I want to return to my people," she continued. "I want to go home."

"You wish to return to a place who sold you to me like you were nothing more than fish?" I shook my head. The little respect I felt for her disappeared. Why anyone would wish to return to where they were clearly unwanted was something I didn't understand. "Why do that to yourself? Have you no pride?"

"I plan to return so I can stop this from happening to someone else," she said. "So no other siren will have to go through this. I plan to get an army, start a war, and bring the heads of the Pascals to my people as a prize."

"What end will I meet in your little fantasy?" I asked.

"I suppose that depends," she said. "What do you plan to do about what's happening? Will you continue to take the sirens given to you, or will you finally stop?"

"I am saving you."

"What of your counterpart?" she demanded. "Why is she leaving at all hours, meeting with Diego Pascal?"

I pressed my lips together. Pepper. Again, Pepper.

"When?"

"The night you stayed on your ship," she replied.

The night Pepper sent Hannah to me. Pepper was behind everything.

CHAPTER THIRTY-TWO

Hannah

I decided to stay clothed in the attire Adrian had given me. I didn't want to wear a dress and risk exposure. This was my one chance to meet with Marcella and discover the truth of my nature and I didn't want to ruin it. What happened at the Consumption still confounded me, and then there was what happened to Claire. A strange sort of contradiction: Adrian's life had been saved and Claire's life had not. If I could trade them…

Guilt wrenched through me. I didn't want to even entertain such a thought. I missed Claire, and felt maybe I could have helped her. But that didn't mean Adrian should die.

I'd missed my time with Marcella that evening and I didn't intend it to happen again.

I couldn't help wonder why she hadn't showed. Perhaps Jonathan Nyx's escape rattled her and she didn't wish to risk exposure.

As far as I knew, Marcella had no affiliation with Ankura society. As an outsider, she might have been questioned and demanded she prove herself human.

All conjecture. I shook my head as I stepped into a pair of dry boots. At least Marcella had written to me and said she still wanted to meet.

I pulled my hair back and braided it, tucking it into my overcoat to hide it. My heart hammered in my chest and my hands were slick with perspiration. The last place I wanted to be was in the Forest of Legend. Though I knew a beast did not kill Claire, I was also aware of my mother's warnings: danger lived in the forest and I should stay away from there.

A strand of hair fell in my face, but I didn't have the time to re-braid it. I tucked it behind my ear and opened my window, preparing to sneak outside from my balcony. I closed the glass behind me, the wind whipping at my face and tugging at my clothing. I pushed back, reached for the tree, and unrestricted by a dress, I shimmied down the trunk with more ease. My magick cushioned my landing.

I didn't bother to look around for guards or lingering people. I was sneaking out more than I was staying in lately, and the thrill of it sparked excitement inside of me. No wonder many women in my position skirted the rules society demanded they should not. The rush, the feeling of making my own choices without asking for permission, doing something bold and independent made me want to do it again.

I passed my mother's fountain and crossed the field, making sure I moved silently. The old coat was heavy and stifling, but it masked me from view. I felt safe wrapped up in its warmth.

As I was about to sneak through the iron gates, I heard footsteps behind me. I straightened.

"No need to stop what you're doing on my account, Ms. Walker," a familiar timbre said. "By all means, lead the way."

Sage Pascal stepped out of the shadows. Standing beside me, he reached my hips in height, but his green eyes were filled with knowledge of every sort—knowledge found in books and gained from experience.

"What are you doing out here?" I asked, keeping my voice down. I wanted to look up at

Diego Pascal's room to ensure he was unaware of my feeble attempt to sneak out, but I withheld from doing so.

"Following you," he said pointedly. "I thought it was obvious."

"Why?"

"We can discuss it on the way to wherever you're going so we can continue to avoid your father's guards," he suggested, nodding toward the west side of the manor.

Shadows crossed the field, indicating the guards were indeed coming. Though they did not speak, their footsteps were not as soft as they could be, even in the short grass.

"Fine," I said through gritted teeth, turning my attention back to Sage. "But you will tell me why you intend to follow me."

He nodded, but said nothing. We slid through the iron gates, and because of his stunted height, he had a much easier go of it than I did. Once we were through the gates, we pushed our backs against the stone wall, hiding from the guards.

We headed down the dirt path that spilled out into the square, keeping to the edge of the building. We needed to take a back road into the Forest. Part of me wanted to head to Blood's Brothel since the Forest was directly behind it, but I refrained. I didn't want to see Adrian, not after what happened yesterday.

Not after our kiss.

"Well?" I pushed, once we were in the square.

Noise pierced the night, masking our words. People stopped to stare at Sage. He was instantly recognized. Some laughed while others slithered away, not wanting to do business with him. A couple of women waved their fingers, smiling, while another was forward enough to walk up to him and kiss his cheek. Apparently, he had a reputation with women of the night, one I tried hard not to pay attention to.

Once he'd charmed the whore into leaving, he cleared his throat. "I heard reports of what happened to your friend," he said. "How there was a good chance her death was accidental due to a beast attacking her, and she was in the wrong place at the wrong time. The problem with that theory is, I've studied Ankura. I've studied the Forest of Legend. I know there isn't a hungry beast in the forest longing to feast on humans. At least, not one known to man. In all my research, I haven't found anything able to attack a human in such a manner."

We turned from the main path down a back road, the tree line of the forest dark and ominous. I stopped, fear prickling along my skin. I didn't want to enter the dread place where my friend was butchered.

"What is it?" Sage asked, looking up at me. "This is…hmm…this is where they found her. You hesitate out of fear?"

"How do you know that?" I demanded. It bothered me this stranger seemed to know more about Claire and her death than I did.

"What?" Sage asked. "About the case? I told you, I am conducting my own investigation.

As a Pascal, I have resources Patrol doesn't have."

"Such as?" I prodded.

“Money.” He lifted a shoulder into a nonchalant shrug. “Everyone has a price, Ms. Walker. You, me, even my brother.” Sage didn’t need to specify he meant Diego. I understood his implication. “My job is to find that price and offer two times the amount.”

“Why on earth would you do that?”

“Because a man bought will flow as freely as water,” he replied. “Well? Do you hesitate out of fear?”

“I hesitate because I am unsure as to what waits for me inside,” I said. I didn’t bother attempting to keep my annoyance with him out of my tone. Instead, I tried to make something out in the darkness, through the trees, in hopes to find anything that might settle my nerves a little.

“You certainly won’t know standing here,” he pointed out, and before I could stop him, he began walking into the forest.

I sighed. Marcella was supposed to be waiting for me here. Marcella was the person I longed to speak with about everything. About the truth of who I was, about my magick, about my mother. There was no one to distract me from finding her, not Adrian conducting an interrogation that almost got him killed, and not Jonathan Nyx escaping from Consumption. The forest provided a cushion against the outside world where we could discuss things and not be disturbed, except by the youngest Pascal brother. I didn’t feel comfortable leading him directly to Marcella. But, unfortunately, if I wanted answers, there was nothing more for me to do about it.

I almost wished I had had the foresight to take him to Blood’s Brothel. Sage might’ve gotten distracted by the women and I could’ve easily slipped out.

We continued to walk through the forest. Where Marcella wanted me to meet her was a guess, but I hoped I would come across her eventually. I wished she had been more specific in her note. A low branch whacked my face, stinging my skin, and I nearly tripped over a thick root. Rays from the moon slipped through the cracks between the trees, allowing me to see my way, but I had to squint and stare hard.

“How long must we wait?” Sage said from behind me.

“How should I know?” I retorted.

“Are you planning to kill me?” he asked.

“Why would I—"

Before I could finish the sentence, we walked into a small field filled with grass and wildfire. The fresh scent of dew and the cold filled my nose and I instantly relaxed. The moon hung low and I could see it clearly—and Marcella. She was young and beautiful, with ink-black hair pulled up into a complicated bun and sparkling brown eyes, which seemed to say she knew much more than what someone might expect from her. She wore a simple red dress, bold for an enchantress. I would’ve expected something more subtle, though her beauty would attract anyone’s attention.

“I am surprised you’ve brought a companion,” she said, her eyes fixed on Sage. “Though

I’m surprised it’s a Pascal and not your Blood Mage.”

I blinked once, unsure I heard her correctly. “I’m sorry?” I asked.

“Your Blood Mage.” She said it simply. “Adrian Blood.”

“I’m sorry,” I said through a smile. “Do you mean to say you believe Adrian Blood is a Blood Mage?”

“Belief has nothing to do with it,” she insisted, though she seemed amused I was having difficulty processing the news. “It is fact. He is a Blood Mage.”

CHAPTER THIRTY-THREE

Hannah

Adrian Blood was a Blood Mage?

I laughed, though I didn't find her statement humorous. I didn't know what else to do, or how to feel. It didn't help Marcella thought it wise to reveal such things in front of Sage. Either she didn't view him as a threat, or she didn't care about him being here.

I took a step back, my equilibrium thrown. I turned from Marcella, but there was no place for me to gather my bearings, not when tall, shadowed trees surrounded me and darkness bled through the spaces, filling them in. The leaves rustled, and even the stronger trees swayed in the brisk breeze. The sky had turned black and the stars and the moon had disappeared. I felt alone even though Sage and Marcella were here.

"Are you certain?" Sage asked.

I blinked. I didn't know if I should laugh or cry. My emotions bubbled in my chest and it pained me to take a breath.

I'd been told such beings existed so I wasn't entirely surprised to hear they were out there. Sage's reaction nonchalant reaction did surprise me. Apparently, he was aware of Blood Mages' existence, which meant there was a good chance his brothers were as well.

"Do you think I would lie, dwarf?" Marcella asked. "What would I have to gain from spitting out untruths?"

"She's not lying." I didn't care if Sage found out about me and my power. I shouldn't risk it, but in the face of what I was learning, and how long I'd waited to talk to Marcella, I didn't have much of a choice. What Marcella said was true—at least, she thought it was. There was no hint of manipulation in her words.

"How do you—"

"I do," I snapped.

Sage closed his mouth and stared ahead into a thicket of trees. If the Pascals were aware of Adrian's truth, Sage was doing a good job of pretending. However, I didn't think that was the case. Maybe Diego knew about him, maybe even Vibora, but Sage had been unaware.

My eyes burned with unshed tears. Magick swirled around me until I felt it pushing out my fingers. This time, I didn't try to stop it. I was not sure if my magick would glow the way it did when I inadvertently freed Jonathan Nyx. I didn't care. I didn't care about exposing myself in front of Sage. I didn't care about risking myself. I didn't care about any of it.

"You seem surprised, little witchling," Marcella said, her dark eyes twinkling with mischievous stars. "I'm certain you knew deep down there was something more to him than what you saw. Something dark. Something dangerous."

Ever since I first met him doing collections with my father, Adrian intimidated me. Everything stood on edge and it was difficult for me to focus around him because I constantly felt the need to protect myself. I knew he was dangerous. I had seen it in him when he was ready to kill that man in his storage room for stealing money from him. I could see his anger. I could feel it.

But a Blood Mage?

The reference to humans in regard to the man who tried to kill him. That he was on his ship the night I sought him out. That he conducted business only at night. Blood Mages were confined to the sea until darkness took over, which meant they stayed on vessels during the day because touching land would kill them. They were similar to Pyrate Mages in that respect, but they fed on life, on blood, rather than possessed magick.

Suddenly, Pepper's comments about Adrian's feeding came to my mind and I bent over and began to gag.

"Apparently, she doesn't have the stomach for such a revelation," Sage pointed out, his tone dry.

Sage reached out as though he was going to rub my shoulder or pat my back. I glared at him with as much ferocity as I could. The last thing I wanted was to be touched by anyone, especially a Pascal.

He caught my look and stopped, drawing his arm back to his side. When I was in control of my stomach, I stood. I had to wipe my mouth with the back of my hand, trying to rid my chin of the excess saliva.

"Are you quite finished?" Marcella asked.

I nodded, still unable to trust my voice. My cheeks pinched in embarrassment. I thrust my hands behind my back, horrified I was so weak and ignorant.

"You foolish girl," Marcella said. "How is it you've bound yourself to a Blood

Mage?"

"You never showed that night," I pointed out, my voice raw and cracking. My gaze found Sage, and I stopped talking. I had already said too much. I didn't think he knew I had magick, but it was clear Marcella did, and Sage was clever enough to read the spaces within our conversation. If I hadn't been so brazen when I left the house, so full of my "independence," getting caught would've never happened.

"No," she agreed. "I had other matters to deal with. Your magick proved useful in releasing Nyx from his confines."

"Magick?" Sage asked.

"You must not say such things in front of the Pascals," I said, raising my voice.

"Just because he's a Pascal doesn't mean he holds the same values as his family," Marcella pointed out. She shifted her eyes to Sage, tilting her head. "Go on, then. Tell her. Will you reveal to the world what she is, and what you've learned here?"

He cleared his throat and glanced away.

"What do you mean, my magick proved useful?" I demanded to know.

"You released Nyx."

I shifted my gaze to Sage. He was clearly interested in the conversation, even if he was holding his counsel. I was grateful he didn't burst into questions about my magickal abilities, but I couldn't help but wonder if he was already aware of it. Could those resources he claimed to have bought be information my sister and my father knew?

I couldn't allow myself to worry about it now, not when there were more pressing matters that needed addressing.

Marcella wiggled her fingers at me, a small smirk decorating her face. "Do you believe me?"

I ignored her. "Mr. Pascal," I said firmly. "Do you plan on telling anyone about me and what is discussed here, whether to Patrol, my father, or your brothers? Because if you do, I will not hesitate to hex you. You think your life is difficult now? I can assure you, sir, I will make it worse."

In truth, I didn't know if I had the ability to hex Sage. However, I could use his ignorance to my advantage. I'd never threatened anyone before. My heart raced, but the sensation I got as my words sunk in caused a shift inside of me. Confidence sparkled at my fingertips. My magick hummed.

Marcella's smirk deepened. Sage was a Pascal, and while he seemed more approachable than his older brothers, I couldn't trust him. I was tired of being afraid. I had magick. I wanted to make it work for me rather than bury it and pretend I was normal and my magick didn't exist. It would be akin to burying a piece of myself and living a lie. An endeavor I would fail at.

"I would never reveal your secret, Ms. Walker," he said. "I swear it."

I held my breath, waiting for my magick to respond. *True.*

I nodded once. Marcella's eyes sparkled.

"So? You mentioned my magick was responsible for Jonathan Nyx's escape?"

She nodded. "Your magick freed him," she said, pointing her finger at me, "but somebody used you to do it."

Regardless of what Kara had said to me at the funeral, I was certain it was her. "Kara," I muttered, my hand on one hip, looking at the way the wet grass nipped at my boots.

"Your cousin who can't seem to get a handle on her own magick?" Marcella shook her head, her soft curls moving back and forth. "No. Kara has much to learn, even though she is powerful. Your magick was used and manipulated in order to free Nyx."

"How?" I demanded. "How is that even possible? Who would know I have magick, aside from my cousins?"

"Who, indeed?" Marcella shifted her eyes. "You must learn about your magick if you are ever to learn about your mother and your aunts, for that matter. Your magick is a gift directly from the Mother. The Father had no hand in it. In fact, the Father loathes all magick. Consumptions are almost like a religious ceremony in honor of the Father, because men are threatened by a woman who can do more than they."

"I must learn?" I asked. "Who could teach me about magick? I doubt Lizzie knows more than I."

"Who, indeed?" she repeated. This time, she turned to a nearby tree and rubbed the trunk with affection.

I closed my eyes, feeling my magick flare in annoyance. "Who released Jonathan Nyx using my magick? And no lies."

"Have I been lying?" she asked. "Tell me, child. You would know."

"How do you know about my abilities?" I asked before I could stop myself. "I haven't told anyone, save for my sister."

"Then you already know your answer," Marcella returned.

I opened my mouth, but there was nothing I could say. Was she implying Lizzie had told her about me? How did Lizzie even know about Marcella unless Marcella lived with my aunt in the coven somewhere in this forest? As much as I wanted to push further, I couldn't. Marcella was right. As far as I could detect, she was not lying. Not about this.

"As to your question about who would want to release Jonathan Nyx from his Consumption, you must ask yourself if Nyx is better off alive or dead," she said. "Would there be a reason why someone would want a Pyrate Mage alive?"

I shook my head. "I… I don't know."

"When you saved Adrian Blood's life in the brothel, what happened?"

"How did you—"

"Answer the question," she pressed, crossing her arms over her chest.

"Well, he said he owed me a debt," I replied.

"Which implies magick is bound by favors and debts," she said. "If someone saved Nyx, he owes them a debt. Find out who saved Nyx, you'll find out who manipulated your magick." She shifted her eyes to Sage. "I must go now."

"Wait. You've said nothing about my mother, about my magick," I cried, throwing my arms out.

"I also said nothing about bringing a guest, but you brought one along." She caught my eye. "I cannot trust my secrets to a Pascal, even the good one. I assure you, child, we will meet again." She reached out and squeezed my shoulder before disappearing deeper into the forest.

CHAPTER THIRTY-FOUR

Adrian

Pepper was quick, lethally so. I lunged for her. She might've been raised by me the minute she was turned, but I hadn't taught her everything.

She dodged my attack. "I'm surprised the great, most intelligent being on the planet did not figure it out sooner," she said through a cackle as she whipped around the bar. "I thought you figured it out the second that damn human came into the bar. I couldn't believe Diego Pascal would send a fucking human to try to kill you."

I jumped over the bar and managed to snatch her top. The fabric split, the rip filling the otherwise silent room. As Blood Mages, breathing wasn't a requirement, and while there were times we engaged in the activity to put humans at ease, we dropped all pretenses when we were with our own kind. She pulled away and I was left with a scrap of her tunic, which I flipped onto the bar.

She didn't hesitate and kicked me across the face.

My head snapped to the side. If I'd been human, she would have snapped my neck. As it was, she stunned me for a moment.

"He wasn't trying to kill me," I said.

She pulled her leg back. This time, when she kicked, I grabbed her ankle and twisted it. She let out a shriek that caused the room to vibrate.

I threw her across the room. She hit the wall directly across from where I was and crumpled into a heap. I dashed over to her and kicked her ribs. She spat up blood.

"He sent me a warning," I said.

"I know that *now*," she managed to get out.

I bent down and grabbed her throat with both hands. I had to restrain myself from squeezing until her eyes popped from her head and bloody tears poured down her face. I needed information.

"Why?" I ground out. "Why tell Pascal anything at all? Why did you betray me?"

"Because you were going to ruin *everything*," she squeaked out. Though she didn't breathe, she most certainly could feel the pressure on her throat as it closed in on itself. She would feel it crush under my hands before her immortality vanished. She tried to paw at my fingers, but the attempt to thwart me was weak, pathetic.

"I… I—"

I loosened my grip but barely, only because I wanted to hear why she would betray me when I was the one who had raised her, taken her under my wing, given her *everything*.

"All you had… All you had to do was follow orders," she said, "and…and you couldn't even d-do that. You were going to ruin everything."

"I was ensuring our survival," I roared. "What do you think happens when Underedge realizes their king was kidnapping sirens and selling them to Blood Mages to be used for feeding and sex? War is imminent because the king can't reveal he was part of the bargain in the first place."

"Bullshit," she said with a hiss. "You felt something, Adrian. Sympathy. You felt bad for them. You wanted to save them, like they're princesses locked up in a tower."

I growled. Feelings were not something I engaged in. They caused too many distractions and reduced the strongest of men to weak children.

"You think you're doing something right," she said. "But what about your own people? What are we supposed to feed on? We can't feed on humans. They'd figure out what we are and then hunt us the way they hunt the damn witches and mages. All they'd need to do was burn our ships while we slept and we'd be dead. That's it. We can't escape the sun the way Nyx can escape every blood prison cell he's placed in. The only compromise is the sirens. Disgusting as they are, they allow us to keep ourselves hidden. They guarantee our survival."

"Tell me, then, why one dead girl looks like she was brutalized by a *fucking* Blood Mage," I bellowed. I pressed harder on her throat, my nails piercing her skin. "You say you care about our survival, about keeping us hidden, and yet you risk everything by your carelessness to feed on one. You stupid fool."

"Adrian… Please." She stopped clawing at me. The pressure was getting to be too much. If I squeezed a little harder, I would put her out of her misery.

Suddenly, my neck burned. I released Pepper and was yanked back. Something was on my throat, something that seared my skin like icy fire. I couldn't even scream. I tried to pull it off, but when my fingers touched it, it burned them too.

"Marcus," Pepper spat out, rolling to her hands so she could breathe. "What took you so long?"

Marcus? Marcus Sawyer had silver on me?

"You know I will kill you, Sawyer," I told him through gritted teeth. "You know I plan to take your face in my hands and rip it in two so you suffer before you burst into ash."

Marcus chuckled behind me.

"Take him to the storage room in the back." Pepper pointed behind me, her voice raw and ragged. "Chain him up to the chair. I'll take care of him personally."

"But—"

"Just do it," she snapped. "Then leave. I don't want you around to fuck this up."

Marcus said nothing and began to drag me backward. I struggled as much as I could, but with the silver wrapped around my throat, there was nothing I could do. Unless a miracle occurred, I was as good as dead.

CHAPTER THIRTY-FIVE

Hannah

The first thing I wanted to do was march straight to Adrian's brothel and demand an explanation. I was hurt and angry and needed a reason why he'd kept who he was from me, especially since he knew I was an enchantress. Instead, I walked home with Sage. I didn't want him to be witness to my confrontation with Adrian as Sage already knew too much.

We barely spoke as we walked home and I was glad. Every now and then, he would tilt his head up and look at me, his mouth open, poised to ask me a question. I never reciprocated the look, never allowed him to have a chance at going through with his question. I ignored him as much as I could and he dropped his head, casting his eyes ahead, not bothering to ask me after all.

For the next two days, I remained home and moped. I tried to do menial tasks to get my mind off Adrian, but each time I tried, I exhausted myself minutes after starting an activity. Even Lizzie thought me uncharacteristically morose and lectured me on my sullen attitude. In truth, I was acting nothing short of pathetic.

"I'm sensitive to your energy," she said, not bothering to hide her annoyance as she took a seat at my bureau and glared at me in the mirror. She had burst in my room demanding I tell her what was wrong because she could not take my sadness any longer.

"Does this have anything to do with the man you sneak off to see?"

I leaned back against my pillow and stared up at my ceiling. There was a shaded spot that stuck out against the rest, and I couldn't help but be drawn to it. Water damage from a particularly bad storm. I laced my fingers together and rested them on my chest.

"Yes," I said. It was easier to lie than to tell Lizzie the truth, and strangely enough, I didn't feel as guilty as I normally did in such circumstances. I was not quite sure what that meant about me as a person. Was I lying so much the truth had gotten lost? Or maybe the truth didn't matter as much in the grand scheme of things. "I learned something about him. He lied to me about what—about who he really is, and I don't know what to do about it."

She grabbed one of my powder brushes from the vanity. Her eyes narrowed at it. How could my sister know the difference between a rapier and a cutlass, but not understand the necessity of a powder brush? "Well, do you care about him?" she asked, turning the brush in her hand.

I lifted my head to look at her. "What do you mean?" I asked.

"It's a rather simple question, dear sister." She glanced over her shoulder. "Do you care about him?"

"Care about him?" I snorted, shaking my head. I shifted on the bed, trying to get comfortable despite the unsettled feeling I had caring about Adrian.

"Yes, care about him," Lizzie said as though it was obvious. "You must care a little if you are sneaking out of the house to see him." She smiled, but for some strange reason, there was sadness in her eyes. "Keep your feelings to yourself if you must, but I know if I cared about someone and it seemed like they betrayed me in some way, I would at least give them the opportunity to explain themselves. I would not assume and ruin a good thing."

My flesh prickled and I realized Lizzie was not talking about me anymore. I peeked at her, tilting my chin up so it grazed my chest. She seemed unduly fascinated by a tool she rarely used.

"You think talking is going to bandage a betrayal?" I asked, doubtful.

"Perhaps, perhaps not," she said, setting the brush down. "But at least you'll give him a chance to explain himself." She turned in the chair, tilting her head so she could catch my eyes. "I think everyone deserves a chance to explain themselves, no matter who they are."

I wasn't so sure. I stared at the ceiling, at the blemish, and let Lizzie's words sink in. Would my sister truly mean what she said if she knew I was referring to a Blood Mage? Probably not.

My best course of action would be to avoid Adrian at all costs.

***

The next evening after supper when our guests had retired, Father pulled me aside. I was less afraid of Diego Pascal now I knew what Adrian was. Diego had not sought me out since catching me in his room, and the times we happened to be in the same room together, he had been polite, though his gaze seemed to follow me wherever I went. If Sage was going to tell my secrets, I was sure he would have done so already. Of course, I couldn't help but wonder if he was waiting for the perfect moment to try to get something out of me. He already had everything. What more could I give him?

"Yes, Father?"

"I need you to go to Blood's Brothel and retrieve his collection," he said. "I must meet with your uncle regarding this Underedge business. The king refuses to send us aid and now we must figure out our next course of action."

As much as I wanted to refuse my father's request, I didn't. He had his own stress he needed to deal with and he was asking me for assistance. How could I refuse him?

"I shall send one of my guards with you," he said, placing his hand on my shoulder. "You must have an escort."

"I need to be able to do this on my own or I will not earn any respect," I pointed out. I didn't tell him I had been about town frequently at night and no one had recognized me. As long as I kept to myself, and was much more careful than I had been the last time when Sage caught me, I would be fine. "Allow me to do this job and earn your trust."

"You don't need to earn it, my dear. You already have it." He dropped his hand from my shoulder and leaned forward. "You will take a carriage with a driver who will protect you, then. He will not go in the brothel with you. If anyone tries anything with you, Hannah, do what you must in order to protect yourself. Do you understand? If you have any concern over revealing certain things, put them to the side and do what you must. I promise I will take care of it."

He knew. He knew about me. There was a good chance he knew about Lizzie as well. It must be why he was all right with her opening her own shop, with allowing us more freedom than other young women in our station. He knew we could protect ourselves if we needed to.

If only I knew how.

"Of course," I said. "Father, is it true you've increased the amount you're collecting from everyone?"

My father narrowed his eyes. "Who told you that?" he asked. There was a darkness on his face I had not seen before, and while I knew it was not directed at me, I could not help but be wary.

"I overheard Patrol," I said, "when I walked Lizzie to her shop."

My father sighed, picking up one of the silver spoons and inspecting it in the light. "Yes, I am afraid that's true. Not everyone is happy about it. With the threat of war, protection taxes must be increased."

"Why is there a threat of war?" I could not help but ask. "I don't understand what Ankura has done to upset Underedge."

"Why worry about that, my child?" He placed the spoon back on the table. "Just take

Blood's collection and then come straight home."

"Father." Typically, I wouldn't push for an answer, but I didn't want him treating me like I was some sort of child. If he could trust me to retrieve the collection in the first place, why couldn't he do the same regarding why we were collecting a specific amount?

You could always check your powers, a voice in my head suggested. *See if he's telling the truth.* I rubbed away a drop of wine that had fallen from my goblet during supper. I promised myself I would never break the confidence of my family members. I knew what it felt like when Lizzie attempted such a thing with me.

I pressed my lips together to keep myself from saying or reacting in a way that revealed my turmoil. I figured he knew I had some spark of magick within me, but I felt sure he didn't know what that magick was. Which meant he did not know I was able to ask him questions and decipher whether he was telling me the truth. Would it break his trust, doing something he didn't know I could do?

Probably. Yet, I was tempted.

"Please," I said, leveling my gaze so it locked with his. "You trust me with your collection. Trust me with this. Please."

"You know the body they found, the one they attributed to Jonathan Nyx?" my father asked. "The one that got him caught finally?"

I nodded. “The waterlogged body.”

“It was an Underedge siren,” he said, his voice low.

Truth.

“Not the first one. Underedge believes we’re waging war on them by attacking and killing their sirens.” I opened my mouth to ask how they died and why they attributed the murders to us, but my father placed his hands on the table and stood abruptly. “I must go. You should as well. I don’t want you out too late, Han. It is already dark.”

The two of us left in separate carriages. It felt strange to me to go to Blood’s Brothel in a carriage when I had been visiting the business on foot the majority of the time. I hadn’t stepped into a carriage since Claire’s funeral.

I smoothed out the wrinkles of Adrian’s pantaloons, swallowing. Guilt still gnawed at me. I worried it wouldn’t rest until I could put her ghost to rest.

An image of the Claire from the mortuary flashed across my mind, and I closed my eyes. The smell somehow lingered in my memory to the point where it felt as though I could taste the rotting flesh of her corpse. I sucked in air, but it was too warm, too clammy. The rocking of the carriage teased and prodded my stomach, causing my head to spin. If we didn’t arrive at Adrian’s business soon, I would spill my guts all over the carriage floor.

At that moment, the horses stopped. I had to grab on to the edge of my seat to resist the forward momentum. I forced myself to swallow, though that didn’t do anything for my nerves.

I waited for the man to let me out. There was something ominous about my surroundings. The driver opened the door and helped me down. I went to the brothel and pulled the door open. It struck me why I felt a chill here

It was too silent. Empty. Deserted.

I headed to the bar, seeing no one, and made my way to the storage room. Perhaps someone would be there, cleaning up. When I saw what was in there, my heart nearly stopped. Adrian was tied up, lying on the cold stone floor.

He was so still I didn’t think he was breathing.

CHAPTER THIRTY-SIX

Hannah

I rushed over to Adrian. His head was tilted back, but his eyes were closed and his body slack. There were cuts all over different parts of him. Some were already healing themselves. From my mother's warnings, I knew the Shadow Magick in a Blood Mage's veins allowed them to heal themselves, and yet, it did not seem to be working for Adrian.

Minor cuts seemed to be clotting as they would in someone like me, but for a Blood Mage, it was uncharacteristically slow. When I reached Adrian, I discovered why. He was in chains, arms hanging limply behind him in his chair, while shackles wrapped around his feet. They were iron, blocking his magick from working. Which meant the iron would block mine as well.

All of my anger and pain at discovering Adrian's true identity disappeared the moment I saw him sitting there. All I could think about was figuring out how to get him free from his shackles.

"Adrian?" I whispered, my hand going to his face.

He let out a muffled groan but did nothing more. His eyelids didn't even flutter. At least I knew he was alive.

I sighed with relief, my eyes scanning him.

Think, Hannah. Whoever did this will be returning soon. You do not want to be here when they do. What will they do to you, a mere enchantress, when they've tortured a Blood Mage?

Since I was unable to use my magick to unbind him, I knelt down and pressed my hand against the chair. It was cool to touch and I was left unharmed. Odd. I always assumed the iron was painful, but maybe it was a deterrent rather than something that administered harm to the magicked entity.

I could work with that.

I reached up and pulled out a pin from my hair. Each shackle had a lock I had to pick. I was used to sneaking into locked drawers or rooms, not undoing iron restraints. I didn't know how long it would take me to free Adrian's right foot, let alone his wrists and his other ankle.

Regardless, I had to try.

I slid my pin into the lock and felt for a latch. I had to go slowly, carefully, and I closed my eyes, hoping it would enhance my ability to find it. If I needed it, my magick would be there when I was ready for it.

"Adrian, can you hear me?" I asked softly. I was desperate to hear him talk, to find out if he was all right.

"Have you… come… to save me again?" His voice was raw and broken. I winced as he spoke, though my heart squeezed with hope.

If he was able to string words together to create a sentence, that had to be a good sign.

My magick flowed through me, insistent, pushing against my fingers. My nerves tingled. I wished I knew how to use it fully. The buzzing energy said there was a way I could direct it somewhere and get it to do what I wanted. If I knew how, I'd be able to think of a faster way to get Adrian out of his restraints.

Focus, Hannah. You do not have the time to—

"Hannah Walker," a voice purred, echoing in the room.

Adrian stirred at the sound of it. I straightened and turned. There, next to the open door, was none other than Pepper, her red hair pulled from her face, freckles like blood splatter across her face.

"Pepper?" I sputtered stupidly. I stood and turned, trying to shield Adrian's body from her gaze. "What are you doing here?"

I glanced over to the door. From my vantage point, the brothel was still empty. I wondered if it was closed on purpose. Perhaps Adrian or Pepper had decided not to open tonight.

"What do you think I'm doing here?" She smirked. "My job."

"I don't understand." I swallowed, my magick tickling the area beneath my skin. Pepper did this to Adrian? Pepper always seemed to respect him. He seemed to trust her more than he trusted most of his employees and considering how she didn't fawn over him made me respect her more than I would have. Why would Pepper do such a thing to him? It didn't make sense.

"Of course, you wouldn't," Pepper said, rolling her eyes as she strolled around Adrian and me. "You have everything you want. You couldn't understand what it feels like to want something of your own. Even now, you wear Adrian's clothes. I can smell him on you. I'm sure your father allowed you to leave home and come here. Let me guess—he needs Adrian's collection payment?" Pepper stopped and stepped toward me. "Does he know what you wear, birdie? Does he know the way Adrian stares at you, like he wants to rip into you and devour you whole? Tell me, why are you the only woman allowed to be out and about at night in a place like this one? Why does your reputation not get tainted as anyone else's would? What makes you so special?"

I swallowed. "I work for my father," I pointed out. I hoped she didn't know about my magick. I still didn't know how I could access it, how I could use it in this moment, but I could try.

"Precisely my point," she said. "You know, my father worked in a tavern. He made dirt, if that, and yet, when I told him about my pay, he sneered. He called me a whore. He said, 'proper women don't work in places like that.'" A pause. "So, I ripped his throat out."

"You're a Blood Mage too?" I asked. Adrian groaned behind me. I winced at the guttural sound.

"It took you long enough to figure it out," Pepper said. "I mean, how much more obvious could I be, at least about Adrian?"

She was right, of course. There were so many clues indicating Adrian was what he was. If I hadn't been so distracted by Claire's murder, I might've picked up on it.

"I wonder if you'll taste as good as your friend did," she mused. "What was her name?

Claire, was it? Did you know she was working for Adrian?"

"You killed Claire?" I took a step back and nearly tripped over one of Adrian's legs. Her other words sunk in. "What do you mean, she worked for Adrian?"

"You stupid fool," she said, disgust evident in her tone. "Do you recall why Jonathan

Nyx was going to be Consumed?"

I shifted, looking at my exit points. I didn't think I'd be able to get Adrian out of here by myself, and I needed a strategy to get us both out alive.

"The girl, the drowned girl," Pepper continued. "She was working for Adrian until Marcus Sawyer drowned her. She was helping the sirens leave Adrian's brothel. That's not part of the deal. Blood Mages need food. If we aren't going to feed on humans, we need some source of sustenance." Her nose wrinkled in disgust. "I wasn't going to go back to drinking pig's blood, to feeding off animals. The Sirens were the next best thing to humans." She grinned. "Then I thought, why not get rid of him and make my own rules?"

"You betrayed him for your own gain?" Contemptuous.

"A deal was made between two important people, a deal we all had to follow." Her expression grew grim. "But because of Adrian's arrogance and pride, he refused to listen. He wanted to filter the damn sirens from the brothel somewhere safe. Your friend was part of it. But I found out and reported it. I was given express orders to take everyone out, including your friend and Adrian. Marcus Sawyer took out the girl. He thought it would be best to make it look like she drowned. But then he got hungry. He couldn't resist her. He killed her after he fed on her and he left a *fucking* mess."

"Why would you kill at all? Why would you want to…to reveal yourselves?" Magick burned through my body as words spilled out of my mouth. I tried to calm myself, but it was no use. "You've seen what they do to Mages and Enchantresses. What do you think they'll do to you?"

"Do you think I wanted this to happen?" Pepper asked, throwing her arms out. "Do you think I want Diego Pascal breathing down my neck because Marcus couldn't keep his cock in his breeches? If I kill Adrian Blood, I cut the head off the snake, and I'll be able to redeem myself. Then, I'll be in charge. I'm certain I'll be able to form a relationship with your uncle the same way Adrian has. The sirens will continue to get transferred to us with the help of your uncle, the Blood Mages' hunger will be satiated, and everything will be as it should be. War will be avoided for the time being."

I sucked in a breath. My uncle knew what was happening?

"You seem surprised, birdie," she said. "Do you honestly believe your uncle and father do not know about Blood Mages? Why do you think your father increased his collection payment? He's taking advantage of the impending war for his own profits."

I swallowed. My father would never do such a thing. He would never be so cruel. My uncle wouldn't be okay with innocent life—even if they were not from Cardonia—consumed by monsters as if their lives were meaningless.

Adrian was silent. I was uncertain whether that meant he had slipped into unconsciousness or if he was biding his time for the right moment to attack Pepper. I knew I needed to think of something, considering he was still clasped in iron.

"Well, I'm done taking orders from a Blood Mage who cares more about freeing fish than keeping his own people fed," Pepper continued. "I'm done feasting from cold-blooded fish. Once Adrian is dead, I'll take over and I'll be allowed to feast on whomever I want, human or not. I have every intention of starting with you."

I needed to buy time. "What do the Pascals have to do with this?"

"Adrian was supposed to die the night you saved him," Pepper said. "He refused to follow orders. Why do you think the Pascals are here? Who do you think provides the mer-folk in the first place?"

Before I could think more on this, Pepper lunged for me. I had never seen someone move so quickly. I'd heard about their speed but didn't realize what it meant until I saw it with my own eyes. I didn't even have time to get out of the way. She pushed me down and I landed on my back, the wind disappearing from my body. I put my hands up, desperate to protect myself. I had never fought before. I didn't even know how to fight. If I survived this, I promised myself I would rectify that.

"You are going to taste exquisite," she said. "I am going to drink you dry and then kill Adrian."

I wiggled underneath her, but she was too solid to move. She leaned forward, tracing my lips the same way she had the other night.

"I am going to enjoy you, birdie," she said.

Without warning, she opened her mouth and extended her fangs. They slid out of her mouth with ease. She lunged for my neck and ripped a chunk of my skin off. I screamed. The pain was more intense than I imagined anything could be. I had to figure out how I was going to get out of there. If I didn't, I would be dead, like Claire.

I thrashed despite the pain. I reached up and clawed at her. My life flowed out of me, my motions sluggish and tired. She leaned her head back and laughter bubbled out, blood—*my blood*—dripping from her mouth and rolling down her chin. Like I was nothing more than a joke, something she didn't take seriously as a threat.

"Pepper," a weak voice said. "Let her go. This has nothing to do with her."

Anger set my blood aflame. Even Adrian's tired voice did not temper it, though I was relieved he was okay.

"I'm done listening to you, Adrian." Malice filled her words, and the way she glared at

him made me shudder. "You couldn't even be bothered to do the simplest job you were given. Feed the sirens to the Blood Mages. No one died. They might not consent to the feeding, but everyone stayed alive and no one discovered the truth about Blood Mages. When I realized what you were doing, I told the Pascals. Diego wasn't pleased to find out you were starting to refuse to offer the mer-folk to the Blood Mages, that you were trying to free them from their duty, using fucking humans to help you. You were no longer following orders."

Adrian hissed threateningly. My head grew light and unfocused. It was hard to grasp her words, even as I tried to push the fog.

"Now, I get to feed on your favorite human," she jeered. She turned her attention back to me, her eyes glittering. "You taste delicious, probably because you're so pure."

She leaned forward. I reached up to prevent her from getting any closer and the room filled with light. The feeling was familiar. It was the same way I felt the night of the Consumption, when the darkness was set on fire as everything changed. I pushed more out, unsure if I was doing it the right way. I wanted to use my magick, to protect myself and Adrian, and to stop Pepper from ever harming anyone again.

I might not have been able to help Claire, but I refused to allow Pepper to do the same thing to me.

Pepper screamed in pain, the sound vibrating throughout the room. I ground my teeth, pushing out my magick, forcing it into her as much as I could. I felt triumphant, victorious as power rushed through my veins and into Pepper. She gave one last horrified scream and then the room was silent. The light from my hands dimmed and I let out a breath, exhausted. If I wasn't already on the floor, I would've collapsed. Pepper was gone. In her place was a pile of ash, coating my body.

"She's dead," Adrian said in a low voice behind me.

I looked down at my hands. Had I done that? No one else was here, so they couldn't have manipulated my magick.

Pain shot down my arm and I groaned. I reached up to touch my wound and felt hot, sticky blood trickle out of my skin. I closed my eyes, wincing.

"Hannah?" Adrian's voice seemed far away. Stars filled my vision.

Hands gently tapped my cheeks. I opened my eyes, surprised I'd shut them. Adrian. How had he freed himself? He slid something into my hair. It must've been the pins I dropped when Pepper interrupted my attempted rescue.

"I need you to drink this," he said. "It will heal you."

I opened my mouth but no sound came out. He placed something against my mouth. At first, my stomach twisted. It tasted like heavy metal but smelled sweet. It almost tasted like blood. The second a drop hit my tongue, however, my body warmed and stretched. I felt stronger. I took more of him until Adrian had to gently pull my head away.

Pleasure buzzed against every nerve and my eyelids got heavy until I floated away.

***

I dreamed of darkness and fields and Claire's smile the night she died. When I woke, I was in my room.

"Just in time," a voice said. It was so close I jumped, only to realize I was in strong arms, pushed up against a broad chest.

"Wh-what are you doing?" I asked. I tried to disentangle myself from Adrian, nearly stumbling over myself as I did. He caught my forearm, helping me steady myself.

"I wanted to bring you home," he said, stepping forward. I tensed. "I wanted to make sure you were safe."

"Who are you?" I demanded.

Before he could answer, someone knocked on the door. Without waiting for my response, it opened. There was no time for him to hide, no time to change out of my bloody clothes.

We were caught.

CHAPTER THIRTY-SEVEN

Hannah

Adrian pushed me behind him. I didn't expect him to be so protective, but I appreciated it. Then again, he believed he owed me a debt, so maybe that was his motivation.

I swallowed, one hand going to his back. Not to push him from me or keep him close, but to connect with him in some way. I wanted him to know I was here if he needed me. Though I didn't think we had to physically worry about my unexpected guest, I didn't want Adrian to think he had to face them alone. Even if it meant tarnishing my reputation.

"Hannah?" Lizzie hissed in a loud whisper.

Relief swept through my body, but it lasted only a moment. As much as I adored my sister, I didn't think she'd approve of Adrian being in my room. Since she had invited herself in, there was no way he'd been able to hide.

"Hannah?" This time when Lizzie said my name it was more of a question about Adrian's presence rather than her checking in on me. Gently, she shut the door, and the click seemed to echo throughout the room.

She stilled in front of the closed door: her gaze fixed on Adrian. There was suspicion in her eyes. I was unsure if she had met him before or if she knew him from his reputation. Regardless, she seemed stunned to see him at all, let alone in my bedroom so late at night. Though she probably would've felt the same way about any man, I doubted there would be a gleam of fear in her eyes not even my fearless sister could hide. "What is Adrian Blood doing in your room?"

"You need not worry, Lizzie," I said, trying to keep my voice low. "I have it under control, I assure you."

"There's a man in your bedroom, little sister," Lizzie said. She seemed to be inching to the wardrobe. "Not a man, but Adrian Blood. I've heard rumors he ravages young women without their consent. I believe I have every reason to worry, especially considering the two of you are rather close physically. I doubt you have it under control."

I pressed my fingernails into my palms. Though I knew Lizzie was concerned about my safety, I didn't appreciate her refusing to listen to what I told her. I needed her to trust me.

"I can assure you my ravaging is always consensual, Ms. Walker," Adrian said.

I rolled my eyes. I didn't want to talk about Adrian ravaging anyone, especially not in my bedroom. Especially not in a voice that caused every inch of me to tense with anticipation.

"What are you doing with my sister?" Lizzie asked. The more she lingered, the less afraid she seemed to be. "Have you come here to—"

"Ravage her?" He paused, turning his head to the wardrobe. I was positive Lizzie had stored one of her weapons there. If so, I hoped she would refrain from taking possession of it. Lizzie had no idea what Adrian was, and I didn't think it was time for her to learn. I also didn't know how Adrian would react if my sister threatened him. He seemed controlled, but that might not make a difference if he believed his life was at stake. "I think we both are aware no one would be able to ravage your sister even if they wanted to, don't you? She's fully capable of defending herself, whether in terms of using her body to physically protect herself or using her words as weapons to injure her opponents. I'm certain she picked up on some tricks from you."

"Don't presume to flatter me or to tell me things about my sister, Mr. Blood. I know her better than anyone else, and pretty words are fragile and meaningless."

Lizzie might be right in general, but my magick told me every word out of Adrian's mouth was true. He really believed me capable of such things.

"You'd like to think you know her, wouldn't you?" Adrian said, stepping forward. Lizzie stiffened at his approach. "Yet it is you who disappears in the Forest of Legend during the day rather than tending to your business. I'm sure Hannah doesn't know about that, does she? Where do you go, I wonder?"

Lizzie's eyes burned with anger. "That is not your concern," she snarled, her fingers curling into tight balls.

"But shouldn't it be your sister's?"

"What do you want?"

"I want to know Hannah is safe under her own roof," Adrian said. Though his voice was low, his tone was like a dagger slicing fragile skin. "The Pascals are a family to be wary of. Your father is so distracted by this war with Underedge he doesn't realize the battle brewing in his own home."

"What battle is that?" Lizzie asked, her tone flat.

"Why are the Pascals here?" Adrian asked. "Why does Diego Pascal want to get married *now*? He is nearly thirty, is he not? Why has he decided to ally himself with your uncle now? Blood Mages have been around for the last ten years, and yet this is the first attack on a human. Why do you think that is?"

"How do you know how long Blood Mages have been around?" Lizzie asked.

The curtains billowed in the breeze. A chill crept into my room and no one seemed to notice except me. I moved from behind Adrian ready to position myself between him and my sister.

"I know far more than you realize," he said. "You are sneaking off during the day and no one thinks to question you because you are hardheaded and hardhearted. You only care about yourself."

"That isn't true," Lizzie snapped.

"You refuse to acknowledge your own selfishness," he continued, ignoring her. "Maybe that's why Brendan Pickard ended your engagement. He finally saw the forest for the tree, and he did not wish to be trapped."

I gasped, horrified. "Don't," I said, my voice low in warning. "Do not speak to my sister that way."

"*I* ended our engagement," Lizzie said in a low voice. "Not him."

He turned to me. "You know every word I say is true. I'm the only person who has never lied to you, has never manipulated you, and you choose to admonish me because I speak the truth?"

"I chose to admonish you because your comment was rude and unnecessary," I said. "Just because you never lied to me doesn't mean you have the right to insult my sister."

His jaw tensed. I supposed that was as close as I would get to him admitting he was wrong.

Despite his rudeness, he was correct. He had never lied to me. He might believe his own lies to make them true, but he never went out of his way to do so. Lizzie, on the other hand, had used her powers to try to see inside my mind. Her magick was much more versatile than mine as she could detect a person's thoughts, not truth and lies.

Regardless, she was my sister. Though our relationship had become complicated, even strained, that didn't mean Adrian could insult her in our home in front of me. Lizzie was blood.

"Lizzie," I said, keeping my eyes on Adrian. "You should go."

"I'm uncomfortable with the idea of you being alone with him," she said.

"Go," I told her. "I know how to handle things on my own. I'm more experienced than you give me credit for. As much as Adrian shouldn't have said what he did, he is not wrong. I would like to finish my conversation with him alone."

Lizzie regarded me the same way she would a stranger. She opened her mouth, probably to try to talk me out of it, closed her mouth, then thinking better of it, and slipped away. When I heard the door click shut, I reached in my pocket and handed Adrian Diego Pascal's parchment.

"I wanted to give this to you the night we were at the mortuary," I said in a low voice so no one, not even Lizzie, could hear.

"The night…" He let his voice trail off. He didn't dare speak it, did not dare utter the truth about our kiss. Instead, he took the parchment from my hand, careful not to touch my skin. He scanned it. "What do they mean?"

I lifted a shoulder. "I don't know."

After another cursory glance, he folded it and slid it in the pocket inside his coat. He dropped his arms, his icy blue gaze moving over my skin, leaving a trail of frost.

"You saved me once again," he said.

"And you saved me," I replied quickly, looking out my bedroom window and crossing my arms over my chest. "When you gave me…" I swallowed. I didn't want to speak the words, afraid Adrian might detect the pleasure I felt drinking from him. That wasn't something I was able to admit it to myself yet. "We're square."

"I wanted to tell you about your friend," he said.

"But you didn't," I snapped. Angry tears filled my vision. Claire died because she was helping Adrian free kidnapped sirens. Though she didn't die by Adrian's hand, looking at him caused my heart to break. He could've told me. He knew and he could've told me. This felt worse than when I discovered he was a Blood Mage.

He stared at me for a long moment. There was something in the silence, in the tension. I refrained from offering an answer. My wound had healed quickly, well enough not even Lizzie had noticed anything had happened to me. It should've relieved me, but it didn't.

"You lied to me," I said. "About everything. About Claire."

"No." He shifted his weight, his entire frame leaning forward. His strength rippled in every graceful movement. "You would've known."

"You didn't tell me what you were. You didn't tell me you knew her, and she was helping you."

"You never asked," he pointed out. "You always assumed I was some sort of monster. Now you know you were right." He paused. "Claire risked her life to help the sirens."

"She died for it."

"She knew the risks."

I wanted to argue with him. I wanted to fight him. But I refused to exhaust myself any more than I already had. I didn't have the strength. All I knew was heavy disappointment was sinking deep into the pit of my stomach.

"What do the Pascals have to do with Blood Mages?" I asked, my voice cracking.

"I don't think it's best for you to know such things, at least not right now." He patted the pocket where he'd placed the parchment.

"You don't trust me?" I scoffed. I shouldn't care, but I did.

"I trust you more than I've ever trusted anyone," he said quickly, his voice filled with frustration. "You cannot possibly understand the lengths to which I have gone for you."

"My friend is dead because she helped you," I shouted, then glanced sharply at my door. I needed to control myself or else Adrian's presence would be discovered.

"The Pascals—Diego Pascal—discovered I was freeing the sirens and planned to get back at me," he said. "Pepper told him. He ordered her to kill everyone involved. Pepper sent Marcus Sawyer to retrieve Claire from the Consumption and kill her in the forest, hoping to put the blame again on Jonathan Nyx. Marcus Sawyer is a regular at my brothel who also wanted to taste human flesh."

I remembered him. The man whose name was announced when I went looking for Adrian the night I went to his ship.

"Marcus lost control and ravaged the body. The human I killed that night was not stealing from me as I thought. He was sent by Diego Pascal as a warning. Diego knew the human would most likely not survive. He would've killed me, but you saved my life. If it were not for you…" He let his voice trail off as I let his words sink in.

"You employ mer-folk?"

"Blood Mages are not allowed to feed on humans because it risks exposure," he said. "My brothel caters to Blood Mages who need sustenance, and we are only allowed to feed on mer-folk."

"These mer-folk are willing participants?" I asked in a voice barely above a whisper. I held my breath, waiting, though somehow I already knew the answer.

"Some, not all," he said, looking away. "It's why I tried to free them."

"Instead, two people are dead, and who knows how many sirens."

"You know nothing," he snapped, leaning forward, glaring at me. "You know nothing of what I must do for my people."

I opened my mouth, ready to argue, but the truth was, I didn't know anything. "Now what?" I asked, my words as broken as I felt.

"Now we part ways," he said. "You are a weakness I cannot afford. It's too dangerous to cross paths. Not when war is brewing. Not when we could be on opposing sides."

"A weakness?" I questioned. When he didn't answer, I forced myself to say, "I thought the war was with Underedge because of their missing mer-folk, who you're using *for profit*."

"I never gave my people allowance to drain them dry," he said through gritted teeth.

"As if *that* makes it better," I pushed back. My magick tingled, at the ready.

He took a step toward me, towering over me, glaring. His eyes dropped to my lips and I sucked in a breath. He going to kiss me again. My heart thudded at the thought. I didn't want him to, yet I was unable to move, unable to breathe, and rooted in place.

He stepped back, and I could breathe again. If he'd kissed me, I wouldn't've told him to stop. My cheeks burned with shame.

"You can sit in your high tower like the gods you worship and pretend you know what it is like to be in my position," Adrian said as he bent to me. His lips were so close I could practically feel them on mine. "But you know nothing." Closer…he came closer still. "But you want to."

Without warning, he dipped his chin and kissed the column of my throat. I stilled under his touch as my heart refused to beat. His lips whispered against my skin, "Perhaps, when you realize this, you will come to me." I leaned back, granting him more access to my flesh. I couldn't pull away. I didn't want to. "And then, I will tell you everything you wish to know."

He stepped back, and before I knew what happened, he left.

I blinked once, twice, feeling the last few minutes were a dream.

I needed to get out of these clothes and wash my face. I needed to return to the Hannah I knew. The good girl who always followed the rules and was polite and ignorant.

The girl who didn't know Adrian could do such things. Who found it easy not to care about him. Who had a sister she could rely on and share secrets with.

I didn't think I'd ever see that girl again.

CHAPTER THIRTY-EIGHT

Hannah

Every night, I dreamed about Adrian. There were times when he was truly a monster, and I woke clawing my throat, afraid he had sunk his teeth into my flesh in order to take my life. Others were more alluring with us walking the docks hand in hand. A few were more vivid than I wanted, with us participating in activities that were much more illicit than holding hands. And, though I didn't want to admit it, even to myself, I relished *those* dreams.

Each time I awoke from one, my eyes always went to my window. I expected to see him on my balcony, a wicked smile on his face and a gleam in his eyes, ready to offer an easy quip about my dream he would somehow be familiar with. However, the glass was sealed shut and I was alone every time.

At first, I couldn't fathom what would inspire such dreams. Was it because Adrian and I had been through an ordeal many people didn't experience? Or was this simply my own truth manifesting in my dreams? I was afraid of him, and yet a darker part of me I didn't want to acknowledge was intrigued by him, by the fact he could be both gentle and savage. I remembered his lips trailing on my neck, and his kiss. My fingertips brushed my lips reminding me the kiss was real even if it felt like a dream.

I wanted to avoid him, and yet I wanted to see him.

I didn't know what I wanted.

If anyone understood the importance of keeping things hidden due to fear of persecution, I did.

I let out a disgusted snort and rubbed my face, cursing my body and my heart. The echo of the taste of his blood hitting my tongue filled my mouth. My stomach turned with the sudden desire to retch, not because I was disgusted with it, but because I was disgusted with myself, with the pleasure I felt upon tasting it. For craving more of it.

Tears pricked my eyes. I wished my mother were here to tell me what to do. Not about my magick, but how to navigate the waters of becoming a woman and experiencing such contradicting feelings for a man—a monster—I knew wasn't good for me. I couldn't go to my father. I couldn't go to my sister. After her confrontation with Adrian, I knew she wouldn't approve. This was something I had to work out on my own.

As much as I hated how Adrian treated Lizzie, he was right. Lizzie had been keeping secrets from me. But then, I'd done the same to her. We should be communicating with each other, especially since there was so much about our magick we didn't know, and she was the only one I trusted. As much as I adored my cousins, I was unfamiliar with what their magick could do, and I didn't think we could find a place to openly discuss it.

Lizzie, on the other hand, was someone I admired, someone I wanted to be. She was fierce, fearless, and proud of who she was. She felt no need to hide herself and earned the respect of the men and women doing their business in the square, even though she was Father's daughter. She was more than a silly girl from an affluent family: she was her own person, confident in her abilities to do whatever it was she wanted. I didn't want things to be tense between us.

A gentle knock on my door interrupted my thoughts and I sat up, smoothing the wrinkles of my dress. I had burned Adrian's clothes the night he brought me home after our ordeal with Pepper. I didn't want any physical reminder of him here. My memories were bad enough.

My room was my safe haven, a port, and Adrian was a summer storm, unexpected and devastating. My purpose was clear, and I had no time for distractions. I planned to learn more about my magick in whatever way I could.

"You have visitors," Roseanna told me.

My heart hitched at the thought it could be Adrian. After the last time I'd been with him, when he put his mouth on my throat, I should be scared to see him again. But I wasn't. I *wanted* to see him again. I wanted… I swallowed, trying to sort through my feelings.

I wanted him to touch me.

And a part of me wanted him to do much more.

It was more than the physical sensations Adrian caused within me. I was worried for him, worried about why Diego Pascal would want to kill him. Worried about the dangers of his job, and if should anyone find out what he was doing with the Sirens war could break out.

He would be in danger, and I would protect him any way I could.

I hated myself for even caring about him.

But I did.

And I needed to accept it.

"Mum?" Roseanna knocked again. "Are you well?"

I shook my head, trying to clear my thoughts. I hadn't been expecting anyone. I glanced at my window. The sun was still out, its rays causing the surface of the sea to glitter, which meant the visitor couldn't be Adrian. "Who are they?"

"Lieutenant Pickard and Lead Davenport."

I froze. Brendan and Henry? What were they doing here? Were they going to question me again? Did they find out what happened?

I stood and quickly readied myself. Once I finished fixing my hair, I left my room and found them waiting in the foyer. Brendan had one hip jutted out, hands at his waist while Henry was looking at the same vase Adrian had peered at what seemed like so long ago.

"Gentlemen," I called as I made my way down the stairs. My heart thudded against my chest, and it wasn't because I was moving so quickly.

"Ms. Walker," they both murmured when they saw me, bowing their heads.

I didn't bother to curtsey. I didn't want to wait to know why they were here. I didn't want to play games.

"Ms. Walker," Brendan repeated, tilting his head at me as he stepped forward. Henry avoided me altogether, which was perfectly fine. I didn't want to indicate we'd seen each other at the mortuary. Brendan's arms were behind his back, looking at me through his rakish brown hair. "I thought you would want the news directly. Claire Turner's murder case has been closed. It was reassigned as an accidental death. Something about the body indicated as much and despite questions that arose, it is settled."

I nodded once, unsure how I felt. I knew the truth, and Brendan suspected as much, but that didn't mean Ankura as a society, or even Cardonia for that matter, needed this information.

"Has Richard been informed?" I asked. "He has been keeping his distance due to your baseless accusations and I wonder if I will be able to see my friend after this."

"You may do whatever you wish, as long as you obey the law," Brendan said. "Whether that means keeping your distance from locked mortuaries and sneaking inside them to see bodies. As long as you refrain from doing anything that would arouse suspicion, you should be fine."

Pompous *and* arrogant.

I moved my gaze to Henry. He tapped the vase, seemingly confused. I should've been angry he was so quick to tell Brendan everything, but I didn't have the energy. They seemed as close as brothers: as close as Lizzie and I had been. I wondered if the nature of their relationship was as complicated as ours had gotten.

"Is there anything else?" I asked, shifting my attention to Brendan.

"Not that I can think of, although if I…." He let his voice trail off midsentence, his eyes going to the stairs.

I was entirely forgotten.

I turned, wondering what it was he saw. When my sister came into view, I bit back a smile watching the astounded way Brendan regarded her, the way his blue eyes softened and sharpened at the same time, the way his mouth went slack though didn't quite open proved there were still residual feelings inside of him.

Lizzie pretended not to notice Brendan or Henry until she reached the bottom step. She nodded at them, giving them a small curtsey. Surprisingly, she was in a simple yellow dress, which fit her body and flared at the hips. Her curls were pinned to the top of her head, a couple framing her face.

"Ready, Han?" she asked. "Father has an announcement he wants to discuss with us at supper."

Pain flashed across Brendan's face, but quickly disappeared. I almost thought I hadn't seen it at all.

"Thank you," I murmured to both of them before following Lizzie into the other room. I knew Harrold would see them out.

We stepped into the dining room. I shouldn't have been surprised to find the Pascals already seated. They were our guests and would remain so until they left Ankura. I didn't want to confront them so soon after everything that had transpired with Adrian and Claire. The men stood upon seeing us enter and waited until we sat before returning to their seats. For a moment, nobody spoke. The servants brought out dishes filled with creamed corn, roasted lamb, and vegetables mixed with spices. A clash of scents tickled my nose and my stomach rumbled. I wanted to grab a sweet roll and assuage my sudden hunger.

"It is official," Sage said, goblet of wine in his hand. "Claire Turner's death was ruled as accidental. Apparently, there was a beast present in the forest not even I was aware of." He glanced over at me, his gaze lingering a beat longer than it should have.

I swallowed, tilting my chin down and bringing my goblet to my mouth. I wanted

Sage to know I understood what he was saying. And while I didn't understand why he was sanguine with hiding the truth, I acknowledged there was something more going on.

The Pascals, and definitely Sage, knew more about Blood Mages than they let on. But why? How? Based on what Pepper said, the Pascals seemed to have created some sort of rule system. There was more to this I planned to find out.

My magick tingled in anticipation. I set my glass down and folded my hands in my lap.

"I am sorry about your friend," Diego said, turning to look at me. His dark eyes were sinister, especially as they looked at my cheek where his cut should still be.

I reached up to feel for it, knowing Adrian's blood had healed it along with the other injuries on my person. I wanted to draw Diego's attention to the fact it was gone. His eyes widened a fraction and his brow wrinkled as confusion spread across his face.

I curled my lips up into a small smirk. "Thank you for kind words, Mr. Pascal," I said, nodding once. "They mean more to me coming from you than you could ever know."

"Here, here," Vibora said, clapping his hands. "Let's get another round of wine, hmm? We have Sage's case closed and we are among friends and family. We have reason to celebrate."

"We do," Diego said, lifting up his glass. "I have come from the governor's manor. I would like to announce, officially, that I and the youngest Beckett will be getting married in three months' time." *Truth.*

I choked on the sweet roll I'd been chewing and everyone turned to look at me, including Diego. I forced myself to lift my glass, hoping it would seem like I supported his announcement. We toasted, but I didn't drink. Diego noticed and cocked an eyebrow at me, which I ignored.

"So, you caught Jonathan Nyx?" I asked, remembering the offer he made to my uncle.

"You have his head for my uncle?"

"His head is as good as mine," he said.

Truth.

My cousin Everly was bound to a villain, and Jonathan Nyx would finally be caught once and for all.

And what of Adrian? What would happen to him?

I will not let anyone, or anything, hurt him. I swear on my life.

For the rest of the evening, I picked at my food. Later, I sat on my balcony and watched as the sun bled into the water, defeated, heavy, life flowing from it, leaving a trail of desolate darkness.

But tomorrow the sun would rise despite its mortal injury.

It would fight another day.

And so would I.

Coming Soon

Bone & Ash

Book 2 in the Shadow and Ash series

ABOUT THE AUTHOR

USA Today Bestselling Author Isadora Brown is a Disney villain addict, a sucker for Persephone and Hades retellings, and a lover of all things dark and forbidden. She believes in happily ever afters, a mystery that leaves readers guessing until the last minute, and stubborn characters set out to achieve their dreams even if no one else thinks they will.

A Southern California girl at heart, Isadora currently resides in a small lake town in Michigan with her husband, four children, and her plethora of fur-babies.

Stay in touch by subscribing to her VIP newsletter:
https://view.flodesk.com/pages/5ec2d2d61bb82200264a1e7b

CONNECT WITH ISADORA

IG: @authorisadorabrown
FB: /authorisadorabrown
BookBub: /authors/isadora-brown

www.BOROUGHSPUBLISHINGGROUP.com

If you enjoyed this book, please write a review. Our authors appreciate the feedback, and it helps future readers find books they love. We welcome your comments and invite you to send them to info@boroughspublishinggroup.com.

Follow us on Facebook, Twitter and Instagram, and be sure to sign up for our newsletter for surprises and new releases from your favorite authors.

Are you an aspiring writer? Check out www.boroughspublishinggroup.com/submit and see if we can help you make your dreams come true.

Love podcasts? Enjoy ours at www.boroughspublishinggroup.com/podcast

www.ingramcontent.com/pod-product-compliance
Lightning Source LLC
LaVergne TN
LVHW091052080826
845145LV00002B/724

* 9 7 8 1 9 5 3 8 1 0 8 7 8 *